SUBURBAN BLUES

SUBURBAN BLUES

Al Pauly
Editor
Charles Campbell

iUniverse, Inc.
New York Lincoln Shanghai

Suburban Blues

Copyright © 2005 by Albert F. Pauly III

iUniverse books may be ordered through booksellers or by contacting:

iUniverse
2021 Pine Lake Road, Suite 100
Lincoln, NE 68512
www.iuniverse.com
1-800-Authors (1-800-288-4677)

ISBN-13: 978-0-595-35684-3 (pbk)
ISBN-13: 978-0-595-80161-9 (ebk)
ISBN-10: 0-595-35684-2 (pbk)
ISBN-10: 0-595-80161-7 (ebk)

Printed in the United States of America

Editor's Note

As copy editor for the manuscript of this novel, I take full responsibility for all raised eyebrows resulting from detection of misspellings, typos and grammatical misadventures within this finished work.

That said, I confess that it became a pleasure to be part of this project, for it gave me the chance to be one of the first to read a truly original, suspenseful and entertaining work of fiction.

CHAPTER 1

▼

Summer 1966

Eddie looked around out of habit before he entered his office. The door creaked, as loudly as it always had, but for some reason on this hot August night, that familiar sound seemed to echo in his head as he quietly stepped in and tried to lock the door behind him. *"Jammed. One more thing to fix,"* he complained to himself as he proceeded with his mission. Friday nights were always packed at 'Eddie's Place' and tonight was no exception. The first show of the evening was about to start. As Eddie made his way to the safe, the dimly lit room began to vibrate with the energy of a bass guitar pulsing out a familiar anthem on the stage at the other end of the building. Sweat began to bead up on Eddie's forehead. Not from the heat, but from nerves. Carrying that much cash always made him edgy even if it was concealed in that unassuming brown paper bag.

Eddie had arrived in Detroit from Tupelo in 1950 on his twenty-first birthday with nothing but a dream—a dream of one day running his own blues club. All he had to do was juggle three jobs, save every penny he earned, and basically go without. One lease, two years, and three overwhelmingly one-sided bank loans later, Eddie had his blues bar. That's when the struggle really began. For the next fourteen years Eddie worked even harder. He had no manual to follow, so building a clientele, dealing with suppliers, coping with employees and lining up entertainment had been a struggle marked by trial and error. But Eddie pulled it off. He wasn't rich. He still stretched to pay the bank loans and bills every month, but 'Eddie's Place' had now become established in Detroit as a prime venue for every blues aficionado in the area.

The safe was just ahead of him behind the steel doors of the gray upright filing cabinet. Eddie opened the cabinet and kneeled down to dial in the combination. As he turned the dial clockwise to the first number and then back left, the throbbing of the bass guitar suddenly stopped. In the dead silence that followed, he heard...something. Eddie couldn't readily identify the source of that brief faint clanking. He hesitated and looked around the room for the source. *"Mice,"* he thought as he completed the final rotation of the dial. He reached for the vault's heavy chrome handle and pulled it down. The bulky door swung open, revealing a respectable pile of legal tender. Eddie reached into the bag and pulled out the receipts for the first show and added them to the stash. He heard the clanking sound again—louder this time. He turned his gaze toward the door. It was still closed. He turned back around and nearly bumped into the legs of someone standing over him. Eddie's monkey wrench was dangling from the intruder's right hand. Eddie instinctively attempted to rise up and defend himself. Instead he heard that clanking again and felt a sharp pain across his forehead that confiscated his consciousness.

Winter 1962

It was cold. Waterford was only thirty-five miles north of Detroit and, for some reason, always five degrees colder. But the chill in the air inspired young Jake to blow frost smoke rings as he walked to the record shop late Saturday afternoon. His winter coat concealed his most prized possession. The only evidence of its existence was a thin brown rubber coated wire that twined its way from his coat to what looked like a hearing aid in his ear. The Zenith pocket transistor radio was tuned to WXYZ and the song was *A Little Bit of Soap* by the 'Jarmels'. Jake knew the words and sang along in between smoke rings. In fact Jake knew the words to almost every popular song and many that weren't so popular.

His hands were in his coat pockets mainly to keep warm but also to protect the two, one-dollar bills, part of the pay he had received for cleaning his father's real estate office. The mountainous snow banks along the sidewalk had become crusty from yesterday's sleet. They were the best kind for climbing. But they would have to wait for another time. The record shop was more important today. He wanted to add to his collection of 45's.

Suddenly all the streetlights popped on, illuminating the crystals of cold damp mist in their range. Jake had never before witnessed the exact moment when the streetlights came on. To him they either were on or they were off. He wondered, *"Is that someone's job? Turning the street lights on just before dark and turning them off in the morning? Would it be the same guy or would there be a morning guy and a night time guy?"*

It began to snow—big soft fluffy flakes of snow coming down one by one in no hurry to land as if they'd rather not find out what the earth had in store for them. Jake understood their reasoning. He too would rather be floating gently in space instead of becoming one with a crusty old snow bank by the sidewalk in Waterford. Jake walked the rest of the way with his mouth wide open and his tongue extended in an attempt to catch them and save them from their fate. He'd eye one at twenty feet and mirror its every change of direction until it would land cold and soft on the tip of his tongue.

Up ahead he could see the old 1940's vintage storefront with its wood lap siding and its green and white striped canvas awning over the front door and showcase windows. Up above the awning was a sign in green and white lettering 'Lakeside Record Shop'. It was a familiar sight. He'd bought most of his record collection there one record at a time for almost a year. But now it seemed somehow different, maybe a little magical being covered in yesterday's snow, with tonight's snow still in the air illuminated by the streetlight as it fell. What a perfect Christmas snow globe.

As he approached the record shop, Jake could see something new in one of the two showcase windows usually reserved for record players, record storage boxes and posters. It was a guitar. Not just any guitar. It was an electric guitar, more particularly an Epiphone Sorrento Double. But what was this color? Jake thought he had seen every electric guitar that Gibson and Epiphone made from his guitar catalogues at home. Yes, he'd seen this style guitar in the catalogues, but only in sunburst, which was a dark brown finish on the edges of the body that lightened to a blond color toward the center. He'd also seen them all blond, which was just a natural wood finish. But green sunburst? Never. It was easy to imagine himself playing the guitar as he stood outside the shop, eyes glued to the showcase, hands still clutching the two one dollar bills, one in each of his coat pockets.

As he looked at the guitar, he thought about that whole year of playing the cornet. Part of a deal he made with his father. "A; You play a band instrument for one full year, B; You start saving your money and C; If you still want a guitar after the year is done we will see about getting you a guitar." Jake had committed his father's exact words to strict memory so that there would be no misunderstanding when the time came. For the last eighteen months Jake worked a paper route and cleaned his father's real estate office and the major share of the proceeds were in his father's control to be spent for this worthy purpose.

While Jake stood in solemn reverence to the Epiphone in the showcase, inside the shop Mrs. Cook, the owner, was discussing the possibility of hiring another student with her only part time employee, Tom Tyler age thirteen. Mrs. Cook had fun running the record shop because she loved youngsters and their music. She was a rickety twig of a woman, and probably sixty or so with short silver blue hair and reading glasses that hung from a chain resembling rosary beads around her neck. Under her navy wool cardigan sweater she wore a faded one-piece blue and white flower print dress. Her homely shoes appeared too bulky for her small feet. They must have been real warm and comfortable because no one would have worn them otherwise.

Tom had black hair combed back except for the part that looked like a Brillcreamed waterfall cascading over one eye, depending on how quickly he turned his head. He was an average sized thirteen-year-old, maybe on the short side but powerfully built like a football player. However, in one way in particular Tom was not by any means an average teenager. He possessed tremendous energy and imagination that was sometimes off the charts—especially when he got the chance to talk music to the customers. When he talked about music, he channeled that energy. His eyes would become wide and wild, while he spoke with industrial strength enthusiasm that would either make them want to buy every record in the store or run for their life.

The store had become increasingly busy. The kids came to the 'Lakeside Record Shop' instead of 'Kresge's Five and Dime' because Mrs. Cook made them feel more welcome. And now Mrs. Cook was in need of at least one more able-bodied teen to help out around the store. Mrs. Cook asked Tom if he knew anyone who could work with him after school and Saturday. Tom thought about it and realized that all his friends had jobs after school, so he told Mrs. Cook he'd keep an eye out for someone to fill the position.

The melting snow on top of Jake's head dripped into his eyes, signaling that it was time to go inside and find a new 45 for his record collection. He entered pretty much unnoticed by Mrs. Cook and Tom, although he did leave quite an obvious trail of semi melted snow as he passed by and went about his search through the bins marked "Rhythm and Blues", "Blues" and "Rock and Roll". The record bins were deep wooden cases with slanted backs resting on wooden counters. The 45s were stacked on edge with the 'A' side facing the shopper so that one could thumb through easily. Usually filed alphabetically by artist or group, each 45 was cloaked in a brown or white paper jacket except for the occasional one with color printing. Those were usually reserved for the most famous artists.

As Jake flipped through the bins in search of *Summertime Blues* by Eddie Cochran, he glanced toward Tom and Mrs. Cook talking to a customer. At first he couldn't make out what they were saying. But it seemed like there was some sort of problem the man had, and Tom and Mrs. Cook were trying to solve it. The discussion soon became so intense that everyone in the store could hear every word. The customer had come in to buy a record he heard at a party the night before. He didn't know the artist or the title. All he knew were a few words to one verse. Mrs. Cook and Tom were engaged in what appeared to be a fierce competition to see who would guess the song first. They each ventured about three or four guesses and played the selections for the customer to no avail. The man said it was a new record, sung by a female. Mrs. Cook said, "What was that verse again?"

The man said, "My heart carries scars it can't hide." Once Jake heard the partial verse, he knew the song. He knew it was by Claudine Clark whose recent big hit was *Party Lights* and the 'B' side was called *Disappointed*. He thought it was better than *Party Lights*. It was a mixture of slow blues with a pinch of soul. It was a really nice tune. He had heard that *Disappointed* was intended to be the 'A' side but 'Party Lights' really caught on. Already in the C's looking for Eddie Cochran, it was no trouble for Jake to flip to Claudine Clark, pull out the record *Party Lights*, double check the flip side and walk it over to Tom and Mrs. Cook.

As Jake walked with the record toward the front counter where Tom and Mrs. Cook were, he noticed a large piece of poster board pinned to a bulletin board. At the top of the paper was today's date followed by Tom and Mrs. Cook's names with some hash marks next to each name. It looked like they had been keeping score for some kind of card game. Once at the front counter, Jake humbly stretched out his hand with the recording and said to Mrs. Cook, "E-e-excuse me but I think you're looking for this record."

Tom grabbed the record and laughed. "This is *Party Lights* by Claudine Clark. This isn't what we're looking for, bud."

Jake paused a little for effect, but then slowly and gently reached out to Tom's hand, which held the record and turned it over. "Try this side," Jake said in the softest voice he could conjure up. Tom looked a little confused.

Mrs. Cook said to Tom, "Let's spin it and see what the boy's talking about."

The song started to play and the customer said, "That's it! That's it! I'll take it."

Tom came up to Jake and put his arm around his shoulder and said, "Man, you're good."

Mrs. Cook cashed out the customer, turned to Jake and said, "What's your name son?" After Jake told her she turned and wrote "Jake" on the poster board and placed a hash mark under it. As Mrs. Cook was writing on the board she said, "You see Jake, almost half the people who come in here looking for a record need our help with the title. The only clues they normally give, are a few words from a verse or they try and sing the song to us. So it's important that we know the words in these songs so that we can help the people find what they're looking for. Tom and I make a game out of the whole thing by keeping score. And now you have one point."

Then Tom and Mrs. Cook both turned to Jake and said in unison, "Want a job?"

Jake's mind was spinning with thoughts of working in such a great place that could actually use his skill of remembering the words to popular songs. A skill that was lost on almost everyone he knew except for Tom and Mrs. Cook, of course—skill that he could sharpen by listening to his Zenith pocket transistor radio—one of his favorite pastimes. This could be his dream job. So Jake asked, "Could you give me a little time to find someone to do my paper route?"

Tom and Mrs. Cook truly thought alike because again they spoke in unison. "No problem."

Mrs. Cook got Jake's full name, address, phone number and all the other particulars an employer would ask a new employee. In addition to their shared interest in music, Tom and Jake found that they went to the same junior high school. As they talked, Jake mentioned that he had been saving up for a guitar while serving his one-year sentence, playing cornet.

Suddenly Tom's arms stretched open with each finger of his hands spread as far apart as was humanly possible. His eyes got wide, his mouth even wider. "You play guitar too?" he screeched.

"Uh n...n...ooh not yet, I'm gonna take lessons once I've saved up enough money to get one," Jake humbly replied.

Tom's arms dropped and his eyes and mouth returned to their normal human looking position. "Well, our band needs a rhythm guitar player, bud, so when you get your guitar, maybe you'd like to sit in with us and learn some songs."

"OK. That sounds great, thanks." Jake said his goodbyes as he backed out of the store, completely forgetting about the record he came to buy.

CHAPTER 2

▼

May 3rd 2002 11:30 a.m.
Michigan

Jake switched on the satellite radio on his desk where it was tuned to music from the 1960's. *Nineteenth Nervous Breakdown* by the Rolling Stones was about half way over.

At 53 years of age, Jake was having trouble with the pain in his neck as he leaned forward and back while tilting his head up and down to see the computer screen through the second to the bottom part of his trifocal eyeglasses. He had learned though trial and error, that the second to the bottom part of the trifocal was the part that magnified things like car dashboards, computer screens and people who came a little too close to one's face for comfortable conversation. It seemed that lately most of Jake's clients were coming within the range of the second to the bottom part of his trifocals and he thought they should have the decency to stay back within the range of the top part. He had a list of unreasonable rules lately that he thought his clients should follow. But he knew it wasn't reasonable for a real estate broker to have the audacity to set rules for his clients. Mostly it was the other way around. And thus it had been for the last 30 years of his life. It just started to bother him about a year or two ago and as the days passed he seemed to notice the dissatisfaction more and more.

Each of the first 28 years of his real estate career was great. He loved the challenge of running his own business and the reward of helping clients make virtually the biggest purchase they would make in their lifetime. Jake was honest, conscientious, and worked long hours to see that the job was done right. His father had taught him. And he let Jake take over the business when he retired. Slowly he built up a clientele and hired salespeople along the way. But Jake seemed to be suffering from burnout. What used to be a pure pleasure for him had become a laborious, monotonous, unrelenting, unrewarding, exercise in futility.

He first noticed a change after the World Trade Center and Pentagon were attacked on September 11, 2001, one of the most tragic days in American history during his lifetime. It seemed he started to care less about the business and was at a loss to know for sure what really mattered. As time went on his attitude began to show in the way he acted toward customers and clients, the way he dressed and even in his office management discipline. He began to look for answers to the problem. That's why he was on the computer today.

The web site was one that offered help for depression and anxiety. He was in the process of ordering a self-help CD on line. Jake typed in each little box, his name, home address (he didn't want the CD to come to the office), credit card number, and phone number. *"Why would they want my phone number?"* he thought. *"I wonder if they are planning some sort of phone therapy for me. Maybe it'll be a computer that calls and says, 'before we begin, please get comfortable. If you are comfortable press one. If you need four more seconds to get comfortable press two. If you would like the selections repeated, please press three. Now that you are comfortable please tell me your symptoms. If you are suffering from agoraphobia press one. If you are suffering from Anorexia press two. If you are suffering from Anxiety press three. Depression, four. Mood swings, five etc."*

Once the CD was ordered, Jake leaned back in his chair, feet dressed in tennis shoes, resting on a wooden pull out shelf that slid out from above the top right hand drawer of his desk. Arms up and hands back behind his head pushing his Titleist golf cap up from behind so that the front came down just enough to cover his eyes. His sweatshirt and Levi's matched. Both were blue and threadbare.

His office was in disarray with unfiled deal folders stacked in piles resembling little leaning towers of Pisa on his desk, the credenza, and the floor. On the walls hung several dusty awards for sales and for service to the local board of Realtors. He would tell you that they were mostly his father's if you asked. But you wouldn't. The names on all the awards bore his name—the same as his father's. Most of his awards were thrown out in a random cleaning episode that lasted one weekend when the phone wasn't ringing. There were two motivational posters that Jake had framed years ago. One showed a cat doing chin ups with the slogan at the bottom "Hang in There". The other poster consisted of a monkey on the toilet. Toilet paper was strewn everywhere. The slogan read, "No Job Is Complete Till the Paperwork Is Done".

The satellite radio started playing *We Gotta Get Out of This Place*. The phone buzzed. It was Jenny, Jake's secretary of fifteen years. "Jake, wake up and turn your radio down. I can hear it out here. You've got Mrs. Stowell on line one."

Begrudgingly rising from his reclining position Jake picked up the phone and said in a most pleasant voice, "Hi Mrs. Stowell, how are *you* today?" She was a rather difficult seller/client that had been referred to him by his good friend and attorney, David.

"It's been three months, Mr. Strong, since we listed my home for sale and all you have done is brought me three low offers. Why can't you get me what I'm asking!?"

On the other line Jenny was talking to her mother. "Mom, I don't know how much longer I can take this. I keep after Jake to shape up, but he just comes in every morning and sits at his desk and listens to those oldies stations on the radio. He's not returning his calls like he used to. I've seen him get a little rude to some of his clients. He's even missed a few appointments lately. He's not at all like he used to be. It gets hard to make excuses for him after a while."

After thinking for a moment Jake said to Mrs. Stowell, "Mrs. Stowell, let me be as clear about the answer to your question as I possibly can, so that you won't need to ask it any more. When I listed your home, I told you that, in my opinion, it would not sell at your asking price. I also told you what price range you could expect. Three different brokers have brought offers all of which I should add, were within that range. But did you accept any of the offers? No. Did you counter any of the offers? No. You told me you were insulted by those offers. Mrs. Stowell, why the hell did you hire me to sell your house in the first place if you aren't going to listen to my advice?"

Jenny's mother said, "Well dear, you know that you could run that business yourself. Now that Jake has sent you to real estate school—you have the license and everything. Why don't you ask him to sell you the business?"

"Yeah, right, and what would I use for money? Anyway, it takes a lot of knowledge and experience to know how to solve problems. I wouldn't know what to do if some big problem came up. I'm not ready, Mom."

Mrs. Stowell was at a loss for words, so Jake continued, "You've got this misguided perception that you can paint the exterior trim on the house with forty dollars worth of repulsive lime green paint and add forty-thousand dollars to the value. What you really need is forty dollars worth of air freshener in that place. So are we done here? Because I'm getting a little backed up." Mrs. Stowell didn't answer; she just hung up the phone. At that moment Jake thought, *"This will not turn out well,"* as he set the receiver down and resumed his previous relaxed position. He sang with the radio, "We gotta' get out of this place, if it's the last thing we ever do."

Jenny's mom reasoned, "Well dear, I'm sure Jake didn't know everything when he started either. You ask him to sell and I'll be your investor."

Jenny said, "Thanks, Mom, but I'm not ready for something like that."

"OK dear, but my offer stands."

"OK, Mom, I gotta' get Jake to finish the floor schedule for me so I can type it up. Otherwise, we won't have anyone to answer floor calls next month."

It wasn't long before Jake was startled by Jenny hammering on the poster next to his door and saying, "See? No job is complete till the paperwork is done. I asked you to fill out this floor schedule for me last week and it's still not done." She glared at him from the doorway tapping her foot and gripping the floor schedule in her hand. Jenny was petite and fragile—much like her self-confidence. In order to compensate for the deficiency, everything else about her had to be strong. She was strong willed and terminally opinionated, with her own way of doing things. She was no slave to fashion either. She wore a pullover sweater and Levis every day. Although it would have been his right as her boss, Jake didn't broach the subject of wardrobe and dress code with her. *"I pity the fool who'd try to make her change,"* he thought, but deep down he liked her just the way she was.

Jake said, "I think you're gonna have to do it for me Jenny. You know how to do it. So *please* just do it."

"But Jake what if the salespeople don't like the way I do the schedule?"

Jake smiled at her and said, "You can handle it—can't you see I'm busy here?" as he went back to singing along with the radio. "He's been workin' and slavin' his life away."

"Fine," she said as she stormed back to her desk.

CHAPTER 3

▼

May 3rd 2002, 9:00 a.m.
Somewhere in California

Tom Tyler lay sleeping in his one bedroom apartment with a view of the parking lot. The movement of the curtains was not inspired by a breeze but rather a noisy window air conditioner whose vibrations were only exceeded by Tom's snoring. His bedroom was a mess. Clothes left in three small piles that appeared to be arranged by design. But it wasn't as if they were separated by color or fabric for laundry purposes. More likely they were scooped together in order to leave a clear path to the bed and connecting bathroom. The walls were covered with old posters of famous musicians and groups from the late fifties and sixties along with authentic photographs of Tom with several famous artists. In the corner was a Fender Telecaster guitar with two broken strings.

A worn out dresser overflowed with an assortment of pocket change, socks, toenail clippers, sunglasses, candy (some wrapped some not), lint, CD's, jewelry, and guitar picks. But in the center of that chaos was a barely visible trophy—a Grammy award that Tom had won for *It's Not About the Money*, a song that his group recorded in 1969. That was the extent of Tom's rise to fame. Since then it had been bars and small converted movie theaters and now a so-called nostalgia tour. Through all this Tom, at 53 years of age, maintained the necessary optimism anticipating that his next break was just around the corner.

Tom was jolted awake by his satellite radio alarm clock. The DJ spoke, "That was, *We Gotta Get Out of This Place* by 'Eric Burdon and The Animals'." Then the radio played with no introduction, *Dock of the Bay* by Otis Redding. Tom slowly gained sufficient consciousness to locate his answering machine and press the proper button to begin playing back messages from the last five days. Tom had been on the road with his band in Seattle and Sacramento. His band had been hired to open the show for 'The Mock Turtles.' It really wasn't 'The Turtles' from the 60's, just a group of musicians put together as a tribute band that played the songs of 'The Turtles'

The first voice on the recorder was that of his tour manager. "Tom, I just heard from the promoters and they're very disappointed by the gate on the tour so far. I guess the turnout hasn't been what they're used to. They're threatening to cancel the tour if we don't do better in Michigan and so far advance ticket sales are pretty unremarkable for the Meadowbrook Theater. Tom, I know your hometown is near there, and I know this is a long shot but, could you call home and see if you can create some interest for the show? Remember, it's the eleventh. Call me." *Beep.* "Tom, this is your mother. I got your Email. I'm glad you'll be coming to town soon. Hope you'll have some time to visit. Don't forget, I'll be moving soon and I need you to help me get rid of all your old belongings. I put them in the garage for you. Love you." *Beep—end of final message.*

Tom rolled over face up, arms spread out wide on the bed. If he weren't lying down, he'd resemble most depictions of Jesus Christ on the cross. His long black hair streaked with strands of gray at the temples sprawled about the pillow and wove its way across his face. He usually pulled it back with a tie of some kind so that it looked less intimidating from the front at least. His beard was black, full and would have been well trimmed except the promoter for this tour thought he should look a little grungy. Tom didn't like the way he was told to wear it, but he was used to this sort of instruction from the people who paid him.

His body was in pretty good shape for 53. He regularly worked out running and lifting weights partly for appearance sake for the tours but mostly because he wouldn't be able to afford growing out of his wardrobe. His closet was filled with leather and denim outfits. They ranged from straight plain black to multicolored, from the blues look to country style. Tom usually added to the collection during better times. The newest article of clothing was now ten years old.

For the last twenty years or so Tom had been touring the country primarily as a singer. A few fans around the country still remembered him from his one album named after the Grammy award winning song. However, those fans weren't plentiful enough to sustain a rock and roll singer's career. Thus, Tom was on the road a lot with whichever group or promoter that would use him. One of his songs from the album was used in a movie a year or so ago. It turned out to be pretty well received and Tom earned residuals from it as well as a small amount from the album.

Tom rolled out of bed and for the first time in a long time the worry in his heart was visible in his expression. Until now even when Tom was alone, he had been able to keep positive. Maybe it was the severity of the road catching up with him, or the emotion surrounding the move his mother was about to make, to an assisted living facility. Or maybe it was the effects of his headache that began to ripen just above the back of the neck. Or maybe in the recesses of his usually most positive mind a seed of doubt about the prospects for success was starting to grow.

He stumbled toward the bathroom, weaving around the piles of clothing on the floor. At the bathroom vanity he located the aspirin among the shaving cream, toothpaste and cough medicine. As he poured a big glass of water, he looked up to notice himself in the mirror. Until now he'd always thought of himself as a young man. But today as he inspected the lines in his face connecting each side of his nose to the boundaries of his mouth, it was no longer clear that youth resided within. He popped the aspirin in his mouth and took a long drink of water from the dirty glass. He placed the glass on the counter and slowly looked again at his image in the mirror.

Pressing his hands at each side of his face, he pulled his skin so that it appeared to remove lines and wrinkles. After trying three or four different stretches on his face, he remembered a movie he saw a long time ago with Burt Reynolds called *The Longest Yard,* where Reynolds played a washed-up professional football player. The scene he remembered was Reynolds looking at himself in the mirror and pulling at the skin of his oblique muscles with his fingers. The skin stretched out at least four inches from his body. So Tom thought he'd see how far his oblique skin would stretch.

While his little experiment was taking place the song on the radio ended and the disc jockey announced the next song. "Folks, here's one you probably won't remember from 1969 by a guy named Tom Tyler. Back then, he was considered one of the best voices in the industry and many times referred to as a cross between Bob Seger and Joe Cocker. And today I couldn't even tell you if he's dead or alive. If any one knows give me, Barry Bass, a call at 888-555-6619."

Tom, still engaged in the skin stretching experiment, scowled at the radio. He thought to himself, *"This truly ain't my day."*

Then he got an idea, walked over to the toilet (because that's where the closest phone was), and dialed the number. While he waited, he seemed to perk up a little listening to the familiar notes of his song on the radio, and not just some local station. This was the new satellite radio that could be heard everywhere—even in Michigan, his home state, where his next show would take place.

Then Tom heard Barry Bass cut the song short and announce that he had Tom Tyler on the line. "Hey Tom Tyler. Is this the real Tom Tyler or is this just a little prank?"

"No Barry, it's really me. Alive, well and still rockin'."

"Hey that's great Tom. Where are you singing these days?"

"Barry, I'm openin' for 'The Mock Turtles' and we just finished in Seattle and on Saturday the eleventh, we'll be at The Meadowbrook Theater in Michigan, my hometown. I can't wait to get there and see some of my old friends."

"That's great Tom. Well, I'm looking for a scoop. Got any plans for a new release?"

Tom froze. He had been trying for more than thirty years to put together material acceptable to his old label and for that matter, any label that would give him the time of day. But there were no takers. He had no real aptitude for song-writing and no one would cut a deal with someone so long out of the spotlight. "Tom? Are you still there?"

"Yeah Barry. Sorry, I dropped the phone for a second. No, no plans that I can tell ya about at this time."

"Well, best of luck on your tour and all you fans in Michigan go out to see Tom Tyler at Meadowbrook." Tom put his thumb on the button to hang up then lifted it to dial Dan's number. Dan was the bass player in Tom's very first rock group called 'The Phogg' back home in Michigan.

"Hello?"

"Hey Dan, this is Tom."

"Tyler?"

"Yeah, you idiot. How the hell are ya?"

"Great man, things are good, work is good and Patty and I sent the last kid off to college last year. And we're lovin' it. How about you? I haven't heard from you in about six months. You doin' OK?"

"Doin' good, doin' good. Hey, I'm gonna be in town next Friday morning to do a show at Meadowbrook on Saturday. I'll be gettin' in at Metro about eleven-thirty and was hopin' we could get together."

"That sounds great! Why don't I pick you up at the airport and we can have lunch?"

"That'd be great. Hey, do ya think you could round up a few people to come see the show on Saturday? I wouldn't normally ask but the advance ticket sales are pretty dismal and..."

"Sure, I'll see if I can get some of the guys from the old band together and the wives and make a big party out of it. By the way, why don't ya stay with Patty and me while you're in town? We'd really love to have ya and we need to catch up."

"Terrific. That is...if it's not too much trouble."

"No trouble at all, man."

"OK, then I'm really lookin' forward to it. Hey, is Jake still sellin' real estate?"

"Yeah, as a matter of fact. I see him pretty regularly these days. We've been golfin' together on Sunday mornings for the last couple of years now. He's done well with the real estate, but you wouldn't know it from talkin' to him."

"What do ya mean?"

"He's not said anything specific to me, but I think he's pretty tired of the rat race. I wouldn't be surprised if he up and retired soon."

"Good for him. Ya know, I never would have guessed that Jake, of all people, would end up sellin' real estate."

"Yeah, well life's funny like that, Tom. Hey, what time did ya say you were gettin' in to Metro?"

"Friday 11:30 a.m. Northwest flight 321."

"See ya then."

CHAPTER 4

▼

Jake quickly reached for the radio volume to hear his old friend's name mentioned on the air. "Tom Tyler's still alive you dumb S.O.B.. Dan said he heard from him about six months ago. On a tour, I think he said. I gotta good mind to give that stupid DJ a call," Jake said to himself. Then, like a miracle Jake was listening to Tom speak to the DJ. "He's coming back to town? Next weekend? Great!"

He hadn't seen or heard from Tom since Jake went off to college. Dan ran into Tom in the early 70's when Tom flew into town to be with his mom during her surgery. They exchanged phone numbers and tried to stay in touch. Dan and Jake had rekindled their friendship after the last high school class reunion. Once the 'Phogg' broke up and Jake (rhythm guitar), Dan (bass player), Darryl (lead guitar) and Doug (drummer) went off to their respective schools of higher learning so to speak, they kind of lost track of each other.

Jake learned that Dan was still in the area when he bumped into him at their thirty-year high school reunion. They got to talking about old times and before they knew it they were as close as they had ever been. It wasn't long before they decided to get together for golf every Sunday morning with David, (Jake's attorney), and Jake's brother Rick.

After high school Tom put together a second band and then a third within a two-year period. The third group was the charm. They had a hit record. A hit record that got Tom the Grammy for best vocal that year. That's what took Tom away from home. According to Dan, that had been the highlight of Tom's career.

Jenny's voice came over the intercom. "Jake, your buddy Dan is on line two."

Jake picked up the receiver and said, "Hey Dan, guess what?"

Dan replied without any pause, "Tom's comin' to town."

Jake said, "Were you listening to the radio too?"

Dan said, "No, is Tom on the radio?"

"Yeah, he was a minute or so ago. That Satellite radio station I listen to. What are the odds?"

Dan said, "Well, I found out from Tom himself. We just hung up. I'm picking him up at the airport next Friday at 11:30. You wanna come?"

"Can't. Got a closing. But tell him I said hello. Hey, do you think we could get together with him when he's in town? I mean do you think he'll be too busy?" Jake asked.

"Well, he said he wanted me to get a group together to see his show at Meadowbrook. Patty and I are goin'. Maybe you, Joyce, Carolyn and Rick would like to come with us."

"Count me in."

"OK man, I'll have Patty call Joyce and make plans. See ya soon."

Dan had been married to Patty now since they graduated from college in 1971. They had three girls, all grown up and out of the house. Jake was with Dan the night he met Patty. 'The Phogg' was playing at the 'Silverbell Hideout' the night the dance got snowed in.

In addition to being the all round nice guy, Dan had always been the curious one. He loved to investigate. In fact, when 'The Phogg' was in full swing, he was the one who all the band members relied upon to do the research for any new audio equipment. They all knew that Dan would do the probe necessary to make the proper buying decision.

After the news about Tom Tyler, the day flew by faster than it had in months. It was five p.m. before he knew it.

The walk from Jake's office to Jenny's cubicle was only fifteen or twenty steps but that gave Jake enough time to conjure up another excuse to get Jenny to take on more responsibility. Jenny had been Jake's most loyal employee. She was smart, a self-starter, honest, conscientious and hadn't missed a day of work since she hired in fifteen years ago. Her one flaw in Jake's mind was that she was afraid to take on more responsibility. She had turned down higher pay for more duties out of an unwarranted fear of failure. Jake thought that some day he'd want her to take over the business like he did from his father. First he'd have to coax her into getting comfortable with the big tasks and the accountability that went with that territory.

"Hey Jen Meister," Jake said as he walked up to her cubicle.

When he called her Jen Meister she knew he was going to ask her to do something she didn't want to do. "Hey Jake Meister", she said in a tone that conveyed her annoyance as she put down her paperback novel. This tone was one well practiced, and Jake always thought it was a put-on but was never really sure.

"I have a closing next Friday on Big Lake Road and I'd like you to take it for me. I'm going with Dan to pick up an old friend at the airport." The Big Lake Road deal was one that took a year to put together and was quite complicated as residential deals go. Jenny had worked on it with Jake and was familiar with the file. It would be the biggest closing this year for the firm. But Jake knew she could handle it and trusted that she would do a good job if he could just get her to step outside her self-formulated job description.

"And you want *me* to close it instead of *you*—without *you* there? Are you on drugs?"

"Jenny, you helped me with all the details from the beginning, you know everything about the deal and I know you can do it. What do ya say? If you start doing these closings there's a big raise in it for you."

"No! I'm not ready for that yet."

"Look, you've attended closings before. All the work's done before the closing anyway. You've proofed a thousand closing statements right there at your desk. I know you can do it. Take the raise."

Jenny rose from her chair and gave Jake a look that could melt steel, shot her index finger at his chest and said, "You have just stood on my very last nerve, Jake Strong. Listen to me. I *am-not-ready*. And, if you personally don't shape up around here, I'm quitting."

He knew she really wouldn't quit, but he knew to back off for today about taking on more responsibility. So Jake surrendered for the moment. "OK, OK Jenny, I'm done pestering you…for now. Have a good week end."

"You too," she said as if there had been no confrontation at all. Then she remembered taking a message for him while he was on the phone with Dan. "Jake, a Mr. Houglan called and wanted you to take a look at his commercial property on 3330 Dixie Highway. He's interested in selling and needs an estimate of value. Here's his phone number."

Jake took the paper with the information, walked out, got into his SUV and turned on the satellite radio to the 50's station this time. Those songs really soothed him. The address Jenny had given him was on his way, so he thought he'd stop by to check it out. Jake liked working with commercial listings more than residential. Owners of commercial properties were usually more rational in their outlook and expectations regarding the process of selling than owners of residential property. Jake figured the reason was that the owners of commercial property weren't emotionally attached to their real estate like residential owners. There weren't any heartwarming Thanksgiving dinners or memories of Christmases past to leave behind. Spending part of one's life actually living in any given property could cause emotional side effects such as severe procrastination and unexplainable fits of mawkishness, but most of all, it fostered unrealistic expectations regarding market value. So, for this assignment, he gladly made his way to the address for a look-see.

The property was located in the same area as his father's old real estate office. A little strip of seven or eight very old buildings with their respective walls built right up to the side lot lines. This gave the appearance that all the buildings were attached to each other, like units in a strip center. Since Jake took over his father's business, he moved its location further south on Dixie Highway to a building Jake had purchased. He would rather have bought the original location, but the landlord wouldn't sell at the time. And now, from the looks of the area, it was clear that Jake had done the right thing by moving. The whole strip was worn out and neglected. Jake walked up to the address he had been given, and noticed that it too was in severe disrepair. The storefront appeared to have been haphazardly remodeled sometime in the past. Water had easily seeped into the many nooks and crannies left by the hasty face-lift. The wood was rotted and appeared to be more of a liability than an asset. Now occupied by a tattoo parlor, any indication of its previous use had evaporated. He thought about how the neighborhood had changed over the years.

Thirty years ago, this little strip of buildings had been the heart of the downtown. Each storefront was bright and colorful and immaculately maintained. He remembered the shoe store where he got his first pair of Red Wing boots. It wasn't just a shoe store either; it was a cobbler shop too. You could go in there and buy new boots and shoes or have your old ones repaired. What a concept. There to the left had been the bakery. At that moment, Jake's mind began to experience the essence of the freshly baked bread and glazed donuts that were offered up each and every morning. He could still hear the bell that rang each time he would open that front door on his way in to get a snack after cleaning his father's office. Now which building did the 'Lakeside Record Shop' occupy? Jake looked right and then left down the sidewalk to get his bearings. He turned around and saw a now rusted and apparently inoperable street lamp in front of the tattoo parlor. He remembered the street lamp being directly in front of the record shop. *"So this is what had become of it? It's a tattoo parlor—the injustice of it all."* The thought of his dear record shop (where he met his best friend, where he got his first satisfying job, and where he'd hoped the blues and rock and roll would be safeguarded forever) having such an unseemly successor, left a pit deep inside Jake's stomach. For Jake, it was as if today's vice had prevailed over yesterday's virtue. As he left, he kept his head down, only looking at the cracked and crumbling sidewalk, not wanting to be reminded of what those storefronts had become.

During his drive home, he found it hard to shake the image of the tattoo parlor as he wondered about what he was going to do to snap out of his depression if the CD he ordered today didn't help. He had thought about seeking medical help but that scared him a little. Once a good friend of his went to see a psychologist, who sent him to a psychiatrist, who gave him some kind of drug that turned him into a zombie. His friend couldn't stand to be that medicated and flushed all the pills down the toilet. A few days later he was fine. No zombie symptoms, no depression. He thought, *"Maybe the pills did work. They probably are designed to make you feel so bad that when you've had enough you resolve to toss the pills and snap out of the depression on your own."*

As he pulled into the driveway, he pressed the garage door button. The door slowly opened. He always focused his eyes on the floor of Joyce's side of the garage as the door slowly came up, to see if she got home first. Once he saw the tires of her car he knew she was home. It always made him feel good to know she was home when he got there. When he'd get home first, the house was always a little colder. Joyce was Jake's wife of sixteen and one half years. She was four years younger than Jake, and had lived in the area all her life. She went to a competing high school, was a cheerleader, graduated from high school and went right to work. Jake was introduced to her in 1984 by one of his salespeople. She and Jake had many things in common. Both had been voted most friendly by their respective senior classmates.

Jake knew right away that Joyce was the one for him and had asked Joyce to marry him four or five times before she finally accepted. Neither had been married before so both had a pretty well developed sense of their own independence. Others thought this might be a problem for their marriage but it wasn't. In fact, because of their previous independence each accepted and respected the other's individuality. It was the perfect foundation upon which their love could grow. And it did. Sure there was a learning curve at first, but surprisingly short and sweet. Jake decided to run his feelings by Joyce at dinner. She had always been his major source of comfort as well as his life's G.P.S.

Inside, Joyce was on the phone with her mother in Florida. She heard the garage door opening and said, "Well mom, I gotta go, Jake just got home and I've got to get dinner ready."

Jake came in the door from the garage and said in a crazy sounding low-pitched voice, "Helloooooooooooooooo," trying to imitate a bit from a *Seinfeld* episode.

"Helloooooooooooooooo," she replied. "How was your day?"

Jake was anxious to tell Joyce about Tom coming into town. "Well, guess who I heard on the radio today?" Jake knew that if she hadn't talked to Patty yet, she would never be able to guess.

"Tom Tyler," she said without hesitation, as she was reaching into the refrigerator for some broccoli.

"So you've talked to Patty already."

Head still buried in the refrigerator and handing the broccoli to Jake, she continued, "Yep. We'll pick them up at eight. We're getting lawn tickets. Your brother and Carolyn are going too. We're all bringing a picnic basket and wine. And then we're going back to Dan and Patty's for a little get-together with Tom after the show. He's going to be staying with them while he's in town. How's that for fast planning?" Joyce was in her element with the planning. A big part of her job at a local auto company consisted of organizing and planning all kinds of meetings for the executives she supported. She really knew her stuff and she enjoyed it.

Jake put the broccoli by the sink, and as he washed his hands he said, "I'm looking forward to you meeting Tom. I guess in a way I'm looking forward to meeting him myself. Even though we were best friends in high school, we never stayed in touch. I'm sure he's changed a lot…given the life he's led. So it'll be like meeting him all over again."

"I'm sure you two will hit it off just fine," she assured him.

Jake set the table—this time without Joyce asking him to do it. She liked it when he remembered on his own. "Well, when Dan and I got back together, we had the history of the band in common. But we also had college and regular jobs in common. With Tom, I'm afraid; the only thing we'll have to talk about is the old times. And then we'll run out of things to say to each other. It's silly, but after all this time I still think of him as my best friend. You know, we really had synergy when it came to music. Every song we did in the band came easy, because it seemed like we were thinking each other's thoughts. It was something…really something, back then. And now, when we find out we don't have *anything* left in common, I'll have lost my best friend for good."

"Jake, I think you're blowing this a little out of proportion. He's an old friend coming into town. You're going to get to see what he does for a living at the show and you'll visit with him later and catch up a little before he leaves town. That's it. You'll have fun and be the better for having had the experience. OK? OK!"

"OK," Jake agreed in order to end that discussion. It felt better not to think about it.

Having put an end to Jake's lament and being the organizer she was, Joyce decided to lay out the upcoming schedule for him. "Remember, we have the party at Rick and Carolyn's tomorrow night and we're going to Maryland to see Brian and Graciela on the seventeenth, so we need to get you some new pants tomorrow afternoon. So I'm thinking, could you clean up the storage area in the basement tonight and try to fix the drip in this faucet tomorrow morning if you're not too busy?"

"You know honey, I've been waiting for you to ask me to fix that faucet all week. And now that you have, my life is complete." Jake had never been good at home maintenance and fixing the kitchen faucet was at the higher limit of his expertise. "What's for dinner?" he asked.

"We're having broccoli, and a nice salad with chicken grilled on the George Foreman Grill."

Joyce was a great cook but she was very busy at work these days and had little time to prepare the time consuming meals she loved to do. And with their latest attempt at getting healthy, the menu had changed considerably. Jake took a minute to remember the way she used to cook chicken—southern fried golden brown chicken with the white meat that was so tender and juicy. "Sounds great," he said as he broke out of his food trance, finished pouring the water and placing the silverware.

Over dinner, Jake explained that his dissatisfaction for his job had been getting progressively worse. He told her about the CD he ordered to help with depression and anxiety. "But, I think that it's more the job than it is me. I'm starting to feel the need for some kind of change in what I do. Even though I've loved it, I chose selling real estate as a way to earn a living. I think I need something more from the job. The work has got to be for more than just paying the bills."

Not much got past Joyce. She had noticed a change in Jake lately and was expecting to have this conversation sooner or later. She'd been concerned by his recent string of bad dreams probably caused by his trouble with work. "Maybe you need to start thinking about closing the real estate business and looking for something to do that involves more creativity and less stress. The office building is paid off and the house is paid off. We have our investments and I'll have my pension when I'm ready to retire. Jake, we've worked long and hard and saved and done without so that we could have choices later on in life. Well, I think we're close to that later on in life. If you need a change, I think you should start looking for what it is you want to do."

"Ha, you're kidding, right?" Jake asked in disbelief.

"No, I'm not kidding," she insisted. "Maybe doing something more creative will be just the thing for you. I don't know what you'd be happy doing but I know you haven't been happy with real estate for quite some time. So why don't you think about it while you're cleaning up the storage area in the basement and I'll do the dishes."

Jake was reeling from the suggestion that he close down his business. As far as being gainfully employed, that was all he knew. Almost all his adult life had been spent selling real estate. As he walked down the steps to the basement the questions mounted. *"Could I bring myself to shut it down? What about Jenny? She wasn't mentally ready and probably hadn't even considered running the company. Maybe I could sell it. What about all the salespeople? This could upset them. What would I do afterwards? I couldn't walk away from real estate without having some project or occupation in place, could I?"* While there were questions that caused him more anxiety, he also felt liberated from a burden. The burden of subconsciously feeling tied to the real estate business against his will, had been lifted by his wife tonight.

The basement was half storage and exercise room and half finished into a family room with a big TV and built in speakers like a mini movie theater. At the bottom of the stairs Jake wanted to turn left into the TV room in an attempt to avoid the job of cleaning the storage area, but his work ethic, developed in real estate, won out and he turned right. One thing that the real estate business had taught him was the meaning of hard work and dedication to the task. In that business you had to keep pushing in order to get a paycheck. All the hard work going into obtaining a good listing or a good buyer, all the paperwork, all the regulations to follow, all the showings in the evenings and on weekends when you'd rather be at home or out with friends—it can be for nothing if you can't get the deal closed.

"You don't get paid for the hours you put in. You get paid for the closings you have," his father would always say, *"In real estate, starting the job means nothing. Finishing the job means everything."*

It was different in high school. Everything Jake did was for fun. The band was a job because he earned money at it, but it wasn't a job to Jake. It was fun. And he treated it as if it were play. Learning to play a new song wasn't hard for him. It was fun and it was easy. But he found out that writing a good song was hard work. He remembered that he had started writing a number of songs that he never finished. It was just too hard for him to tie all the verses together with a common chorus.

The basement storage area was piled pretty high with items that should have been disposed of long ago. It was Jake and Joyce's goal to make a space in that area big enough to walk around in safely. In order to do that, things had to be tossed. The first box Jake picked up looked pretty old so he opened the lid to check its contents. It was filled with old photos. *"Joyce and I will have to go through this one together,"* he thought as he started to close the lid. But one photo caught his eye so he took the lid away again and picked it from the pile. It was one that his brother Rick took of Jake's band at Mount Holly, a local ski hill that held dances in its large lodge on the weekends. As he held the photo and looked at it through the many creases he began to remember 'The Phogg'.

Darryl's cinder wall basement was painted in dark gray, dimly lit and filled with cigarette smoke that night after school. The amplifiers were all lined up near the east wall divided by Doug's drum set. The four red standby lights, one from each amplifier, shown brightly through the noxious cloud. It looked like the tail-lights of a semi truck in a midnight fog. It was 11:00 p.m., time for their weekly strategy meeting. They all relaxed in the lawn chairs that had just last week been brought in from the patio for the winter.

It had become clear in recent months that 'The Phogg' was becoming popular with the crowds at many local venues. 'The Pack', however, still remained the favorite band in town. Tomorrow night both 'The Phogg' and 'The 'Pack' were slated to play Mount Holly. 'The Pack' did two things extremely well. Every time a new song was released they learned it and seemed to always be the first to play it. The other thing was that they liked to do original tunes. They had two members who wrote songs on a regular basis. 'The Phogg' was as good at learning new songs but in order to rise to the level of 'The Pack', it was clear that they were going to have to start doing some original tunes.

The group was listening to Jake pitch a song that he thought would be great for 'The Phogg' to do. They had been expecting to listen to the song Jake had been writing for the last two months. Unfortunately, Jake hadn't finished the song and wanted to downplay the problem by introducing the band to a new song not yet released in the United States. Jake held the arm of the cheap record turntable over the record he was about to play. Crudely wired to Jake's Fender Tremolux amplifier, this turntable was the means by which the band learned the popular songs. The band members rarely used their limited ability to read music. Before he placed the needle on the record, he said, "Well, because I still haven't finished the song you guys are waiting for, I think tomorrow night we should open with this song. It's by 'Them', an English group, and it's popular in England and Australia. I know it'll be a huge hit over here in a matter of months. Rick got this copy today in the mail from his short wave buddy in Australia. I think it'd be cool to be the first band in America to play it. And by the way, 'The Pack' has never played a song on stage that hasn't yet been released in the U. S. A."

Jake's hand slowly brought the needle down and the song *Gloria* by 'Them', featuring Van Morrison, started to play. The members of the band all moved their lawn chairs closer to the record player. The only one plugged in was Dan on bass. Jake used his Epiphone hollow body to learn the rhythm part. Darryl had an old acoustic to play the lead. Doug attacked the chair with his drumsticks and Tom sang. The band picked up the song almost instantly and accurately, to the note of the record, as if it were second nature. The band listened and played to it three more times. Darryl said, "I like it. Let's do it. I think 'The Pack' is in for a little one-upmanship."

Everyone agreed and Jake said, "Let's see how it sounds plugged in."

The next afternoon 'The Phogg' and Jake's brother Rick drove up to the ski lodge at Mt. Holly to set up. Mt. Holly was a big place. It was so big that two bands could actually perform at the same time without the sound from one stage conflicting with the sound from the other. The snow had not arrived yet. With no snow and no skiers, the massive parking lot was almost empty. It reminded Jake of a small airport. Inside the lodge you could see the huge wooden beams of the roof open to both dance floors and held together by massive steel plates with bolts that resembled those of a colossal aircraft hangar. It looked huge now but in a few hours the place would be crawling with teenagers packed tightly enough to restrict any free movement, including dancing. The stage designated for high school bands like 'The Phogg' and 'The Pack' was the upper level of the lodge they called the loft. The main stage on the lower level of the lodge was reserved for rock and roll groups who had cut a record. Tonight the 'Rationals' would appear. Their hit single was *Respect* later covered by Aretha Franklin.

'The Phogg' had just completed their set up and sound check and was tired and sweaty when 'The Pack' came in. They were empty handed and dressed as if they were going to a party. No band member was carrying any equipment—not even their own guitars. Six huge football player type guys lugging all their equipment followed them. 'The Pack' did their best to copy the English clothing style.

In fact, if you were to walk into a high-fashion clothing store in Liverpool and see five well tailored male mannequins you could be looking at 'The Pack'. They seemed to be just a little too elitist for 'The Phogg'.

At the sight of 'The Pack', dressed in their finery followed by their goon roadies, 'The Phogg' rose up and extended their sweaty hands to greet them. The lead singer of 'The Pack', who was faking an English accent said, "Well, well what do we have here? You chaps look to be in a bit of a fog. Therefore, you must be that ensemble of the same name. How do you do?" But none of them extended a hand in return.

'The Phogg', one by one instinctively dropped their hands that had been extended in friendship. With the two groups standing face to face, the contrast was about as subtle as a train wreck. It was the Bowery Boys meets the Osmond Brothers. Tom Tyler mocked, in his best English accent, "Well if it isn't 'The Pack Rats'. Howdjado?"

The ominous silence that followed, as the two groups stared at each other intensely, would make any onlooker start planning an exit strategy. And then, all of a sudden as if it had been rehearsed, the two groups started laughing and slapping each other on the back. All the band guys in school knew each other well and got along great mainly because they had common interests. Sure there was competition and each band wanted to be the best. But they all were friends first and it was clear that mutual admiration was overflowing.

Each member wished each other luck as 'The Phogg' left to allow 'The Pack' to set up. As 'The Phogg' walked away Tom said, "I think we're gonna surprise 'em a little bit tonight."

Everyone in the group said, "You got that right."

That night 'The Phogg' and 'The Pack' were to do two sets each. After 'The Pack' played two flawless sets with no new songs, it was 'The Phogg's turn. Tom Tyler took the stage in front of the group and without introduction pointed to Doug to set the beat for *Gloria*. Jake came in with the rhythm guitar plugged into his Fender Super Reverb on one side of the stage and also plugged into his Fender Tremolux on the other side. Having two amplifiers on each side of the stage for the rhythm guitar was a unique element of 'The Phogg's signature sound. Then Darryl came in with his Fender Jaguar guitar playing the lead.

The crowd was into it. Jake could see the mesmerized masses moving to the meter of the music. That was a good sign. The lead singer of 'The Pack' was listening from the back wall of the loft and Jake could see the confused look on his face. Jake could almost hear him thinking, *Now what's this tune? Did 'The Phogg' finally come up with something original?*

Then Tom Tyler began to sing. A flash went off as Rick snapped a picture with his Honeywell Pentax. The crowd cheered, whistled and clapped to keep the beat right through the end of the song. Before the next song, the lead singer of 'The Pack' came running up to Tom and said, "If that's an original, you've got a hit, man."

Tom didn't have time to adequately respond to him before the next song and just said, "Thanks, man."

Jake came back to his senses, laid the picture carefully back into the box as if it were the most delicate Faberge egg, and began to clean out the storage area as Joyce had asked.

CHAPTER 5

▼

The following evening Jake and Joyce arrived at Rick and Carolyn's house party and were greeted by Carolyn. They all exchanged the normal regards and Jake presented Carolyn with a bottle of her favorite Sangiovese. Carolyn and Joyce walked off toward the crowd in the living room while Jake struggled to take off his shoes. No one else had taken off their shoes. The host was wearing shoes. It was a nice evening. It wasn't raining. There was no sign that said, "Please take off shoes." However, Jake took off his shoes whenever he entered almost any house. In the real estate business, one way to show respect for someone's property was to remove your shoes when you entered, and Jake was just in the habit. Joyce knew this and always saw to it that Jake had new socks. No way was he going to be taking off his shoes in front of a client for them to see his big ugly toe sticking out from a hole in a ragged sock.

As he was rising from placing his shoes neatly in the corner of the foyer Jake noticed a framed photo on the foyer wall. It was the same photo that he had found last night in his basement—only much larger. Rick had taken the photo. He took all 'The Phogg' photos back then. He had been a great photographer since high school and was still taking great pictures. In fact over the years, he had won several awards in various photography competitions. As Jake examined it, his mind was immediately transported to that simpler time where it seemed everything was easy and fun. He would have been happy staring at the photo all night. But then an older gentleman dressed in a light blue jogging suit tapped him on the shoulder. "You're Jake Strong, aren't you?"

"Yes," Jake said with a smile, and wondering how this man knew his name.

"I'm Jim Conroy, your brother's neighbor down the street. I see your commercial with your picture at the theater all the time. You know the homes in this neighborhood seem to be selling very fast, so I thought you might like to swing by my place tonight and let me know what you think it's worth. I have it listed for sale with Max Rose of Century 21 right now but he doesn't understand how really special the house is. So I thought you…"

Jake put up his hand indicating that he would like to respond, this time forcing a smile as best he could. "Look—Mr. Conroy, is it? I'm very happy to meet you. And I'm sorry that your broker doesn't understand that your house is 'special'." Jake, with a hint of mockery, held up two fingers, semi curled on each hand indicating quotation marks. "But I'm really not inclined to take time away from my brother's party to help you second guess your broker tonight. I know Max Rose. I've known him a long time. He's one of the best in the business. I really don't see why you need me on a Saturday night, without an appointment I must add, to explain to you what I'm sure Max has already explained. Mr. Conroy, just what is it that *you* do for a living?"

"I'm a urologist, why do you ask?"

"Well, Doc, my urologist doesn't understand my prostate gland like I think he should, you know, and since you're already here at the party and all, how about if I lean over this chair here and you can give me a second opinion."

"Well, I'm sorry I bothered you. Goodnight," Dr. Conroy said as he hurried toward the front door.

Just then Joyce, Carolyn and Rick stepped into the foyer after having heard the exchange. "Well, Jake," Joyce scolded, staring daggers at him, "I can't believe I've ever seen you that rude to anyone, ever. Rick and Carolyn, I apologize for Jake. He hasn't been himself lately."

Rick and Carolyn didn't seem upset at all. Rick handed Jake a glass of wine, started to laugh and said, "Old Conroy wasn't invited. He heard we were havin' a party so he decided to crash it I guess. I've been tryin' to get rid of him for an hour. As a token of my appreciation, I'm gonna give you strokes tomorrow at golf."

Joyce said, "Fine, but that's no excuse for Jake's behavior, he was rude and I'm very sorry."

Jake said, "She's right, I used to be able to cope with people like him, but lately it's become a real chore. I'm starting to think it might be time to get out of the business…Strokes? How many strokes?"

"Never mind that, are you talking retirement?" Rick asked.

"I don't think so. I don't want to retire, as in 'not work'. But, I wouldn't have a clue what I'd want to do either. I'm just now deciding what I *don't* want to do. Just how many strokes are you thinking?"

"You know what I think?" Rick said, purposely ignoring his question regarding strokes.

"What?"

"I think you should take some time off to get your head together before you chuck your business. That's a big step for anyone to take. Maybe just take up a hobby. You used to love music. Maybe you should look in that direction. Dust off your old guitar. Learn a few tunes and just sit and think about what you want the rest of your life to be like. Remember what you had to do before you got your first guitar? Dad demanded you commit a certain amount of time on the cornet. A year wasn't it—a year of playing the cornet before you could get a guitar? And he wouldn't consider even one day sooner. He was hoping you'd get attached to the cornet like he was. But that didn't happen."

Jake said, "You know Rick, I think dad wasn't so bent on getting us to play the cornet as he was trying to teach us to see something through to completion."

Rick said, "Maybe so. I guess I hadn't looked at it that way. I guess what they say is true. The older we get the smarter our parents get."

As Rick spoke, Jake went back in time again. It was 1963 and he was alone in the small bedroom with the knotty pine walls he shared with Rick. It was almost dinnertime and the aroma from the kitchen indicated pot roast. The small record player was playing a 45 from Jake's collection. *Be Bop A Lula* by Gene Vincent and his 'Blue Caps'. Jake was facing the window singing along with the recording, playing his Daisy air rifle as a substitute for a guitar. If he thought anyone was watching, he wouldn't have added the extreme choreography. But there was someone watching—Jake's father.

To Jake, his father was huge. But in reality he was only 5'7", stocky build, dark complexion, dark brown almost black hair and dark brown eyes framed with glasses. The show was pretty good so he temporarily put off the matter for which he had come. He leaned up against the doorjamb smiling and laughing to himself quietly so Jake wouldn't hear as his son continued the performance. The song was winding down and to complete the routine Jake did a complete three-hundred-sixty degree spin and caught his father watching from the doorway. His father applauded as Jake's complexion promptly transformed to the deepest shade of red one could imagine. "Hi dad," came out in a breathless whisper as he struggled to keep his balance after the extreme conclusion of his performance.

"Hi there, Jacob," his father said. Even though Jake made it clear that he wanted to be called Jake, his mother and father failed to accommodate the request until he turned 18 years of age. So it was Jacob and that was that. "I have something to discuss with you," he indicated.

Jake said, "What is it, Dad?" As he put down the Daisy air rifle he thought to himself, *"Something to discuss? Sounds like I'm in some kind of trouble. I wonder if he found the 'Playboy magazine' in the crawl space—no, that can't be it, I loaned it to Tom."*

"You know Jacob, last week I noticed the calendar and saw that you've been practicing the cornet for one year, today. And as I told you one year ago, if you stuck to the cornet for one year and saved your money we would consider employing the savings you have entrusted to me, toward the purchase of another musical instrument."

Jake was polite and pretended to continue to listen, but as his father spoke, Jake was thinking, *"Not another musical instrument. The words he used were, 'If you still want a guitar after the year is done, we will see about getting you a guitar.' Those were the exact words. I have them written down somewhere."*

His father continued, "Therefore, I took the liberty of purchasing another instrument for you. It's in the living room if you'd like to see it."

As Jake ran past his father to the living room he formulated a plan that entailed confiscation of the receipt for what ever brass piece of crap his father bought, go get his money back, buy a guitar and run away from home. But as he approached the living room from the hallway he saw an open case. This case was very familiar to him. It was the standard hard shell case for an Epiphone guitar just like in all his catalogues. And resting comfortably in the plush blue velvet lining was not just a genuine Epiphone electric guitar, but an Epiphone Sorrento Double with the Royal Olive finish—just like the one in the showcase window of the record shop where he worked. For a moment Jake couldn't think. He just ran one hand over the soft plush velvet lining in the case and the other over the smooth satin finish on the instrument. Jake was so excited that he spoke at the top of his lungs. He wasn't screaming, just real loud conversation. "Dad, how did you know that this was the exact guitar I wanted? I mean, we never discussed anything about which guitar or how much to spend. So how'd you know to buy this one?"

"Your friend who works at the record shop, Tom told me about it. I called over there last week to get some advice from Mrs. Cook on where to shop for a guitar and Tom answered the phone. Mrs. Cook was on a lunch break and so I asked Tom. He made it pretty clear that any other guitar would not be accept-able. By the way you were $87.50 short. But why don't we call it even?"

"Thanks dad. I'm sorry I didn't wanna keep playing the cornet."

"It's O K Jacob, you kept your end of the bargain, and I think you're learning about staying the course, and completing what you start. I hope you apply that lesson to your music. Such as it is. Do you even know how to play that thing?"

"Nope, but I'm gonna learn."

CHAPTER 6

▼

It was an eerie morning—darker than usual for this time of day. The clouds were a mixture of dirty yellow and gray as if a bad storm was brewing. Each one as it moved along seemed to hold an unrecognizable yet somehow familiar shape against the glowing firmament. The satellite radio was playing *Tarantula* by the 'Tarantulas', a haunting electric guitar instrumental from the early 1960's. Jake was late for a closing. A condominium transaction that both buyer and seller wanted rushed to coincide with their busy schedules. Things were not in order, as Jake would have liked them to be. There were loose ends.

As Jake sped along an unfamiliar serpentine road that curved erratically around a steep canyon his cell phone rang. It seemed much louder and more piercing than normal. He tried to keep his eyes on the road as he felt for the ringing phone somewhere on the passenger seat among the closing papers and file folders. A sharp turn loomed as he found it and brought it to his ear. It was the title company concerning the closing. The closing manager was telling him that the condominium association dues hadn't been paid. He dropped the phone in order to use both hands to negotiate the sharp curve and avoid the oncoming semi truck whose horn was blasting relentlessly. As he recovered, he noticed that he was sweating. His hands, chest, neck and forehead were all dripping with sweat. It began to rain. He fumbled for the windshield wiper knob on the end of his turn signal and flipped them on high to fend off the driving droplets drubbing the windshield. He reached for the phone that had fallen on the floor of the passenger side, recovering it just in time to hear the line go dead. He fumbled for a pen from his sweaty shirt pocket and looked down to write a note on the file folder resting on the passenger seat. "Pay the dues," he scrawled in almost unrecognizable script. *"I'm never going to get this deal closed,"* he thought as he returned his attention to the road. But it was too late. In a blast of horns, groaning steel and screeching tires, Jake's SUV crossed the centerline of the road, burst through the heavy guard rail and sent it flying and spinning as if it were a piece of tin foil. He and his SUV shot into mid air in what seemed like slow motion among the dirty yellow and gray clouds. His heart was in his throat and he couldn't catch his breath as the sensation of falling overwhelmed him. The rocky terrain hundreds of feet below quickly came into focus and began to spin.

Suddenly Jake sat up in bed, sweating, heart pounding and gasping for breath. Joyce, having been disturbed by his thrashing, rolled over to him and said, "You had the dream again, didn't you?"

Jake said, "Yeah. I'm OK, I'm OK," while holding his chest and trying to make sense of it all. He glanced at the alarm clock to see that it was time to get up for Sunday golf.

Joyce rubbed his back as she had done each time the dream occurred in a successful effort to soothe him while repeating her suggestion that he seek professional help. "Oh, I'll be OK," he said as he got out of bed to get ready for the morning of golf. "But you know, I just wish I knew what it all meant."

It was now 6:30 a.m. and the sun was coming up. As Joyce tried to go back to sleep, Jake wandered toward the breakfast nook TV and flipped on the weather channel. While he was waiting for the local weather to come on, he poured himself a bowl of cereal and sat down in front of the TV to stare at the colorful maps.

Jake couldn't explain why he would want to check the weather forecast when the sun was shining and he'd be golfing in a matter of 45 minutes. The rule was that if it's not raining when you get up, we will play golf. So checking the weather today was only force of habit.

Once dressed, Jake grabbed his golf clubs and tossed them into the SUV, set the satellite radio to the 50's station and was on his way. Sunday morning golf was one of the few things Jake really looked forward to these days. A chance to get away from the drudgery of work as well as any other problems currently in mind. The group played at Heather Highlands in Holly, Michigan, a short drive from home. Usually Jake would pick up David and they would drive out together to meet Dan and Rick.

Driving on Sunday morning was a pleasure because there were few people on the road at that hour. The more people on the road the more thinking one had to do and therefore the more stress one had to endure. Jake thought, *"Why couldn't I have a nightmare about driving on Sunday instead of a workday? Because then it wouldn't be a nightmare. Oh yeah."*

As Jake backed into David's driveway he saw that David had already put his golf bag out. That meant this would be a short stop. No waiting. It was no time before Jake saw David's garage door start to open in his rear view mirror. After loading his clubs in the back, David appeared at the passenger door wearing tan Dockers, a yellow Polo shirt and a navy pullover sweater. Compared to the way the rest of the group dressed, David would win the fashion award. The rest looked like they found what they were wearing in the laundry basket instead of the closet.

Jake greeted David with, "Hey Dave, what's up?"

And David greeted Jake with, "Hey, I've got a bone to pick with you, pal!" David was usually mild mannered, a little sarcastic every once in a while, but lacking the intimidating bone in his body that most attorneys like to show off. But today he had a pretty big bug up his butt about something.

Jake thought for a while and then he knew what this eruption was about. Mrs. Stowell, the client David had sent Jake, most likely told David about the exchange she and Jake had on Friday. So Jake said, "Oh, so you talked to Mrs. Stowell."

"Yes, we had quite a long and pointed discussion about the fate of her listing and what should be done with her insolent Broker." David was not as upset as he could have been or should have been because he was aware that Mrs. Stowell was a pigheaded and difficult seller. "Jake, I did everything I could do to keep her from canceling her listing, but she's asked me to instruct you to cancel it as of Monday morning. And if you need something in writing I'll fax it to you Monday. You know better than to talk to a client that way. Did you really suggest that she buy air freshener?"

"Yep."

"You don't sound too contrite about the whole thing."

"Nope."

"Well, if you want to stay in the real estate business and if you want me to continue to send you clients, you'll have to regain some sense of decorum and diplomacy. Sure she's a bitch and sure she doesn't take your advice, but she's a client. She's the person you represent. You just can't talk to clients that way and expect them to stay with you. Think of all the bad word of mouth we'll both get now. I can just see her now. She's probably in church, bearing witness to the evils of Jake Strong and David Williamson. Do you realize how many people are in that church she goes to?"

"Nope."

"Well, a lot, I'm sure. And by now they've all gotten an earful about us."

"I really don't think she's at church yet, Dave," Jake said, as he pointed to the time displayed on the car radio.

"Well, when she gets there, that's what will happen. Do you feel like telling me your side of it, or are you gonna just sit there going Yep, Nope, Yep for the whole trip?"

Jake took a deep breath, starting to feel that Sunday golf was not going to be the escape from reality it usually was. The sanctity of Sunday golf was at risk if this kind of talk continued. Jake, being a big *Seinfeld* fan, remembered a scene where George was upset that Jerry, Kramer and Elaine wanted to include Susan (George's Fiancé) in their group of friends. George was against the idea, explaining that his relationship with Jerry and Elaine should be separate from his relationship with Susan. You see, there were two worlds for George. There was world #1—relationship George (with Susan). Then there was world #2—independent George (with his friends). If you bring Susan from world #1 into world #2 where George is independent, this would destroy independent George. So Jake said to David, "Dave, do you know what happens when you bring stuff from business world into golf world?"

"What are you talking about?"

"You're gonna destroy golf world, Dave. You're gonna destroy golf world."

"Jake," David said as he laughed, "you are one sandwich short of a picnic my friend."

"I'm sorry Dave, I'm just not myself these days when it comes to my job. I still want the positive things about it, but can't endure the negative things about it lately. They seem to overwhelm me anymore. And the time this job eats up—evenings, weekends. You know why I play golf early on Sunday morning? Because that's when I get the fewest calls. But on my way home from golf, almost every Sunday at eleven-thirty, I'll check my messages and there'll be someone calling me about business. I'm beginning to hate it, Dave. How old do you need to be to have a mid life crisis?"

"Well, if I ever knew someone who needed a break from his job it would be you, I guess. Why don't you just take a break? You have people who could fill in for you. Take a few weeks. Take a month. I know you can afford to do it. In fact, I'm thinking maybe you can't afford not to do it. You could be running into more problems if you keep up the way you're going."

"I've been considering it lately," Jake confessed as they pulled into the golf course parking lot to meet Rick and Dan, who were already putting on their golf shoes.

The first thing Dan said as the group walked to the pro shop was, "Hey David, would you and Janet like to go see Tom Tyler at Meadowbrook next Saturday night? We're all goin' and I can pick you guys up a couple of tickets if you want. They're only eight bucks each."

"Who's Tom Tyler?" David asked as he opened the clubhouse door.

Dan, Rick and Jake, who all had a higher appreciation for rock and roll than David, just paused for an instant and looked at each other. Jake spoke what both Dan and Rick were thinking. "You don't know who Tom Tyler is?" Jake proceeded to answer his own question. "He's the only famous person from the Waterford Kettering High School class of '67'. He sang *It's Not About the Money* back in 1969 or so and got a Grammy for it."

"I don't remember that song by name. How does it go?" David made the mistake of asking.

As if on cue, Jake, Dan and Rick began to sing *It's Not About the Money* as the clerk behind the counter in the pro shop rolled his eyes with David. Jake saw that it was embarrassing David so he led the guys through two more verses. After the singing was over, the clerk said, "I guess we'll have to post one more rule of conduct up here," as he pointed to the sign that listed the club rules. Dan and Rick were surprised that Jake could remember all the words after thirty-five years.

"OK I remember the song now. Thank you for reminding me…I think. So you guys must know Tom Tyler, having gone to school with him," David surmised out loud.

Dan said, "Yeah, we sure do. Jake and I were in a rock and roll group with him in high school called 'The Phogg'."

"Dan, I knew you were musically inclined. I've heard you play the harmonica at a few parties, but I can't picture Jake being in a rock and roll group."

Dan filled David in on 'The Phogg'. "Jake used to play guitar. He was the rhythm guitar player. I played bass, Darryl Walker, (who now lives out west somewhere) was our lead guitar. Doug Denton was our drummer and I believe he's a doctor in Florida. Tom was our singer. We were together three or four years and played a lot of the local dances. Jake even wrote some songs for the band."

Jake jumped in for accuracy's sake and said, "Well yeah, I did some writing for the band but I don't remember the band ever playing any of my songs. Come to think of it, I don't really remember ever finishing any of the songs. Huh, I guess I was too busy having fun." As he spoke, Jake's voice seemed to trail off as if talking about this had struck a nerve with him.

Dan jumped back in to remind everyone that Tom would be staying with him and Patty that weekend and there was going to be a party at their house after the show so everyone could catch up. "David, I know you'd really like Tom. And Jake, you haven't seen Tom for what…almost thirty-five years now?"

"That's about right," Jake confirmed.

They all paid their green fees and pulled their carts to the first tee of the par thirty-one precision course. The group loved this little course because it was challenging and they could play nine holes, grab a bite in the clubhouse and be home before noon. Only a hard rain or highly important family matters ever caused any one to miss Sunday golf.

The conversation touched on many subjects as it always did, but David was intrigued by the fact that he had known Jake for going on ten years and Jake never mentioned anything about the band, much less his knowing the likes of Tom Tyler. Jake and David always spoke so freely about everything that he couldn't reconcile the lack of detail about this part of Jake's life. This piqued David's curiosity to the point of asking, "So, Jake," David began as they approached the fourth tee, "how come your rock and roll days have never come up before?"

Jake searched for the answer and didn't have one. "I don't know. That was a long time ago." Jake thought about the words to Don McLean's song, *American Pie,* which seemed to sum it up although only metaphorically.

A long long time ago
I can still remember how that music used to make me smile.
And I knew if I had my chance
That I could make those people dance…

But something touched me deep inside
The day the music died

Jake couldn't really explain why it hadn't been a topic of discussion for the ten years that he knew David. He had talked a little about the band days with Dan at the class reunion, but it was nothing either had dwelled on after the fun ended and real life began. He had labeled that time in his memory 'Do Not Disturb' for some reason. But the news of Tom coming into town coupled with the decline in interest in his life's work of over 30 years had triggered one big nostalgia trip. Jake tried to continue the explanation to David. "I think probably because it's just something so insignificant and irrelevant to me, now that I'm *supposedly* an adult, that it just never came up."

David got the sense that Jake was a little uncomfortable with the probing and decided to accept that explanation and let it go. But the impending visit from Tom seemed to inspire Dan's memory of those days. So Dan began, "Jake, do you remember?"

Jake pleaded, "Oh no, here we go with the nostalgia."

Dan continued, "Do you remember the night we went cruisin' on Woodward Avenue with your mom's Tempest Lemans?"

"Don't you mean the night I dropped my mom's transmission all over Woodward Avenue?"

"Well yeah, that would be a more accurate description of that night, I guess," Dan confessed. "But up until then we had a riot." As Dan told the story Jake was thrust back in time once more.

It was a summer evening in 1966. The band was doing a full weekend with another group at 'The Fire Place'. They just finished their last set for that Friday night. The other group got the honor of performing the final set so 'The Phogg' was done a little early. Usually the band would be facing about an hour and a half of packing equipment before they could leave. But, because they were playing both nights, they got to leave their equipment intact.

Tom was in the mood to celebrate because he just sold his old car for five hundred dollars that morning and his pocket was bulging with a roll of twenty-dollar bills. Out of necessity, Tom was the hardest worker in the group. After his sister got married, Tom paid his mom rent to help out. All schoolbooks, clothes, car insurance, gas and food were Tom's responsibility. So Tom not only sang in the band, he worked in the record shop and at the car wash to keep up with expenses. His old 1950 Plymouth was in need of lots of repair. He really needed a newer car with fewer problems, but couldn't afford to buy one without selling the Plymouth. The Plymouth was his down payment. He had his eye on a 1960 Chevy and was glad to see it was still available now that the Plymouth was sold. Tomorrow he would go to the owner and tie it up with the five hundred dollars and his mom was going to sign for the loan.

Dan suggested, "Let's go out and get somethin' to eat."

Darryl said, "Sounds good. How bout the A & W on Woodward?"

Tom proposed, "Hey Jake, if you drive, I'll buy your dinner." Jake was driving his mother's new, red, 1966 Tempest Lemans, and Tom just wanted to ride in a new car for a change. Everybody wanted to take the Tempest. It had the GTO body style but, of course, none of the beef the GTO's had. It was an automatic shift with red leather bucket seats. It was sharp but it was not a GTO.

It was settled. Jake would drive. Tom would buy Jake's dinner and they'd all cruise Woodward in the imitation GTO.

Their arrival at the A & W was quite timely. It was about 11:00 p.m. and the place was crawling with kids on dates, kids looking for fun, and kids looking for trouble. The band pulled into one of the parking spots set up with the menu. It was a clear warm evening with a slight breeze. So, many of the kids were mingling in the parking lot with their fries and root beer. The car hop came up to take their order. She was about 20 years old and wore the short brown skirt with a tight white blouse, a brown and red plaid scarf around her neck and a big name tag that said 'Laura'.

She was about to take the order when a senior from West Bloomfield named Larry something recognized Tom in the car and walked over to say hello. Tom introduced the guy to the rest of the group. Then Larry said to Jake, "I bet this sled here is a real dog. Couldn't you afford a GTO sonny?"

As Larry's defiant stare was piercing Jake's timid little brain, Tom jumped in with, "Well Larry, between this Tempest and your rusty old Falcon, I'd say *you* were driving the dog."

Larry said to Tom as he continued to stare a hole through Jake, "I think we should find out which one is the dog, don't you?"

In a nervous attempt to avoid what he thought was about to take place, Jake stuttered, "Well, Larry, we'd really like to find out which car is the dog, but it's been missing real bad and we were just on our way to have that looked at. So maybe another time."

"Looked at? You're gonna have it looked at tonight? What mechanic is open at eleven at night?"

Darryl, who was sitting behind Jake in the back seat leaned up to Jake's ear and said quietly even though Larry could hear him, "You really need to work on those excuses, Jake."

Then Larry said the four most feared words on Woodward Avenue, "I think you're chicken."

Tom responded, "OK Larry, look, we were trying to save the new fuel injection system for the drag strip Sunday, but since you insist, we don't mind racin' ya. But, we'll have to make it worth our while. How's about we race from Fourteen Mile to Lincoln and we let Laura here hold the money. You OK with five-hundred dollars, Larry?" Tom handed the big stack of twenty dollar bills to the car hop and looked at Larry as if he made these bets two or three times a night. "Larry, you OK with five-hundred?" As Tom calmly waited for an answer from Larry, who was standing there with his mouth open, all the guys in the band were sitting in the Tempest with their mouths open. Tom said for a third time, "Larry, you OK with five-hundred, buddy? Lets go, we haven't got all night, Larry. What's it gonna be?"

Larry was still standing there with his mouth open when he looked down at his left wrist where he wished he had a watch and said, "Oh man, look at the time. I gotta get back to the, the, the thing. Yeah, so listen, I'll see you guys later. Good luck on Sunday," as he turned and ran to his car.

All the guys and even Laura waited till Larry sped off to start laughing. Jake said to Tom, You just saved my ass. That was one fine bluff, Tom."

Dan, trying to catch his breath from laughing asked, "So Tom, what would we have done if Larry said OK?"

Tom, maintaining that calm confident persona that saved the day said, "We woulda had to race the creep for five-hundred dollars, what else?"

The group ate their dinner and then decided to cruise Woodward a little before going home. They spent the whole ride talking and laughing about the way Tom pulled one over on Larry. All the while, Jake was thinking how Tom put his neck and his new car money on the line for him that night. Who would do something like that except your best friend?

On the way home they stopped at the light at Woodward and Fourteen Mile Road, the spot where Tom suggested they race. In an attempt to memorialize their close call with Larry, Jake decided to pull a hole-shot when the light turned green. At night it was easy to see when the stoplight was going to turn because you could see the glow of the yellow light facing Fourteen Mile Road. Once that yellow light facing the cross street appeared, Jake put the Tempest in neutral and stepped on the gas to rev up the engine. Tom protested wildly, "What the hell are you tryin' to do, wreck your Mom's car?" Jake didn't listen. Once the light turned green, Jake popped the shift into low and burned rubber until a loud noise from the transmission was heard. It was a weird combination of clunking and grinding that none of them had ever heard before. In a panic Jake pulled the car to the side of the road, turned off the ignition, got out and lifted up the hood.

He had no idea what he would find and wouldn't have known what to do. But he opened the hood anyway because that's what you were supposed to do. A light foul smelling puff of smoke emanated from the under side of the motor. When he turned around, Tom, Darryl and Dan were all peering bewilderedly into the engine compartment along with Jake. Tom said, "You guys wait here and I'll walk to the gas station and see if I can get a tow truck."

Jake said, "First, let's see if it'll start up. Maybe I can drive it home." So they closed the hood and all filed back into the car, taking their previously occupied places and braced themselves for the ignition. Amazingly enough, the engine started up with no problem. So Jake applied the brake, put the gearshift in Drive, let up on the brake and pressed the gas pedal. There was the sound of the motor purring along. However that sound was accompanied by a ticking sound and the car was not moving.

"Oh shhhhhittt," someone said. Jake, undaunted or out of sheer panic decided to try another gear and moved the gearshift to low. The ticking subsided and the car began to move. Everyone was silent as Jake pulled slowly onto Woodward. Except for the radio, the trip back to 'The Fire Place' was a quiet one.

When Dan finally finished the Woodward story they were on the ninth green. David said to Jake, "So Tom risked his car money to keep you from having to race Larry and probably getting in trouble for it."

Jake responded, "He did."

And David retorted with a hint of his brand of sarcasm, "But he couldn't save you from doing something stupid on your own."

"That would be correct," Jake confessed, as everyone laughed.

David said, "I think I'd like this guy."

"Then it's settled, your comin' to the show and the party afterward," Dan declared.

As Jake started to add up everyone's score he said to Rick, "How many strokes did you say you were gonna give me?"

After golf was over and Jake dropped David off, Jake thought about the Woodward story that Dan told. Sure it was entertaining and had its tense moments, but the rest of that night and the next morning facing his father were what Jake remembered most.

It was almost 1:00 a.m. when he and the lame Tempest coasted, with the lights off, into the driveway. He didn't want to wake anyone and have to explain things that night. He wanted time to think about what he would say to his father about the problem with the car. If he opened the garage door, that could wake someone. *"No…Better go around to the back door and use the key."*

He felt that one hurdle was accomplished as he slipped into bed not having turned on one light. He didn't even try to go to sleep the rest of the night. Lying awake, Jake tried to anticipate every question that his father would ask and then formulated an answer—the truth, of course. But there are ways of telling the truth that can soften the impact of strictly raw data. He also contemplated the penalty for the act as well. The penalty phase of this ordeal might not be known tomorrow. It may be after the estimate for the repair to the Tempest comes. That could take days. The more it cost to fix, the greater the punishment. *"OK, I know how I'm gonna approach this thing,"* he thought as he rolled over to look at the clock—6:30 a.m.

His father would be up sitting at the kitchen table, having coffee and reading the paper. It was a familiar view from Jake's perspective. On the table was a steaming cup of black coffee next to the soft pack of Lucky Strike cigarettes. The newspaper that covered everything else, except his thick fingers grasping each side, quivered as he breathed. The smoke from his cigarette streamed up from behind and over the top of the paper forming a cloud at the ceiling. His father loved Saturday mornings. On Saturday his office didn't open until 9:30 a.m. and that gave him time to relax before starting the grind. Usually this was the best time to talk to him. So Jake marched right up and said. "Dad, I messed up mom's Tempest last night," completely disregarding the strategy to supplement the raw data.

Jake's father 's newspaper was covering his face at the time, but without much delay the newspaper slowly descended revealing the look. Yes, the look. He had a look he gave to any one of his four children upon seeing or hearing of their misdeeds. The 'look' consisted of the piercing eyes looking over his glasses that he placed a little lower on his nose with his right hand just for this purpose. "You did what?" he said, not as if he didn't hear Jake—No. He was really asking for details.

"Well, I did a really stupid thing. I was on Woodward last night eating at the A&W. So on the way back, I pulled a hole shot at a light and messed up the transmission I think. It only goes in low. There's a sound that it makes in drive and it won't move in drive. Whatever it costs, I'll pay it, if it takes me all year. It was my fault and I'm really very sorry." Jake kept talking to get it all out at once so that the anguish of the story being prolonged by a series of slowly probing and meticulous fatherly questions would hopefully be avoided.

"So, what were you doing at the A&W last night? I thought you were playing out at 'The Fire Place'."

That was not a question that Jake had anticipated. "Well, we finished a little early at 'The Fire Place' and since we didn't have to pack up, we thought we'd go get a bite to eat. It was sort of a celebration. Tom had just sold his car and…"

"So Tom was with you?" his father inquired with a hint of protest in his voice.

"Yes, and Darryl, Doug and Dan too. We all went out to get something to eat." Jake correctly decided not to tell the story of the race that was avoided.

"Tom has an influence over you that I'm not so sure I'm happy with," his father revealed, in what seemed like an effort to somehow shift the blame from his son, the guilty party, and place it on Tom. Maybe he didn't think his son could do something so stupid without the encouragement of some hooligan as he liked to call bad kids. Which, of course, Tom was not. "Everything is, 'Tom said this', and 'Tom is teaching me that' and 'Tom's gonna be a big rock star some day'. I think you're going down the wrong road with that Tom, Jacob. You better keep your nose clean. You've got one more year before you're going to college and yes you are going to college. I *am not* going to let Tom's influence over you ruin those plans, son. Do you hear me?"

"Sure dad, but Tom didn't..."

"I really have heard all I want to hear from you right now. I'll be taking the car into the dealership today and I'll give you a copy of the bill when it's been repaired." His father calmly but deliberately folded up the newspaper, laid it down by his empty coffee cup, rose from the kitchen table and walked off shaking his head forgetting his cigarette, still burning in the ashtray.

Jake reached over the folded newspaper to crush out his father's forgotten cigarette. "OK dad," Jake offered sheepishly, wondering if his father heard him. And that was all Jake said because he knew from experience that any more discussion after the punishment was handed out could result in added penalties. He felt bad that he was afraid to properly defend Tom. The good thing was that he got off easy. He could have pulled the plug on his rock and roll career right then and there. Jake thought his father might have considered the fact that Jake was making a surprisingly substantial contribution to the college fund from playing in the band. The simple fact was, the band was a really good job for a kid like him back then. His father's practicality regarding economics must have saved him that morning.

CHAPTER 7

▼

Detroit Metropolitan Airport was bustling the day Dan came to collect Tom. Travelers laden with baggage were lined up for their turn with one of the many busy ticket agents. The seats were all filled with the weary while their children ran everywhere, weaving among unsuspecting pedestrians. Dan peered up at one of the monitors showing the arriving flights, their time of arrival and expected gate number. He was holding a scrap of paper on which he'd written the flight number and time. Assured that Tom's plane was on time he headed for the baggage area to meet him.

Dan had a spring in his step today. He was looking forward to seeing Tom after so many years. Dan followed Tom's career with great interest and they would call each other once or twice a year to catch up. Tom regularly mailed Dan promotional items from each tour—a pin, a T-shirt, posters and such. Even though Jake and Tom were best friends in high school, Dan was the one who knew Tom best now. Dan was wearing an old black ball cap that Tom sent him over twenty years ago that displayed the letters TT in front. It was a promotional item for one of the many rock tours Tom had done. He thought Tom would get a charge out of seeing that he'd kept it. He had kept this and each and every item Tom sent him.

Since 9/11, people coming to the airport to pick up travelers were no longer allowed to wait for them at the gates. As Dan made his way to the baggage claim, he noticed that the line of passengers passing through metal detectors was long, but seemed to stream along quickly. As Dan watched the busy airport security, he thought how this country had changed since 9/11. He, like everyone in America, was changed. With Dan, he became closer to his wife. He stopped letting work get in the way of their relationship. He had been up for a promotion that would have taken the family away from their hometown again and put him on a seventy-hour-work-week. He was contemplating taking the position when the towers were hit. Within two weeks Dan turned it down and that's when the change took hold. In fact it wasn't only his wife he began to appreciate more, it was all human beings. It truly was a life changing experience for him.

Dan continued down the long corridors and rode the pedestrian conveyer each time he got a chance. After what seemed like a mile of walking and riding the conveyer, he finally arrived and took his place among the other people waiting. From the monitor above, he knew that Tom's plane had arrived. One by one the 190 passengers streamed slowly into the baggage claim area. Tom wasn't flying first class so he finally appeared near the end of the procession.

When Dan saw him, he stood up and walked up to Tom, waited for him to put down his carry on and gave him a big bear hug. "Good to see ya, Tom."

"Good to see you too, Danny-boy."

"How was the flight?" Dan asked, getting the small talk out of the way.

"It was good. I got some sleep." To Tom it was only about 8:30 a.m. California time and he had been flying for about four hours. A 4:30 a.m. flight to Detroit could be brutal, but it was a lot less expensive.

"Are you hungry?" Dan asked.

"As a matter of fact, I am. I slept through the meal."

"Well, on the way down here, I noticed a few restaurants where we can get a burger and a beer. Lets grab your luggage and then we'll get somethin' to eat."

"Sounds great."

As Dan and Tom walked toward the baggage carousel, Dan noticed that occasionally a few people would look their way and point. No one actually approached Tom to say hello or ask for an autograph, but Dan was sure these people recognized Tom. *I bet they think I'm someone famous too. Hey, this is pretty cool,* he thought to himself.

They found Tom's one suitcase without much trouble and were soon in Dan's car headed for the restaurant. "Hey, thanks again for pickin' me up and lettin' me stay with you and Patty. I've really been lookin' forward to seein' you all again."

"So have we," Dan added. "Hey are you gonna need a car while you're here?"

"No. I got that handled. My band manager will be droppin' a rental off for me at my Mom's tonight so if you don't mind, I'd like to spend tonight with her."

"Not at all, man. How's your mom doing, by the way?" Dan added, feeling that he should have asked about her much earlier.

"She's doin' fine. She's movin' to a new seniors complex right in Waterford. She said it's really a nice place. I know she'll miss the house though." Tom was raised mainly by his mother and older sister who took care of him in between part time jobs. Tom's dad passed away early in Tom's life so he had it pretty tough as a kid. The rest of the guys in the band all had the normal suburban life styles with two parents, father who worked, mother who took care of the kids and two cars in the garage.

They pulled into the bar/restaurant and took a quiet booth so they could drink some beer and do some catching up. The place was empty. They knew that wasn't always a good sign in a search for good food. But they were looking for privacy, and they figured that empty is about as private as it gets. The place smelled as if they didn't regularly clean up beer that spilt on the carpet. Both Dan and Tom were used to places like this. The old 'Dan' had spent a lot of time in the bars as a way 'to keep his sanity' as he put it. Funny, he hadn't been in a bar for almost a year now.

Tom had many meetings in these bar room booths with bar owners to plan performances and talk money when he was between managers. The comfort of the environment was conducive to productive reacquainting, so they got right down to it. "So Tom, what's it like being you?" Dan wanted to know if he was talking to the Tom he used to know.

Tom said, "It ain't for everybody that's for sure Danny boy. The road has made it hard, but I love singin', I love the applause, and I really don't know anything else."

"Tell me the truth. Are you happy doin' what you're doin'?"

"I do love it. I really don't know what I'd do with myself if I weren't singin'. I know some day I'll have to give it up. I just hope it's later rather than sooner." Tom was looking straight into Dan's eyes when he talked and that confirmed for Dan that Tom was the same person inside that left town so long ago. Tom always had a way of making whoever he was with feel like the most important person in the world. The little things he did when he was talking made them feel he was interested in what they had to say. He had a good memory and would bring up points they had made in the past that they wouldn't have expected him to pick up on much less remember. And he would want to talk to them about what they said and what they meant by it, all with that eye contact that made them feel connected to him like a brother. He would always listen to their questions and give them straight answers. Just the fact that he turned his cell phone off when he sat down in the booth told Dan he hadn't changed.

"So, I noticed your hat. I sent that what…maybe twenty or so years ago, from one of the tours. I bet you don't remember, but that hat was for Patty, not you," Tom pointed out.

Dan thought for a moment and said, "Are you sure? I remember you sent me a letter with it but now I guess I couldn't tell ya, for sure, why you sent me this. Really? It was for Patty?"

Tom put his hand out for Dan to give him the hat. Dan took it off and handed it to him with a puzzled look. Tom took the hat and pointed at the under side of the brim. There was an inscription that said, 'To Patty from Tom Tyler. Get well soon.'

"Remember? Patty was in the car accident and broke her leg. She was in a cast for six weeks."

Dan put his head down and shook it in disbelief. "Yeah, I do remember now." While he thought, *"I shoulda been the one to remember that."* Changing the subject Dan asked, "Tell me what things you're plannin'. Are you doin' any recordin'?"

Tom, with a hopeful look said, "I'd like to do more recordin' than I have lately. I've done some backup studio work for a few newer artists. That's always fun. But, I'd really like to do one more album before too long. I'm not gettin' any younger as you can see." Tom still called them 'albums' that showed his age too.

Dan asked, "What's keepin' you from doin' it?" not really having a clue why he couldn't just go to a studio and cut a record.

"Lots of issues. Good affordable material is hard to come by. Record labels don't seem to be lookin' for old rock and rollers lately, so it's hard to get the support you need from any of 'em."

"What about settin' up your own web site and sellin' recordings that way?"

"Well, believe it or not, I'm lookin' into that and should have somethin' up and runnin' soon." Although he didn't show it, Tom was getting a little uncomfortable with the questions because the answers weren't the ones he'd like to be reporting. So he asked Dan, "Tell me about Darryl and Doug. Do you stay in touch with those guys?"

"No. I haven't heard from 'em in years. I hear Doug is a Dr. somewhere in Florida and Darryl's somewhere out west."

"I miss those guys. We sure had fun back then," Tom recalled. "Tell me about Jake. I know you said you wouldn't be surprised if he retired soon. Has he done anything with music since high school?"

"Not one thing that I know of. At golf yesterday, I was surprised to find out that his friend David didn't even know he was in the band. He's been friends with David for at least ten years," Dan reported.

"You know, I miss the times he and I had. We were so tight back then. We did everything together. I thought we'd be close like that forever. Funny how close friends drift apart. How we let geography and careers get in the way of that friendship." Tom expressed his puzzlement. "It's hard to think of Jake any way than how he was in high school. He seemed to make everything we did in the band, well…fun. He didn't seem to have one worry in the world. And the music seemed to come so easy for him too. Man, the dreams we had. He was gonna write the songs. I was gonna sing 'em and we were gonna be rich and famous. He sure was wild, idealistic, and imaginative."

And Dan added, "And now he's rational, realistic and reasonable. All good traits though—just different."

"Yeah, about 180 degrees different," Tom revised.

"You know, his dad had a lot to do with his goin' to college and then into real estate. He probably was concerned, like any parent would be, for his kid's future. And now he's achieved the American dream—a home, a business, a great wife, and the health to enjoy what he and Joyce have worked so hard for all theses past years. I think his dad just forced him to grow up."

"You're right, Dan. All those times I tried to get him motivated to write songs—I was probably in a tug of war with his dad."

"It's only natural for a guy like that to do what his parents want, even though he had a lot of faith in you," Dan said.

"Back then I put a lot of faith in him too," Tom remembered

Dan got up and said, "I'm gonna hit the can. Be right back."

As Dan left Tom thought about the faith Jake and Tom had in each other when it came to friendship and music. He thought back to the night they all got snowed in at the 'Silverbell Hideout'.

CHAPTER 8

▼

None of the band members ever listened to weather reports. If there was a date to play out, that's what they would plan for. No contingencies. So when Mother Nature began piling the snow over the roads like someone layering icing on a cake, no one seemed a bit concerned. They just trudged on through the snow and ice, coatless and gloveless in their Beatle boots and polka dot shirts, hauling the band equipment from the station wagon and the trunks of their cars into the 'Silverbell Hideout #5'. Once the equipment was safely inside, and the snow shaken off their heads, the band members with their footwear in hand looked for heat registers so they could warm up and dry out.

Without a thought to the duration of the storm, they set up as patrons of like mind swarmed into the parking lot and through the front doors of the 'Hideout'. The rest of the band was on stage plugging in, tuning up and testing their P. A. system, while Tom sat alone in the lounge going over the words to a song that 'The Phogg' was working on. He looked through the window and noticed a very long very black 1966 Lincoln Continental with suicide doors pulling up to the entrance of the 'Hideout'. The driver dressed in a long black cashmere overcoat, black silky scarf and chauffeur's cap got out and opened the rear door. A very short balding man in his late thirties or early forties dressed the same as the driver except for the cap, materialized from the back seat through the thick veil of swirling snow.

Tom thought it odd that a man his age and apparent wealth could enjoy the teenage brand of music being offered. Tom's interest waned and he returned to the words of the song. Having committed them to memory, he folded the paper and picked up one of the many unfinished songs that Jake had written. The words *Suburban Blues* posted at the top were scrawled out in pencil and barely legible, having been compromised by the wet snow. This song was about a guy from suburbia who was tormented because he wanted to write a blues tune. But because he had an easy suburban life and had never been exposed to any poverty or suffering that would inspire a blues tune, he couldn't write it. Although it remained unfinished for almost two years, Tom thought its clever premise made it one of Jake's best attempts yet.

Soon Dan came in to let Tom know that he had ten minutes until show time. This had been a ritual between Tom and Dan for the last year or so. Dan knew that Tom liked to get psyched up for the show and needed a little time to get into the zone. So Dan took the job of giving Tom the heads up. Tom would thank Dan, lean back, close his eyes and usually imagine he was Otis Redding, Roy Orbison or maybe Joe Cocker working the crowd. Tonight for some reason, he decided to be Tom Tyler working the crowd. It worked. He was up for the show when he heard Darryl's introduction and ran up on stage.

The crowd was electric that night. Perhaps the kids in the thundering crowd were just glad to be in where it was warm and dry. Perhaps they were happy to be done with school and looking forward to the weekend. Tom didn't know what it was, but they were the best audience he'd experienced in a long time. And that made Tom want to be the best he could be—and he was.

Before the last song of the set the 'Silverbell Hideout' management had announced that everyone should think about leaving early due to the snowstorm. The storm was not letting up and the roads were getting worse by the minute. Jake knew that the band wouldn't get all their pay if they didn't play the three sets that they had contracted for, so he had and idea. Jake turned to the band as the kids started for the front doors and the long bank of pay phones to call their rides. Jake told Tom and the band to play one they had been working on, *Let's Spend the Night Together* by the 'Rolling Stones'. This was the flip side of their hit *Goodbye Ruby Tuesday*. Many in the crowd decided to postpone their exodus for just one more tune. And when the band sang the chorus, 'Let's spend the Night together now,' they made it their theme song for the evening and stayed without regard to the storm.

As the song wound down, Tom noticed the man he'd seen, through the window, earlier. He was standing in the back of the crowd intently watching 'The Phogg' perform. Tom was again reminded of how he thought this man looked so out of place. The song ended and their first set was over.

The snow had impeded the plans of those that chose to leave. There were several cars in the parking lot stuck in the snow. Tom went back to his spot in the lounge to look out the window at the struggling crowd all lit up by the full moon, while he waited for Dan to give him the heads up for the next set. Cars were creeping and sliding as they were being pushed over thick globs of wet snow by their intended passengers who were being sprayed relentlessly with slush by the spinning tires. The exhaust from all the cars rose up through the thickening snow and made the parking lot look like a miniature factory town with all their smokestacks simultaneously engaged. Tom was immersed in the winter parking lot Capades for about twenty minutes when the man in the black coat approached him from behind.

Except for the light from the one window, the room was dark and the pillars that held the building up cast shadows everywhere. "Those kids risked getting snowed in just to hear you sing, Tom," the gentleman remarked.

Tom hadn't heard the man enter the lounge and was surprised that there was anyone watching him. Tom hadn't noticed Dan, who had followed the man into the lounge. Dan didn't want to interrupt so he stood in the shadows and waited. As the conversation continued, Dan thought he should leave but didn't want to move and make a sound that would give him away. So he stayed and listened. "Well, I don't think anyone really thought the snow was gonna be this bad," Tom humbly remarked.

"No, they were headed for the phones and putting their coats on and getting ready to go when you started singing again. And they stopped what they were doing and were drawn back to you as if you had cast some kind of spell just for them."

"Well...no. Actually our rhythm guitar player figured we weren't gonna get our full pay if we didn't do somethin' to keep 'em here. So he thought that song would do it. How do ya know my name?"

"It wasn't the song," the man said, "It was how you sang it. And for that matter, how you have been singing now for the last year."

Tom got a little nervous and instinctively stood up and looked around the room for an exit just in case. "You know me?" Tom asked in surprise.

"I've been following you and many of the Detroit area groups now for some time. My name is Maurie Best," the man said as he handed Tom a business card. "I've put together a band, hand picked from the groups I've been following. They are all on my payroll. I just acquired the rights to a song written by Chase Richardson that I think will be a real big hit. It's good enough to go national overnight. It's called *What's the Point?* and I'm calling the band, 'It's About Time'. I want you to be the lead singer."

Tom's legs went a little weak so he sat back down. He certainly had heard the name Chase Richardson many times before. He was a prominent songwriter with a following. The lights from the parking lot beamed through the window illuminating his business card. It read Maurie Best Promotions, Inc. Maurie Best President. Tom thought that this guy must be for real with the big Lincoln, the driver and the suicide doors and all. "Wow!" was all he could come up with at the moment. Then his eyes narrowed and gave his thoughts away. As Maurie Best watched, Tom's face changed from surprise to a conciliatory frown, and he knew that Tom wouldn't be joining his band.

Tom spoke politely and with all the respect a person like Mr. Best was due. "Thanks for the offer, Mr. Best but I already have a band—'The Phogg'. We've got a songwriter too. And he's good. He'll be finishin' up on somethin' very soon and my goal is to be singin' his tunes in the very near future." Tom extended his hand and repeated his appreciation for the offer.

At that Maurie Best said kindly, "I applaud your loyalty to and your faith in your friends Tom, but I think you may be making one of the biggest mistakes of your life." Mr. Best shook Tom's hand, smiled a little sadly, turned and walked away. Tom put his head down and pretended to look out the window as he left. The offer he had received was slowly sinking in. Sinking into Tom and Dan too, who was still standing unnoticed. Dan couldn't believe what he'd just heard. Tom turned down a big band promoter to stay with 'The Phogg'. He wanted to talk to Tom about what just happened but thought better of it. *"This may be somethin' Tom'll want to keep to himself,"* he thought. So Dan waited an appropriate amount of time. Tom's usual pre show ten minutes for psyching up had passed so he couldn't give Tom the normal heads up. Dan walked up to Tom and said, "Sorry I'm late. It's show time. We better get goin'."

CHAPTER 9

▼

"We better get goin'," Tom heard Dan say again as he came out of his daydream of that night at 'The Hideout'. "Are you OK?" Dan asked as Tom slowly came back to the present.

"Yeah, I'm OK. I was just rememberin' the night we got snowed in at the 'Silverbell Hideout'. Do you remember that night?" Tom asked.

"Oh yeah," Dan replied, "That was the night Jake broke up with his girlfriend, the night I met Patty and the night you got Ah..." Dan stopped in his tracks. He was about to say, *"The night you got the offer from Maurie Best,"* but he remembered just in time that Tom didn't know that Dan knew about it. And since Tom didn't know that Dan had been eavesdropping that night, Dan had to make up something fast.

Tom said, "The night I what?" with more than a little curiosity in his voice.

"The night you got so drunk we had to walk you around in the snow till the sun came up," Dan reported nervously.

In disbelief, Tom said, "I don't remember that."

Dan said, "Of course you wouldn't, you were drunk at the time and it was thirty-five years ago." Skillfully reorganizing the subject matter, Dan continued, "Hey, I almost forgot to tell ya. Joyce and Patty are plannin' a party at our house after your show on Saturday. Jake's friend David and his wife Janet, Rick and Carolyn, will be there too. I hope you don't mind."

"Mind? I can't wait to see everybody. That'll be great!" Tom raved. And the subject of the 'Silverbell Hideout' was closed.

Dan was relieved that Tom didn't question him further on what he knew about that night. It was ancient history. But Maurie Best became one of the most prominent and publicized music moguls in the business. And the band that got him there was 'It's About Time' and yes their first of many big hits was, *What's the Point?*. And no, Dan had never heard Tom ever mention to anyone that Maurie Best gave him first shot at being the lead singer. Dan thought, *"That's got to be tough to carry around with you all these years."* The two paid the check and headed out to drop Tom at his mother's house.

As they turned off the highway onto the street where Tom grew up, both were filled with memories of their high school days. All the members of the band loved Tom's mom. She always encouraged them to gather at the house and stay as long as they wanted. Tom's garage was where they originally practiced. When Darryl joined the band, the practices were moved to his house because he had a basement. This allowed the band to practice all year round. Dan always thought that Mrs. Tyler would have preferred that the practices weren't moved because she missed all the commotion. Dan missed meeting at Tom's house but being able to practice more was a much needed benefit. And as it turned out, Darryl's parents were great supporters of the band too.

Mrs. Tyler really encouraged Tom and the members of the band to do their best and work hard at becoming professional even after the band moved to Darryl's. Maybe she saw talent in Tom and the group. Maybe it was because she knew she couldn't afford to send Tom to college. Well whatever the reason, she had done good with Tom.

As they pulled into the gravel driveway of the modest white wooden 1929 bungalow, they both noticed the For Sale sign in the front yard exhibiting a SOLD sticker. Even though they both knew that Tom's mom was only moving, they turned and looked at each other as if they were going to a funeral. Tom said with a telltale frog in his throat, "There were some great times in this house, Dan."

"I know. Do you remember when Jake and I'd ride your bus from school on the days we rehearsed?"

"Yeah, I was just thinkin' the very same thing. You've got to come in and say hi to mom," Tom demanded, knowing that he couldn't keep Dan from coming in anyway.

As they walked up the steps, Tom's mom came to the door, opened it and greeted them both as if they had just gotten off the school bus. "Tom, you need a hair cut. And that beard! What am I going to do with you? And Danny, oh my goodness, Danny. Is that really you?" she said as she hugged them both at once.

"Yea Mrs. Tyler, it's me. How have you been?" Dan asked.

"Well, I can't think when I've been better. How are Patty and the kids?" she asked to Dan's surprise. Dan didn't know she knew about Patty and the kids. Tom must have kept his mom up to date.

Dan said, "They're all fine."

"Well you boys come in and sit down. I've got some roast beef in the fridge. I'll make you two a sandwich. Would you like some ice tea? I just brewed it this morning. Dan, you like yours with sugar, right?"

"Right. You remembered," Dan said. Neither Dan nor Tom was hungry, having just come from lunch. But neither wanted to disappoint her by turning down her offer. So they both ate lunch again. As they ate Tom got the details of his mother's pending sale and the planned move to the senior housing complex.

She said to both Tom and Dan, "I'm looking forward to the move, but I'll miss this house. We've had so many good times here and all. It's just so hard for me to keep it up. The place needs paint inside and out. New windows would cost a fortune, you know. And I'll be getting a brand new place where all the work is done for me."

"Yeah, It sounds like you're doin' the right thing, Mom. Can I help you to get ready while I'm home?" Tom offered.

"I've got the movers scheduled and they'll take care of everything except your things out in the garage. I was hoping you could take what you want before I have the yard sale."

"OK mom, I'll get on it right after lunch," Tom agreed as if he were still her boy in high school.

After lunch Dan said his goodbyes to Mrs. Tyler and Tom for the time being, so that Tom could get busy in the garage. Tom lifted the double garage door expecting to see tools, yard equipment, old pieces of lumber, and lots of miscellaneous. But there was nothing at all like that in the garage. It was as empty as a donut hole with the exception of a four-foot square area in the middle of the floor. That's where Tom's mom had someone stack Tom's belongings. There were cardboard boxes filled with everything from Tom's childhood and teen years. From kindergarten crayon drawings to old 45's and record albums. There were black plastic bags filled with clothes, model cars, sports equipment and even old toys. There was some music equipment too—his old microphone stand, his old Dan Electro guitar and a Fender Princeton amplifier.

Tom was curious if the old guitar and amplifier worked. So he sat down on the amplifier while he tried to tune the guitar. After getting it pretty close, he went to the back storage compartment of the amplifier for the cord to plug it in and to see if there was a cord for the guitar as well. While looking for the cords in the back of the amplifier, Tom pulled out two brown legal sized envelopes that had been rolled up to fit in the back compartment. He tossed them aside and found the cords he was looking for. Once plugged in, Tom began to play the guitar. Even though Tom didn't play an instrument in 'The Phogg', he had taught himself guitar, the bass guitar, piano and harmonica over the years. His mom had always preached to him about being well rounded and versatile. Tom's interpretation of that message was to get well rounded and versatile in music, even though he really knew her statements were meant in more general terms. Nevertheless, Tom had been able keep up with the best of them on those instruments. He debated, *"Do I keep the guitar and amplifier and try to get it back to California or do I let my mom sell it in the garage sale?"* Having no immediate answer he put the guitar down and started to go through the rest of his belongings.

Then it occurred to him. He had given the amplifier to Jake not quite forty years ago. Jake had given it back to Tom right before he left for college. *"So, I wonder what's in those big envelopes?"* he thought. He turned around to look for them on the floor among the plastic garbage bags, spotted them and picked them up. He sat back down on the amplifier to get comfortable. After unrolling the dusty faded envelopes he reached in and pulled out a stack of old lined school paper with words written there in pencil, like poems. No, they were songs. As Tom carefully leafed through the pages he came upon one page with the words *Suburban Blues* at the top, somewhat faded and water stained.

Tom remembered reading the verses that night at the 'Silverbell Hideout'. He hadn't thought of that night for years and now twice in one day he was reminded. There were twenty-two songs in all—none of them finished or even signed. He knew they were Jake's, of course. He picked up *Suburban Blues* again and read the two verses he had there and no chorus. *"The chorus was always Jake's downfall. The chorus is what holds a song together. It's the common thread that stitches the song into one cohesive piece. Why this part was so hard for Jake to conquer, I'll never know,"* Tom thought. The day Tom gave the amplifier to Jake was the same day he first heard these few verses to the song.

It was sometime in August of 1964. Tom was late for practice at Darryl's house that afternoon. It wasn't common for Tom to be late, but he had to make a stop first. He'd been on a mission to keep Jake in the band. It was early in 'The Phogg's existence and they were only at the practicing stage. Jake wasn't able to afford the proper equipment he needed to be a member of 'The Phogg'. Yes, he did have a great guitar. But that was all he could afford at the time. Even though he still worked at the record shop and cleaned his dad's office, his father was holding back a portion of the money to pay for Jake's college. Therefore, he hadn't saved up enough money to get a suitable amplifier. He had been plugging into the second channel of Darryl's Twin Reverb since he joined the band. This wasn't acceptable for the sound they wanted to project and the rest of the band had finally put a consolidated foot down. The ultimatum had been issued. Get an amplifier of your own, or be fired.

Tom and his mom drove up the driveway to Darryl's house. It was about four-thirty in the afternoon, but the sky was so dark that it seemed like nine-thirty. Rain was pelting the hood of his mom's car so hard that even the radio couldn't be heard. Tom's mom turned off the ignition so that she could give Tom the keys. She said, "Tom, put your parka hood on and try to stay dry." Tom accepted the keys so that he could get the cargo from the trunk, put the parka hood over his head, unlatched the passenger side door, and paused as if to mentally prepare for the impending shower that awaited him.

His mom took that opportunity to ask one more time, "Tom, are you sure you want to do this?"

"He'd do it for me, Mom," Tom replied as he pushed open the car door and ran around to the trunk, fumbled with the piece of chrome hinged over the trunk lid's key hole, and opened the trunk. As if he had rehearsed every move, he ran to the driver's side door and handed his mom the keys through the vent window so his mom wouldn't get wet. She gave him a barely visible wave from behind the foggy droplet covered window. Tom ran to the back of the car and with one hand pulled a Fender Princeton amplifier from the trunk, slammed the trunk closed with the other and lugged it to the shelter of the back porch of Darryl's house. His mom backed down the drive as Tom went inside.

No one heard Tom come in. There was a lot of commotion in the basement. Tom set the amp down on the landing of the basement stairs, took off his parka and shook the water out of his hair. He carried the amplifier down the stairs and set it just outside the practice room. Jake was playing the song he had been working on. Tom entered the room as Jake was singing DA, DA, DA, DA, DAA, DA, DA. As a substitute for the words to the chorus he hadn't yet written. The song ended and Jake said, "What do you think of it so far?"

Darryl took the lead for the group and cut to the chase, "Look Jake, that may be a fine tune, some day, but this isn't about your songwriting or the way you play guitar. You're good, man. It's about you, not having the equipment. You know we can't play out and sound good with both of us plugging into my amplifier. You need your own amp, man. You were supposed to have one by today and ya don't. So we've got no choice but ta find someone else—someone with his own amp. I'm sorry, man. I wish things were different." Darryl hung his head and turned to see Tom standing behind him. Darryl looked at Tom as if he'd lost his best friend, shrugged, and looked away. The commotion had subsided and no one said a word as Jake unplugged his guitar from Darryl's amplifier.

Just then Tom casually spoke as he slid the amplifier in from behind the doorway. "Hey Jake, I picked up your amp for ya. Why don't ya try it out?"

Everyone in the room turned and looked at Tom and then at the amplifier and then at Jake and then back at Tom. Jake hadn't mentioned that he was getting an amplifier today. But no one cared about that. They were elated that Jake was staying in the band. Dan spoke up and said, "Jake, that's a nice one. Hey we're burnin' daylight. We've got some songs to work on."

Darryl had a better idea, "While Tom and Jake set the amp up, lets see if there's anything in the fridge." That room cleared out as if someone yelled "fire".

After the guys left, Jake said, "Tom where did you get this?"

"Pawn shop—picked it up today."

"Thanks, Tom. Hey, I have money in lay-away at Pontiac Music and Sound on a Super Reverb, but I'm not even halfway to paying it off. I'll get my money back and give that to you tomorrow and I can make payments to you till this is paid off. OK?"

"Jake, keep paying on your Super Reverb. If I'm right about our band, you'll be needin' it pretty soon.

"How'd you come up with the money to get this?"

"Oh, I've got a friend at the pawn shop who owed me a favor and he let me have it."

"What do you mean, he let you *have* it? Nobody lets you *have* a perfectly good two hundred dollar amplifier. What's going on Tom? I wanna give you the money you spent on this."

Tom grabbed Jake by the shoulders and gave him a friendly shake. A shake that rattled Jake's skinny frame, to emphasize the point he was about to make. "Listen to me! It's not about the money." Tom let go of Jake, switched on the amplifier and said, "Well…play something."

Like a kid with a brand new toy, Jake was at a loss. "What should I play?"

"That song you were playin' when I came in. And by the way, you better finish that song or I'm takin' the amp back."

Jake began to play, his face displaying serious contemplation. But as he progressed with the tune, the contemplation faded and a big smile formed in its place. Tom picked up the paper with the words that Jake had written, turned to the microphone and sang them as the rest of the band appeared, manned their instruments and joined in. It was a good practice.

Tom found himself sitting in the garage with no work done. *"I wonder if Jake would appreciate havin' this amplifier? I'm sure he'd want the songs. I'll worry about the rest of this stuff later."*

CHAPTER 10

▼

The Big Lake Road closing was taking place at the buyer's attorney's office in Birmingham, Michigan. Even though it was a 1.5 million dollar transaction, Jake thought it was a little pushy on the part of the purchaser's attorney to insist that the closing be held at his office to the inconvenience of all the other parties needing to attend. There was the mortgage representative, the title company closing agent, the purchaser, the purchaser's broker, the sellers, and Jake. Jake had planned to object to this tactic and told his client. He knew from experience that when a purchaser or his representative insisted on any particular closing venue, it was because they wanted home court advantage. Having home court advantage made it easier for the purchaser's representative to intimidate the sellers if they found it necessary. But the seller said that he didn't want to make an issue of something as unimportant as the place where the closing was held.

The attorney's office building was one of the most conspicuously opulent buildings Jake had ever seen. He didn't want to appear to be a bumpkin. He had to force himself not to gaze up at the twelve-foot high mahogany paneled ceilings, supported by mahogany walls, accented with huge gold-framed oil landscapes. It was even harder not to be in awe of the Italian marble floor that covered every inch of the place, as they were led into one of several gigantic conference rooms. They were invited to sit down at a large granite conference table surrounded by plush leather executive type swivel chairs. At one end of the room sitting on top of an antique buffet was a silver service for twelve set up and in operation for the occasion.

The closing seemed to be going along fine. Jake had attended to all the particulars well in advance. Even though he had been neglecting his people skills on occasion, his attention to the detail of a closing had not suffered. He had personally seen to it that all the changes in the agreement had been followed up with fully signed addendums. Every nuance of the transaction had been tied down in writing. Jake had meticulously flyspecked all the closing documents in advance and previewed the documents personally with the sellers the day before. All calculations were accurate. There was no stone left unturned. No surprises. That's how Jake handled all his transactions.

The title company's closing agent, who presided over the closing, was carefully explaining the mortgage document to the purchaser and his pinstriped attorney, a Mr. John Klein. The sellers had not yet signed their documents. Jake was listening to the sellers articulate their plans for the home up north in a whisper so as not to disrupt the purchaser's discussion with the closing agent. They were all moved out of Big Lake Road and had the keys and the garage door remote controls to their soon to be former home laying on the closing table in front of them. It was obvious that they were happy to be moving and were anxious to get on the road up north to their retirement home.

As the last mortgage document was signed, the title agent placed it to her left face down on top of the two-inch thick stack of freshly signed closing documents. As the closing agent picked up the closing statement in order to clarify it for the purchaser prior to signing, Mr. Klein, his attorney interrupted with a comment as he placed his heavily gold ring-laden fingers on the document. "There is just one small item that my client would like to remedy before we finalize our purchase today."

As Mr. Klein spoke, the sellers ended their discussion of the place up north to listen with some concern. Jake calmly looked up but instantly knew full well that this dirt bag was planning on pulling something. Jake knew that dirt bags can appear in an instant and can take many forms. This one wore a pinstriped suit and gold rings. Most attorneys, just like most real estate agents, are fair and honest and usually only want what's right for their clients. But dirt bags want more than what's right for their client or themselves. They're more interested in "winning". Which means that the other side has to lose something they hadn't counted on. And Jake knew something else. The loss usually would come out of the broker's commission. It was always the easiest target. The aggressor party always figures that the brokers don't want to risk losing all their commission due to a failed closing. So they figure that brokers will generally take less than their previously negotiated fee just to keep the peace. Another calculation they make is that the cost to the broker or seller to hire an attorney to protect their interests would be equal to or more than what they could settle for at the closing table.

While Jake listened, he quickly added up in his head that the attorney probably would be charging the purchaser about five thousand dollars for his services. He'd probably attempt to extract that five thousand dollars from the seller or brokers, for the purchaser. Jake guessed he would be asking for about ten thousand dollars based on some trumped up concern figuring that it would be negotiated down to the five thousand dollars. So Jake waited for the bomb to drop from the mouth of this smartly dressed dirt bag.

"It seems," the dirt bag continued, "that on his walkthrough of the property this morning, my client noticed to his dismay, that the boat dock was severely worn and rotted. This will cost my client approximately twelve thousand dollars to correct. Therefore, we would like to deduct this amount from the purchase price in order to compensate for the problem." The purchaser's broker was listening, in surprise, because he had been on the walkthrough and the purchaser mentioned nothing about the dock. Prior to entering into the purchase agreement, the purchaser had examined the entire property and noticed the rotting dock along with the seller's disclosure form disclosing the condition of the dock in detail. The purchaser's agent also remembered that during negotiations the purchaser had mentioned the dock and that he had intended on removing the old dock and replacing it with the modular dock he currently owned. The purchaser's agent also remembered telling Jake about the modular dock.

Jake remembered all the pertinent facts about the dock and the disclosure and discovery that had taken place prior to the signing of the agreement. This was a clear and quite bold attempt to intimidate the seller or broker to pay for the purchaser's attorney fees. Although no one could tell from his demeanor, Jake was seething with rage. This was at the top of his list of things that he hated about the business, and he made up his mind then and there not to put up with it. So Jake responded to the request made by the purchaser's attorney. "Counselor, I'd like to take my clients out into the lobby to discuss your request."

"Be my guest." Mr. Klein offered, "But just for clarification…it wasn't a request."

"Not a request?" Jake thought. *"You make me sick, you fat pinstriped S.O.B. You think I'm too afraid of not getting paid on this transaction to contest your blackmail tactics. You think I'll frantically beg the seller to agree to this, so that his plans won't be delayed. It's no secret to me that you're using your position as a license to steal. A year or so ago you would have gotten away with it. I would have caved in. I would have folded like a cheap lawn chair and chalked it up to the cost of doing business. But you know what? I'm not afraid anymore. I'm so tired of this business and people like you, that suffering consequences has lost all meaning. Today, I'm gonna kick your ass*

for all the times your kind has put me in this position and for all the times I've caved in to keep the peace." Of course if Jake had said this out-loud he would have lost the needed element of surprise.

As calmly as he would ask someone to pass the salt, Jake said, "I'd like a minute outside with my client and we'll be back shortly." With that, he picked up his file folder, turned to the sellers who, at this point, were not only enraged but baffled at how their smooth closing went to pieces. Jake didn't speak; he only motioned for them to walk toward the door as he did his best to muster up a smile that would reassure them. Jake turned and left the room and the sellers followed. Upon reaching a quiet corner of the palatial lobby, Jake asked his clients to be seated. The husband spoke first. "Jake, we disclosed the condition of the dock in that disclosure form that the purchaser signed. How can they come back and ask us for anything at this point?"

"Technically, they can't—he knows he can't. But they're counting on us to cave in and pay, just so that we can proceed with the closing."

"I can't believe that the purchaser would be a party to this kind of thing. He seemed so nice," the wife lamented.

"It isn't likely that this was the purchaser's idea," Jake assured her. "However, we're left with the decision on what to do about it."

The husband said, "On the one hand, I don't like being taken advantage of. But on the other hand, we've made plans to get up north and if we stay, we go back to a house with no furniture. It's all in the moving van on its way up north. And the amount they're asking is less than one per cent of the purchase price."

"That's true, but the purchaser has all his belongings in a moving van sitting in your old driveway, just waiting for the keys, so he can unload. He's kind of in the same boat. With your permission, I'd like to try something. If it doesn't work, you can stay at my house until we resolve the problem." They listened as he mapped out the simple plan of action.

As they filed back into the conference room, the purchaser's attorney rose from his plush swivel chair. The air was thick with tension. The closing agent from the title company had her pen poised in order to revise the closing statements to reflect the blackmail money. She was waiting to see if Jake would have the guts to try and negotiate the amount down at all. She had seen agents in this position get mad at the request and throw a fit in front of all the attendees. This usually caused the seller and purchaser to be more at odds and they would tend to dig in. Then no solution would be reached without litigation. Sometimes the agent would try to reason with the attorney. That seldom worked because reason was not the basis for the demand in the first place. She knew of no good way for a situation like this to be resolved without the attorney getting his way. The rest of the waiting group was on the edge of their seat wondering how the money was going to be cut up so the closing could proceed.

Jake got to the table first and began picking up the balance of his paperwork. As he calmly and gracefully stacked it neatly and slid it into the file folder he simply said, "My clients have decided not to sell their home to you. We apologize for any inconvenience this may cause the parties involved." The tone in Jake's voice was calm, unaffected, and graceful—similar to the message you might hear on an answering machine. And when he promptly and deliberately turned and left, so did his sellers, carrying the keys and the garage door remotes. The balance of the attendees was astonished at the sellers' decision and their resolve in the matter. The purchaser's attorney fell back into his chair. The closing agent started to gather up all her papers with just a hint of a smile. She had never seen such a simple, bold and direct answer to the blackmail problem. The purchaser's broker wanted to contribute something constructive in order to resolve the crisis but was too upset to speak.

They were at the conference room door when the purchaser yelled out, "Wait! This dock issue isn't all that important to me. If it's a problem for you, why don't we just forget about it? And finish the closing," he pleaded.

Jake looked back over his shoulder toward the purchaser and his now seated attorney and paused for what must have seemed like an eternity to them, and eventually asked, "That OK with you Counselor?"

The purchaser's attorney in a feeble attempt to save face said, "It seems to be all right with my client, so I suppose the issue can be overlooked."

They all resumed where they had left off and let the closing agent finish her job while the attorney excused himself and left the conference room. And just like that, Jake had won. David had defeated Goliath. But, he shouldn't have had to fight in the first place. It was highly distressing to him that such an uncivilized act could occur in such a respectable looking place. Further more, Jake didn't feel like he had won. There was no rush or feeling of euphoria that normally followed that kind of victory. Instead all he felt was emptiness. A void inside created by more than thirty years of the same. He knew then that his days in this line of work were numbered.

CHAPTER 11

▼

Saturday afternoon Tom and his mom were having some iced tea in the kitchen when he heard a car drive up the driveway. Tom said, "That'll be the road manager with the rental car. I should be goin'. I've got a sound check and rehearsal to do before the show tonight."

"All right Tom, I'm glad you could spend some time with me this trip."

"Me too, Mom."

"Thanks for the tickets. I can't wait to see you perform."

Before long, Tom was in his rental car with the satellite radio tuned to his favorite station heading for Meadowbrook for the set up, rehearsal and sound check. He was amazed at the amount of traffic and how it had increased since 'The Phogg' traveled these roads. You could race up and down and barely hit a traffic signal. Now, with all the cars and stoplights you couldn't reach the speed limit, even with all the new lanes that had been added. Meadowbrook wasn't hard to find. There were big green and white signs all along the way offering travelers the proper direction. Then he saw the giant billboard with his name posted next to today's date.

As he turned into the parking lot, he heard a familiar song on the radio. No, it wasn't one of his. It was one by 'It's About Time'. The first song they did, called *What's the Point?* Tom never really liked listening to that song. It reminded him of the chance that was given to him by Maurie Best years ago. And lately he'd been reminded of it too much. He was about to turn the channel when the DJ broke in over the music and reported, "I've got some big news for all you 'It's About Time' fans out there. After almost thirty-five years, everyone's favorite group of all time is going to the Rock and Roll Hall of Fame. That's right, after thirty-five years and thirty platinum albums they've made it. Along with the string of hit tunes supplied by their genius promoter originally from Detroit, Maurie Best, this group is without question one of the greatest legends in American music history. *It's about time* these guys were honored for their contribution to the industry."

The song was still playing when Tom finally turned the station and parked his car. He sat there in the parking lot and listened to the radio playing somewhat appropriately, *You've Always Got the Blues* by Mickey Newbury. Even though Tom had a big list of things to do in preparation for the show, he just couldn't move. He had, over the years, successfully suppressed that night at the 'Silverbell Hideout'. To dwell on such a huge miscalculation could devastate anyone's self-confidence. So he just never indulged himself with the questions. What if he had taken Maurie Best's offer to sing for the group? How would his life be different if he'd just said yes? And now after hearing of the band's entry into the Hall of Fame, he was fresh out of willpower to resist. The slide was almost comforting in sort of a depraved and twisted way as he slipped into a coma of self pity sped along by the sad and hypnotic rhythms of Mickey Newbury. Lucky for Tom that the song was over quickly and the next song was much more hopeful in constitution and cadence. Tom recovered from his coma and soon realized he had his own hand of life's cards and he needed to get back to the business of playing them.

Joyce was in the kitchen frying chicken. And to Jake's surprise it was the unhealthy kind that he loved. It was for the picnic they had planned for the lawn party at Meadowbrook. So Jake knew he wasn't going to get chicken for lunch. He'd just returned from showing some homes and was off for the rest of the weekend. He went straight to the refrigerator, opened the door and stared inside. It usually took fifteen to twenty seconds of peering among the shelves before Joyce would ask if she could make him anything to eat. It didn't work this time. So he began pulling items from the shelves in an attempt to show some intent to make lunch himself. This of course was designed only to get Joyce's attention. "It's a little late for lunch," she finally told him.

"I know, but that showing lasted way longer than it should have and I'm too hungry to wait for the picnic tonight."

"How did your closing go Friday?" Joyce asked while she gathered the ingredients for Jake's lunch.

"Fine," he reported, not wanting to burden Joyce this weekend with more *why I hate this business* talk.

"So yesterday you had the biggest closing you've had in years. You didn't mention it last night when you got home, I ask you about it today, and all you can say is *fine*? What happened at that closing that you're not telling me? Did it close or not?"

"Oh, it closed all right," he said with just enough flair to get Joyce curious.

"What do you mean? Was there a problem?" she probed.

"Let's just say that we almost had the sellers coming here to live with us for an indefinite period."

"Oh no! What happened?"

"The Purchaser's attorney wanted a little blackmail money is all." Jake filled her in on all the gory details of the ordeal and how they had bluffed the attorney.

After the story had been told, Joyce just shook her head and said, "I'd have never guessed you would take a risk like that. Not with what was at stake for both you and the seller. What was your share of the commission on that one, twenty—thirty thousand?"

"Forty-five."

"Forty-five? Forty-five thousand dollars?"

"Yeah."

"You are the Indiana Jones of the real estate business. You basically bet forty-five thousand dollars on the turn of a card," she shrieked in surprise.

Jake tried to correct her perspective on the risk and said, "Well, not Indiana Jones. More like Doc Holiday, I suppose…and not really on the turn of a card. The odds were more like betting forty-five thousand dollars on red at the roulette wheel."

"Whatever got into you, that would cause you to even try such a thing?" she asked with a renewed fascination toward her husband of so many years.

"Well, my dear, I guess I just had one too many bad experiences getting pushed around by that kind of person. You cave into those dirt bags just in order to close the deal and then you walk away from the closing feeling violated and small. Really small," he said as his voice trailed off, as if he were talking to himself. He paused, took a deep breath and continued with renewed authority in his voice, "I just couldn't let that happen to me one more time. And, fortunately for me, the sellers went along for the ride. Fortunately, every thing worked out fine. But a guy really can't afford to operate in a way that puts his client at risk like that, especially for his own twisted sense of satisfaction. Yeah, I won that one, but I don't even want to think about the downside if the plan had failed. And you know Joyce, the way I feel, I'd be tempted to do something like that again. And that's just not the way your friendly neighborhood Realtor should be."

"It's just another reason to try something new," Joyce asserted.

Dan and Patty were busy putting the house in order for their guest of honor and for the party following the Meadowbrook show. Dan was busy skimming the pool, spraying down the lawn furniture and making sure the mosquito zapper was in good working order. Patty was restocking the refrigerator and bar with all the essentials. She could see Dan in the back yard sweating in the sun. *"He still looks pretty good for fifty-three. I think I'll keep him around for a little longer,"* she joked to herself and thought about their marriage and the life that they had shared. She thought about the night they met at the 'Silverbell Hideout' dance.

CHAPTER 12

▼

She had come to the dance with her best friend Denise. They had never been there before and got lost trying to find the place. The snow was worse than predicted and they both harbored visions of being found by bloodhounds at dawn, frozen in a snow bank. Although late getting there, they were excited to see the lights of the parking lot. The plan was to meet two guys that evening. Denise had been dating Roger for about three months and his cousin Eric was up visiting from Pennsylvania. Denise wanted to see Roger that night, but Roger couldn't leave Eric home alone in front of the television while he went on a date. And thus the plan for the double date was hatched. Patty wouldn't have agreed to it for anyone else other than Denise. It just wasn't her style. It did help a little when Denise explained that Eric was tall. Patty being five feet eleven inches was self-conscious about dating guys shorter than herself. Not so much for her sake as her date's. She had mastered every item on the list of things that tall girls don't do to tower over their dates. Never wear heels, never wear your hair up, and if all else fails, slouch a little.

It seemed a little odd that there were so many cars leaving. They had no idea that the 'Silverbell Hideout' management had broadcast the snow warning. As they got out of their car they could hear music coming from the building and figured the party was still going on. As they approached the front door, they spotted a long shiny black Lincoln Continental parked by the front door with the engine running. The driver, dressed in black, was holding the right rear door open for two people who were quickly getting in the back seat. It was an older, rather short balding man with a woman too young for him. She had the longest straight black hair Patty had ever seen. The driver got in and the Lincoln began moving toward them. She remembered thinking that it seemed odd for a car like that to be at a place like the 'Hideout'. They both stood by the curb waiting for the Lincoln to pass by hoping to recognize who was inside. Denise stood close behind her in an effort to stay warm. Patty leaned in a little closer to catch a glimpse of the occupants of the Lincoln as it rolled by, not noticing the deep pothole filled with slush directly in front of her. The huge car slowly drove past her. First the front tire dropped into the pothole with a jarring thud, spraying slush all over her. She was covered with the cold wet dirty slime. Unfortunately her coat was not buttoned and had been flapping in time with her gait toward the curb. Consequently the slush found the front of her brand new, golden brown, sleeveless Patty Woodward corduroy jumper, with the deep U-shaped neckline. She stood paralyzed and horrified just long enough to become the target for the rear tire's volley of slush that glopped a thick second layer on her from head to toe. The slush on her legs slid in a serpentine pattern down into her brown leather boots. Her new white long-sleeve Baltman and Co. lambs wool knit sweater that she wore under the jumper was saturated beyond redemption.

The crowd was so busy leaving that no one but Denise noticed Patty get slushed. As Patty looked down at her outfit she saw globs of frozen ice so completely covering the gold tone buttons on her jumper, that the raised anchors stamped there were no longer visible. She wanted to run back to the car and go straight home, but Denise insisted that they go inside and try to clean her up and get her warm before any decision to leave was made. So Patty walked toward the building with Denise's arm for support. They both stepped in that big pothole together on the way in. Patty did it to demonstrate that nothing could make her feel worse than she did at that moment and Denise, because it was the noble thing to do in support of her friend.

They went through the big entry door together and got the back of their hands stamped after paying the admission fee. The imprint was an illegible mark in lime green glow in the dark ink. She remembered that the kids did their best to preserve the stamp for Monday when they got back to school. It let the other kids know that you were cool. And even if you weren't cool, it showed that your parents did actually let you out once in a while. The girls asked directions and made a beeline for the restroom. Patty went into a stall while Denise stood near by. Then the clothing appeared draped over the stall door. First came the jumper, which Denise gathered up and took over to the sink. She rinsed off the residue of the dirty slush, wrung it out and hung it over the hand dryer. Her lambs wool white knit sweater was next. Denise was more careful with this in order to preserve its shape even though it had been ruined. The panty hose was the last item that came over the stall door. While the clothing was drying on all three hand blowers, Denise was handing soapy paper towels over the stall door so that Patty could wash off the grime that remained after the slush was wiped away. It took a long time to clean and dry everything, including Patty, but forty-five minutes later the two were ready to join the throng.

They emerged from the restroom warm and dry to find about half as many patrons as they expected. Many had fled due to the snowstorm that was now raging. The plan was to meet Roger and Eric at the snack bar. They wove their way around the building looking for the snack bar. Along the way they stopped near the front of the stage to listen to 'The Phogg' sing *You Really Got Me* by the Kinks. With the thinning crowd, it was easy to get a spot up front. Along with most of the other girls in the crowd, Denise had her eyes on Tom and was very impressed by what she saw and heard. Patty had her eye on Tom until she noticed Dan the bass player. The first thing she considered from a practical standpoint was that he towered over the rest of the group. Dan was only six feet, but compared to the rest of the group who averaged five feet six inches, he seemed like a giant. The next thing she noticed was the kindness in his eyes and the quiet confidence he projected. Dan was singing back up through most of the song, but it didn't register with her. Her focus on him became so intense that she couldn't hear the band at all. She would have stayed there indefinitely except for Denise pulling her arm leading her toward the snack bar. Just as Denise grabbed Patty, Dan looked down and noticed Patty being dragged off. Denise said, "Patty, come on, we have to find the guys." Just as they left 'The Phogg' started to play the last song of their last set.

They walked into the snack bar and didn't see Roger or Eric. So they bought two Cokes and described their dates to the cashier. The cashier said she had seen two that fit that description. Unfortunately they left about twenty or thirty minutes ago. "They probably waited as long as they could before getting caught here all night like you two," the cashier informed them.

"What da ya mean, caught here all night?" Denise asked.

"Haven't you girls heard? There's a huge snowstorm and we're right in the middle of it. No one still here is going anywhere tonight."

Denise said, "Well, we can't stay. We have to get outa here. My parents are gonna be insane over this."

"Honey, there's no way out," the cashier explained. All the roads are closed. They'll probably come and dig us out in the morning."

The two looked at each other bewildered and sat down at a booth in the snack bar to map out a plan. "Well first we have to call Roger and let him know where we are and what happened. Then we should call our parents. They're gonna be pretty upset if they aren't already," Denise calculated.

Looking on the bright side, Patty said, "Well, at least it can't get much worse."

At that point a young stocky man with a flashlight walked up to the two girls, briefly examined them sitting there and said, "How did you two get in here tonight?"

Denise and Patty turned and looked at the man gripping the flashlight, which must have commanded a lot of respect at the moment, because the girls both spoke right up, pointed toward the front doors and said, "Through there, sir." They both were a little intimidated by him and a little confused by his question.

"Did you pay to get in?"

They both said, "Yes," and raised their wrists up toward the man's face to show him the lime green glow in the dark stamp they had received earlier.

The man looked down at the back of their hands and said, "OK ladies, very funny, but I'm afraid I'm going to have to ask you to leave the building."

"What for?" they both asked, now more puzzled than ever.

"Well, ladies. It's obvious to me you haven't paid the cover charge and you're going to have to pay or be escorted from the premises."

"But we did pay, sir," Patty repeated. But this time she took a look herself as she offered her wrist to the man once more. The stamp mark was not there. She quickly looked at her other hand. No. Not there either. She grabbed Denise's wrists and looked for any sign of the lime green glow in the dark ink. Gone. "I bet it got washed off when we were cleaning the slush off," she surmised out loud. Patty and Denise began to tell the man about the Long Black Lincoln Continental, the pothole and the slush that ruined her clothes, but he wasn't impressed.

"Yeah, and I think we found your glass slipper in the lost and found too," he said with a smirk, as he holstered his flashlight as if it were a sidearm. He scolded them for sneaking in, with one hand on Patty's shoulder and the other pointing at Denise and then at Patty and then back again. "It's gonna be six bucks—three bucks each if you want to stay. Otherwise, you two are history."

The girls looked at each other dreading being thrown out into the snow with no chance to make it home. They dug into their purses to find two dollars and thirty-seven cents between them. Denise looked at the two cups of Coke on the table. Attempting some dark humor she said, "Well, if we hadn't got the Cokes, one of us could have stayed warm tonight."

Patty didn't see the humor and neither did the man with the flashlight. "Well, ladies, it's time to go," he said as he helped them up from the booth.

"Pete! Hey man! What are ya doing with my girlfriend there, Pete?" The voice came from the snack bar doorway. All three turned to see who was speaking. It was Dan.

Pete, the man with the flashlight said, "Are these girls with you, Dan?"

Patty, all five-feet-eleven of her, stood up out of the booth, and asked in more of a statement than a question, "Who else would we be with?" She looked pretty bad standing there with her clothes all puckered up from her recent slushing. But she looked good to Dan. And that's what really mattered.

Dan looked at Patty and gave her a sly smile as he said to Pete, "And ya have Tom's girlfriend in your other hand Pete."

"Well, I didn't know, Dan, they didn't say they were with the band and they didn't have a stamp. So I just figured they crashed the dance," Pete explained.

Dan said, "You were right to stop 'em. No matter what we do, we can't get these girls to say they're with the band. They say it doesn't project a wholesome image. They probably used the, 'we washed it off' excuse didn't they?"

"Right, they did," Pete said, as if Dan had just made the whole story make sense. "I'm sorry for the inconvenience to you girls. I'll be on my way now. Dan, see that they get stamped. OK?"

"OK Pete," Dan promised.

One of the few perks of being the entertainment for the 'Hideout' was that you could get a limited number of your friends in for free. This was the first time Dan had exercised this privilege but after hearing their exchange with Pete, he could see it was for a worthy cause. Dan said, "Come on girls, let's get ya stamped or re-stamped whichever one it is."

Denise and Patty looked at each other and smiled, not believing their luck, and hurried to catch up with Dan. On the way to get stamped Patty said, "Thanks for helping us out of that jam. I'm Patty and this is Denise. And it really is re-stamped by the way."

Dan said, "I know. No one could make up a story like that on the spot. Hey, we just finished our last set and it's gonna be at least eight hours before we can get out of here, so why don't you girls join us. Tom's grabbin' the band a good spot next to the fireplace."

So they all spent the rest of the night around the fireplace talking and getting to know each other. Dan and Patty were inseparable since that night. And the rest is history, so they say.

CHAPTER 13

▼

God couldn't have created a more beautiful evening for Tom's show. The sun was melting into the horizon and broadcasting its crowning glimmer of orange and yellow from behind the tall pines that sheltered the attendees from the outside world. Blankets and miniature lawn chairs were laid out in random patterns all over the hill. More than enough picnic baskets filled with delectable summer fare and plastic glasses of wine were on hand to complement the music and company of good friends. Tom's band was up first. His group was the warm up for 'The Mock Turtles'. 'The Mock Turtles', with no real resemblance to the original. Everyone in Jake's party was wondering how drunk one would have to be to come up with that name. They probably thought it was pretty clever at the time.

First Tom's backup band walked on stage to scattered applause and began a short tune-up session. This component consisted of eight members. To the far left the keyboard player, dressed in a shark skin jacket and pants, was standing under a spotlight equipped with a three-color carousel filter. As the spotlight filter turned, it created a rainbow of colors reflecting off his sharkskin suit. He had three keyboards. Two keyboards directly in front of him, one over the other while the third was at his right perpendicular to the other two. To the extreme right, up on a three-foot high platform, were three female backup singers dressed in long shiny black eveningwear. Each dress was cut differently from the others but made from the same material. They were gorgeous creatures that moved with poise and grace. The drummer was in the back among a full set of Slingerland drums. Each component was individually miked. The bass player looked like George Harrison as he appeared on the *Let It Be* album; tall, skinny, shoulder length hair and mustache. A vintage Fender Jazz bass guitar from the early sixties was slung over his shoulder. The lead guitarist, dressed in sequined bellbottom overalls, was a short scruffy looking lady who resembled Janis Joplin. She had a small army of guitars among which were one Paul Reed Smith, one Taylor 914 acoustic, two Fender Stratocasters, and one Fender Telecaster. Her bank of effects pedals looked so complicated that a brain surgeon must have assembled it. The eighth member, a huge guy weighing in at over 260 pounds and wearing another sharkskin suit played the saxophone, harmonica and conga drums.

It wasn't long before they all got organized and started an instrumental that was a cross between Chicago blues and rock and roll. Immediately the crowd rose to their feet and cheered. It was clear the unimaginable talent that was being displayed surprised them. Dan, Rick and Jake looked at each other with eyes wide and smiling in amazement. It was clear that they were comparing what they were hearing with how they remembered the sound of 'The Phogg'. No contest. They knew they were in for an amazing treat. It was easy to tell that each and everyone in the party was glad they came and eager to see and hear Tom perform.

The song ended to a cheer that probably was heard in the next county. Without delay and oddly no introduction at all, the band began to play *It's Not About the Money,* Tom's Grammy winning tune from the late sixties. It was a hard rocking cross between Chicago blues and rock and roll, like the first tune. Jake, Rick and Dan all had copies of Tom's album stashed among their collectibles for safekeeping until they heard Tom was coming into town. Since then, they had been playing the tunes from the album regularly so that they would be able to sing along if the urge struck.

While the intro to the song was played for the second time Tom walked out on stage to the thunder of applause, grabbed the mike and began to sing. His voice was awesome. The years of entertaining might have taken a toll on his 53 year old body, but it had aged the blues/rock voice within, like the finest of red wines. He was incredible. Each member of the band backing him up was more together than any of the big name groups Jake had seen in concert over the years.

Night had fallen and the stars lit up the crystal clear sky. It was a perfect backdrop for Tom's next song. It was a Bob Seger tune about a rock and roller's life on the road, called *Turn the Page.* It was a haunting song accented by the plaintive lament of the saxophone made famous by Seger's saxophonist at the time, Alto Reed. Already mellow from one glass of wine, Jake laid back on the blanket, propped up by his elbows. A paper plate of Joyce's potato salad and fried chicken was perched upon his lap. He thought, *"Is it just the wine, or is Tom as good as I think he is? You only find that thickness in the voices of the greats. I think Tom really needs to be re-discovered."*

Dan leaned over to Jake and said, "I thought he'd be good, but I didn't really expect him to be this good."

"I was just thinking the same thing. I can't believe there isn't a bigger crowd here tonight," Jake answered.

"Me too."

After that song Tom stopped to thank everyone for coming out and said that he was glad to be back in Michigan. While the stage hands rolled a big black baby grand piano to center stage, he introduced his mom who was sitting in the pavilion. She stood up to a cheering crowd. Next he introduced the members of the band with a little history on each one. Then he introduced himself and sat down at the piano. Jake, Dan and Rick looked at each other as if they'd just discovered the Pope was Jewish. They knew that Tom could play a chord or two on the guitar back in high school but had no idea he could play piano. *"Was he really going to play it?"* they wondered.

Before the song began, Tom said, "This song is dedicated to some very good friends of mine I know are here tonight. I'll be seeing you guys a little later."

The piano was turned in such a way that the audience couldn't tell if he would actually be hitting any keys. The only lights shining on stage were one on Tom and one on the three back up singers. Not a sound could be heard. Tom began to play the intro to the song. The piano sounded as if they had a concert pianist stashed backstage somewhere hammering out this masterful and melodic prelude so intricately, that no one in the crowd could tell what the song would be. As Tom played on, the piano began to rotate. It had been rolled onto a turntable built into the stage. There was no longer any question that Tom knew how to play piano. Everyone could witness it for themselves. Tom and his piano eventually rotated back to the point of beginning. As the intro progressed the melody became unmistakable. It was, *With a Little Help From My Friends* written by John Lennon and Paul McCartney. He began to sing it like Joe Cocker did.

"What would you do if I sang out of tune?
Would you stand up and walk out on me?
Lend me your ears and I'll sing you a song.
I will try not to sing out of key."

Then the back up singers joined in with their ten-thousand watt voice power singing 'The Beatles' version of the chorus.

"Oh, I get by with a little help from my friends.

Mm, I get high with a little help from my friends.
Mm, gonna try with a little help from my friends."

Everyone there was blown away. *"How could these guys be a back up band, to those 'Mock Turtles'?"* Before Tom's performance was over, he had sung most of the songs on his old album, many old familiar blues tunes by John Mayall and Eric Clapton, and covered several 60's popular tunes. He and his band exited to an eternal standing ovation that was extinguished only when 'The Mock Turtles' appeared. 'The Mock Turtles' were a letdown after Tom's performance. And since Tom had planned to head right over to Dan and Patty's after his show, it wasn't long before they left to start the mini reunion.

They had ridden to the concert together in one big SUV that Joyce borrowed from work. The buzz on the trip back to Dan and Patty's signified their collective amazement at what they had just witnessed.

Patty left a note on the front door saying, "Come on in. We're in the back." They were all gathered around the pool, drinks in hand. The 50's and 60's music was emanating from Dan's old strategically placed ADS speaker cabinets when Tom appeared through the back yard gate in the stockade privacy fence. He carried a twelve-pack of Miller Lite under one arm and a wrinkled brown paper bag with contents unknown under the other. The group was stunned for a moment, somehow not expecting his understated attire. Instead of his sparkling show clothes he wore a fairly nondescript outfit of old, well worn levis and a promotional T-shirt fresh from the night's concert. Tom stood in the light of a tall bamboo torch as he surveyed the crowd. Each one was wearing that same promotional T-shirt in his honor. Tom smiled and said, "Well, I guess we won't be needin' these," as he dumped the contents of the paper bag onto the patio for effect. It had contained ten more promotional T-shirts.

Dan jumped up from his lawn chair, walked up, gave him a hug, grabbed the twelve-pack from his hand and introduced him to David and Janet. Patty followed and put her arms around Tom, gave him a big kiss on the cheek and said, "I'm so glad to see you. We've really missed you Tom."

"I've missed you guys, too. I can't believe you're still puttin' up with Danny Boy," Tom joked.

Rick followed and Tom gave him a big bear hug and said, "It's great to see you, Rick. Are you still into the photography and short wave?"

"I'm still doing the photography, but I gave up the short wave and started brewing beer in my spare time. I brought some for you to try later too. I'd like you to meet my better half. Carolyn, this is our old buddy, Tom."

Tom gave her a hug and said, "It's very nice to meet ya. Ya know you've got a good man there."

"Oh, I know," Carolyn said with a smile.

Jake walked up with Joyce at his side. After hugging Carolyn, Tom turned to see Jake and said with a little mist in his eye, "It's been way too long Jake." As Tom extended his hand, Jake stepped forward and put his arms around Tom.

"Way too long," Jake agreed as they each tried to find a way to hug the other, to show that they meant what they said.

No words were exchanged for the longest time, until Joyce tapped them both on the shoulder and said, "OK, OK break it up you two."

Jake and Tom let go of each other, both wiping their eyes with the back of their hands. Jake cleared his throat and said, "Tom, the referee here is my wife Joyce."

"It's a pleasure to meet you," Joyce said as she extended her hand to Tom.

"Come 'ere," Tom coaxed as he gave her a big hug too.

"You really put on a great concert tonight," Joyce complimented.

Then, as if they all felt bad for not being the first to praise Tom's performance, everybody spoke at the same time with their individual accolades.

Dan opened Tom's twelve-pack and gave him a beer, and like a good host, put each of the remaining beers in an ice chest next to Tom's designated lawn chair. They all mingled and reminisced around the pool for a drink or two. David and Janet made their exit first and began their goodbyes to everyone. Tom and Jake had just found the time to settle down to have a serious one-on-one when David and Janet came up to wish Tom well. "It was nice to meet you, Tom, and we really enjoyed ourselves at your concert tonight. And Jake, don't be too late tonight. You know we have golf in the morning," David nagged. "Tom, why don't you go golfing with us tomorrow?"

"That's a great Idea," Jake agreed.

"Oh, I can't golf," Tom pointed out.

"Neither can we. We'd love to have you suffer along with the rest of us," David said.

"Well you're not getting any strokes from me," Rick shouted from across the pool.

As they turned to go, Jake and Tom settled in to do some catching up. "Man you were great tonight Tom." Tom opened his mouth to modestly deny the use of the term great, but Jake held up his hand for permission to continue. "I've been to lots of concerts—seen a lot of the greats—right up close, you know? And Tom, you are absolutely without question head and shoulders above all of 'em.

It's so great for me to think back to those days when 'The Phogg' was playing and now be able to see how you've perfected what I thought was perfection back then."

"Wow," Tom blushed. "You should be my publicist."

"No Tom, I really do mean what I'm saying. It's not just me either. Everybody else thought you were fantastic too. And I guess I'm wondering why you've only done the one album."

"I love doin' what I'm doin'. I really do. But don't be fooled man. This is a tough business. If you don't fit the mold, for one reason or another, you don't get the breaks. The music I do is geared to people like us. The people buyin' the records today are young, man. Have you heard what they're buyin' today? That stuff isn't me. So I'm happy to be able to play for the baby boomers and leave the generation X and Y's to someone else."

"But Tom, aren't the baby boomers a much bigger segment of the market than either the X or Y's?"

"Yeah, I think so, but the record companies aren't caterin' to us." Tom wanted to get away from this subject, so he said, "I heard from Dan, that he's gettin' the impression that you might retire from the real estate biz pretty soon."

"I've been giving it some serious thought recently", Jake admitted. "I wish I could get into something creative. Something I enjoy. Where it wouldn't be like work, ya know? Oh, I've had a pretty good run with real estate, and believe it or not, I do love the business for the most part. It's just that the older I get the less tolerant I am about all the crap that comes along with the good stuff. For example, just yesterday I had a pretty big closing. At the last minute the buyer's attorney wanted to change the deal and basically blackmail my sellers into giving up an extra twelve thousand dollars. What a dirt bag."

"No kiddin'? What did ya do?" Tom asked intently.

"We walked."

"Walked—as in left the building?" Tom asked in astonishment.

"Yeah. Well, we got as far as the conference room door before the purchaser caved and called off his pit bull attorney. It was a lot like when you bluffed that Larry guy at the A&W, so I wouldn't have to drag race him on Woodward. Remember?"

Tom nodded and said, "You've got some guts there, buddy. Larry wasn't exactly your high-powered attorney; he was just another stupid teenager. It seems a little risky to me to just walk out like that."

"Well, that's my point. I need to be more level headed for my client's sake. But my temperament these days is to cut the crap and plow right through, without regard to the consequences. I think it's a sign of burn out. That can be a problem long term, if you know what I mean."

"I guess so. But ya know, I wondered what kind of man you'd turn out to be and I'm really impressed. The way you've stuck with this real estate gig and become a success. That's good stuff. You've grown up, my man. I bet your dad is real proud of ya."

Jake remembered the struggle with his dad regarding his playing in the band and how that conflicted with his dad's plans to get him to college. "Yeah, I guess he is. He taught me everything he knows, along with his work ethic. I found out it isn't easy to survive out there unless you're willing to focus on a goal and work your butt off for it. But for some reason, my heart just isn't in it anymore and I want to do something else for a change. Something I'll enjoy."

"Well, look at it this way. Ya gave it thirty some years. You not only did it well enough to survive, ya did great at it. And now ya don't need to do it any more. I only wish you coulda picked up on that work ethic thing, back when you tried your hand at writin' songs. I really think ya had some talent there, man. If ya had applied yourself with the discipline you've shown in the real estate game, who knows what mighta happened."

"You know, Rick thought I should take some time off, given my attitude about work lately. He actually suggested that I take up music again," Jake offered as he contemplated the light reflecting off the ripples in Dan's swimming pool.

"Well, why don't ya?"

Avoiding the direct question from Tom, Jake said, "Funny, back in high school I used to dream of becoming a big successful songwriter. To me, the words to the songs were always the most important part. And today I'm still listening to the oldies and singing along with all those old songs. I amaze myself at how many songs I know the words to."

Tom took a minute to process Jake's comment. Regretting not having the talent to write music himself, but appreciating what it takes to grind out a tune with potential; he just couldn't let his friend's frivolous remark go unchallenged. With a hint of disdain in his voice, Tom said, "I don't think, just knowin' the words ta old songs is gonna get you too far in the songwriting biz, bud," Tom pointed out as he took a long tug and emptied his beer. Tom reached into the ice chest and fished out two more beers, twisted off the tops and handed one to Jake. "Even if a person had a tremendous amount of talent, there's a hell of a lot of hard work that goes into writin' a song." Jake tried to jump in and qualify his comment but it was too late. Tom was on a roll and would not be interrupted. "Here's a 'what if' for ya. What if you've wanted to be a songwriter all your life? You wake up one mornin', you're 53 years old. More than half your life has passed ya by, and ya haven't even put in the kind of effort it takes to finish one song even if it's a bad one. What if that's what's buggin' you? What if you're a little mad at yourself for choosin' the path you're on and now ya wonder if it's too late to make that kind a change? Ya wonder if the talent ya had is still hidin' somewhere inside ya or if it died from thirty-five years of starvation. What do ya do about it? Turn the radio on and sing along with the oldies and let thirty-five more years go by, or start payin' your dues? Come on man, I think I see a window of opportunity here."

Jake wasn't prepared for the verbal slapping around that he just received and tried to find a way to release some of the pressure that Tom had just applied to his ego. "I think if you twist my arm just a little harder it'll break off and then you can use it to beat me over the head."

"OK, Jake, I know I'm gettin' in your face a little and I'm sorry if I'm makin' you uncomfortable, but man, ya have a chance to find out if ya have what it takes to write songs. Just think for a minute." Tom enumerated the reasons. "One; you're burnt out on your job and you need a break. Two; you can afford to take time off. Three; song-writin' is about as creative a job as there is, and Four; ya have the chance to find that one thing in life that ya live for, instead of somethin' ya do for a livin'." Tom's eyes opened wide as he spoke. His arms were stretched out and each finger of both hands was spread out as far as they could go. It was reassuring for Jake to see that Tom hadn't changed the way he expressed himself. Through Tom's eyes, Jake could visualize that dream, because music was Tom's dream and Tom was living it. Was it Jake's dream too or was it just a dusty old memory?

"You make a pretty strong case. Maybe I'll give it some more consideration," Jake said, not really sure if he meant it.

"Would it help ya if I could give ya a head start on your song writin'?" Tom asked.

"What kind of help?"

"Do ya know where all your old songs are right now?" Tom asked.

"I'm sure they found their way into the trash long ago—too bad too. It woulda been a big help to have them and all my notes from back then."

"Did ya know my mom's movin' into senior housing?" Tom asked.

"Yeah, Dan told me. How is she, by the way?"

"She's fine," Tom said quickly—wanting to get back to his point. "I was there yesterday and she asked me to do somethin' with all the things I left at her house over the years. So I was goin' through all of it and came across that Fender Princeton amp that ya used in the band."

"No kidding," Jake beamed. "Hey, I remember the day you brought that amp over to Darryl's. They were about to kick me out of the band because I didn't have an amp and you…" Jake stopped a moment to fight back the sudden erupting emotion he felt from that memory. "You got that amp for me so that I wouldn't be kicked out."

"That's the one," Tom confirmed. "Well, ya gave it back to me when you left for college. So there it sat over at my mom's house all these years."

"I bet it's in pretty good shape. Going through all your stuff must have been like opening a time capsule."

"It really was," Tom acknowledged. "In fact it was like openin' *your* time capsule when I pulled all *your* songs out of the back of that amplifier," Tom reported.

"You have the songs?" Jake asked in disbelief.

"Yep. They're sittin' in my Mom's garage right now."

"Well, I'll go pick 'em up after golf tomorrow."

"That's OK, my road manager is goin' to drop 'em off at your house in the mornin' if that's OK."

"Sure. Thanks."

"Do ya still have your guitar?" Tom asked.

"Yeah. It's in a closet somewhere. I think I've had it out maybe twice since college."

"That's a shame, man. Why don't ya pull that ol' Epiphone out, blow some of the dust off and see if ya remember how to play a 'C' chord?"

"It sounds like a good idea Tom, but after all these years, trying to learn the guitar all over, and writing songs. It just seems like an uphill battle to me. I do want to do something creative, but it might take me the rest of my life to be any good at songwriting. I may never make any money from it and all that time would be wasted."

"I'm sorry," Tom said facetiously. "I thought ya were more interested in the creative part than the money part." Tom was tired and had had enough of Jake's resistance for one night, so he threw up his hands and said, "Suit yourself man. I tried. The ball's in your court now, bud."

CHAPTER 14

▼

For Jake, golf supplied as much entertainment as he could stand in a week. So Tom's show the night before, the drinking, plus golf this morning was bordering on mayhem. Tom, Jake, Rick, David, and Dan were all present and accounted for on the first tee for no other reason than they had committed to it while under the influence the night before. A five-some. One really hung over five-some suffering from last night's festivities.

Dan pulled his driver out of his golf bag and placed it on his shoulders behind his head, grasping each end with his hands. He began twisting his torso to loosen up. When he turned, he groaned as if he were in labor. Each golfer had his own way to loosen up. Jake would spread his legs out to shoulder width and bend down to touch the grass with the palms of his hands. David executed several swings holding his driver and three wood at the same time. Rick knelt down on one knee with his other leg extended forward and leaned into his outstretched leg. The four of them groaning one after the other put Tom in mind of a very busy maternity ward. Tom hadn't golfed since he appeared in a pro-am tournament in Carmel back in 1971, so he just sat there on the dark green wooden bench watching the others and trying see the benefit of such a routine.

Dan teed off first into the pond about thirty-five yards out and to the right. So he took a Mulligan. His second shot went exactly where his first one went. Rick followed with a swing and a miss. His next effort sent the ball straight up in the air about twenty feet. The ball came to rest not more than four feet from where he was standing. David and Jake didn't fare any better. Tom was about to take his turn when the wind picked up and the sky turned dark. Tom looked up and said, "Please God, all I need is one drop and maybe a little lightnin'." Just then the golf course siren blasted, signifying thunderstorms coming and advising all golfers to get off the course. It was truly a miracle. In no time the five golfers were in the clubhouse ordering breakfast.

They took a table by a window that looked out on the ninth green of the regulation course. The rain began pelting the window in waves so that it was hard to see the flag. Usually after golf, the guys would gaze out the window at the ninth fairway and watch the golfers play the hole. It was a standing tradition to mock the golfers as they played even if they did well. This time they had to entertain themselves by making conversation.

David was anxious to hear about the history of their high school band. "So Tom, how long did you guys play together in 'The Phogg'?"

Tom surveyed the group for help remembering and said, "Well, our first gig was the Moose Lodge on Dixie Highway in 1964, I think." Jake and Dan both nodded their agreement. Not because they could confirm it but more likely, their memory wouldn't support any better account.

"Do you remember those baby blue 'V' neck sweaters that Darryl's sisters picked out for us to wear?" Dan asked.

"Don't remind me," Jake added.

Rick jumped in with, "Don't forget the little white dickeys they made you wear."

"We never liked those matchin' outfits. I think that was the first and last time we wore those sweaters," Tom said.

"So you guys were together till graduation," David surmised.

"We broke up in 1967 when everybody went to college," Tom answered.

"After you gave up the baby blue sweaters and little white dickeys, what did you guys wear?"

Dan fielded this one. "We dressed pretty eclectic as I remember. Tom was more of a greaser and Doug, Darryl and I were frats. Jake was a frat one day and greaser the next. Sometimes he'd mix and match so you really couldn't tell what he was."

David looked confused and said, "Refresh my memory. What was the difference between a frat and a greaser?"

Jake offered an explanation for David. "You know how James Brown looked in the sixties?"

"Yeah."

"Little Richard?"

"Yeah."

"The Righteous Brothers?"

"Yeah."

Jake used his index finger as if he were pointing to each invisible big name and said, "Grease, grease, grease. Now do you remember The Beach Boys?"

"Yeah."

"The Rolling Stones?"

"Yeah."

"The Animals?"

"Yeah."

Pointing again, Jake said, "Frat, frat, frat."

"OK. Thanks for the education." David continued the prodding. "Did you play mostly around the Waterford area?"

"We played in most of the places around town. We played in Detroit and up north too. There were some places that catered to just the greasers and they wanted only the soul groups. We played 'Stones', 'Kinks', 'Animals', 'Beatles', Chuck Berry, you know, mostly rock and roll. So we weren't welcome in the soul places. I never really got that. Soul and rock and roll both came from the blues. I love it all. I never got why they thought they were so different—except for that one place in Detroit, on McNichols. That was a bar that didn't mind one bit. They let everybody play there, no mater if ya were blues, rock and roll or soul."

"Remember Prudenville?" Dan asked. "We played the Music Box. I think it was probably July or August of 1966—up by Houghton Lake."

"Yeah," Rick said. "You guys were really riding high that weekend. Remember on the way up, we had the radio tuned to their local station? We heard the ad for the Music Box. They said that 'The Phogg' from Detroit was going to play that night."

"That was the only time I ever heard the band's name on the radio," Dan said, with a big grin on his face, "Jake, do you remember Lizzie Turner?"

Jake hadn't heard the name for years. Yet, the sound of it sent a sharp hot pain through his body that culminated in his forehead producing little beads of sweat while his hands turned to ice. Maybe it was his hang over causing the sudden simultaneous rush of pain, heat and cold. Even so, he didn't want to be reminded of her. But he knew that to show any emotion over a girlfriend from over thirty-five years ago wouldn't play well at the breakfast table. So he played this one like he did the Big Lake Road closing—cool and calm. "Yeah, I remember Lizzie. All you guys couldn't figure out what she saw in this superior example of manhood," as he pointed to himself with his thumbs.

"Well, do ya blame us?" Dan said. "She was at least twenty, maybe older. She was tall and she looked like a movie star. You were seventeen, five foot five and covered in zits."

After the laughter died down Tom said, "I remember figurin' she was trouble right from that first night at the Music Box. She got her claws into you pretty deep." Tom and Jake gave each other a look that indicated they remembered how much trouble she caused.

"Was she from Prudenville?" David asked. "Maybe they don't grow them too smart up there."

"Funny, Dave. Well no, I don't think she was," Jake said. "But now that we're talking about it, I don't think I ever knew where she was from or where she lived. Do you guys remember?"

"No, all I remember is that she would show up at our gigs and hang around you during the breaks," Dan recalled. "I don't remember ever running into her after you two broke up."

"Tom, what about Jake's songwriting?" David asked curiously. He hadn't gotten any answers from Jake, so he decided to prod Tom a little. "I hear from Dan that Jake had potential."

"Hey fellas, I'm still in the room here," Jake protested, fearing that his past shortcomings were about to be revealed.

The table became silent for a moment while Tom tried to formulate a response. Jake didn't know what else to say so he just busied himself sipping iced tea and waited with the others. "Yeah, I'd have to say he had potential back then. But potential really ain't enough to get the job done." Tom looked straight at Jake as he spoke. "You have to apply yourself. You have to have a work ethic that most people just don't have. Jake didn't have it back then. I tried all through high school to motivate him, but he just wasn't ready to make that big a commitment I guess." This time Tom wasn't successful hiding his ancient disappointment in Jake. Everyone at the table sensed that Tom had really been frustrated because Jake hadn't made the effort he could have back then.

Jake, feeling the need to defend himself said, "Look Tom, back then I was just a kid having fun. I didn't know what commitment was all about."

"No, Jake—ya knew what it was all about. Ya just didn't care to commit. That is, until your dad made ya commit…to college."

"OK…OK, you made the choice to go into music and my dad made the choice for me to go to college, so what's so wrong with that?"

"What's so wrong with that? I can't believe ya have to ask me? Jake, take a close look in the mirror and tell me. Who's the one dissatisfied with the path they're on? What really gets me, though, is that your solution is just starin' you in the face and you're too stupid or too scared to see it."

He knew Tom was right and he could have taken the comment if spoken in private. But, because it came in the form of an announcement in front of his closest friends, Jake was humiliated. He didn't want to get into a full-blown argument with Tom. *"How do you argue with someone you know is right?"* he thought. Escape was the only solution he had for this set of circumstances. So he slowly stood up and dropped a twenty on the table and said, "I'll see you guys later."

While the group sat silent, Jake turned and walked away through the pro shop, out the door and into the morning's rain. Dan picked up Jake's twenty-dollar bill, held it up so everyone could see it and said, "I think he's mad. He only had iced tea." Nobody laughed.

Tom said, "I'm sorry, guys. I shouldn't have done 'em that way in front of everybody."

Rick tried to console Tom, "He'll get over it, Tom. I'm sure he's not going to stay mad at you forever. Anyway, it might do him some good. You never know."

"Being drenched with rain seemed appropriate somehow," Jake thought as he loaded his golf clubs into his SUV. There was something about humiliation and being rained on that just seemed to go together so well. While driving through the rain, he tried to adjust the speed of his wiper blades so that the rain would be swept away from the windshield as it fell. Too fast and the blades would rub and bounce against the windshield. Too slow and the rain would blur the view of the road. Once he found the appropriate speed he fiddled with the satellite radio dial to busy himself, so that he wouldn't have to think about what just happened. But with all the effort at distraction he couldn't get Tom's words out of his head. He knew Tom was right.

As he pulled into his driveway, Jake noticed something sitting on the porch. As he drove closer, he could see that it was a brown box the size of a large suitcase sitting there, protected from the rain by the porch roof. He realized that it wasn't a suitcase. It was the old Fender Princeton amplifier he and Tom had talked about last night after the concert.

CHAPTER 15

▼

Jake lifted the heavy brown protective sheath that covered the amplifier. The amplifier looked as if it was just a few years old. Waiting in the darkness, unused, it was as if it had been sheltered from time. Its cabinet was covered with the original brown vinyl called Tolex. The wheat-colored grill cloth looked new and behind it was one little Jensen ten-inch speaker. It sure looked small to him now. It only had four brown knobs on the control panel: volume (no gain), tone (no treble, midrange, or bass), speed and intensity for the Tremolo effect (no reverb). It was your basic amplifier. Sure he had gotten bigger and better amplifiers after this one. But back then it was the one that kept him in the band. After he replaced it, he kept it at home to help with the songwriting until giving it back to Tom.

Then he remembered that Tom had found his songs in the back of the amplifier. The thick envelopes were there all right. He could see them through the opening in the back. They were just laying there in plain view, waiting for him to open them and get inspired. But instead of grabbing them and checking their contents, he decided to put the cover back on the amplifier and take it inside. It may have been out of spite for what Tom had said to him that morning. Or it may have been that he was afraid to look at the songs. If he looked at them he might be tempted to try and finish them—and then what. What if he couldn't do it? *"Fear of failure? Where did that thought come from?"* he wondered.

Joyce had gone grocery shopping as she always did on Sunday mornings. The house was empty. He never liked the feeling of being home without her. He wasn't afraid to be alone. It wasn't uncomfortable to be solitary. But Jake had become accustomed to the sounds in the house that she created as she went through her daily routine. He didn't have to be in the same room with her to sense her company. The sound of a cupboard door or her soft steps on the hardwood floor making her way from one room to another. Even the delicate fragrance of the shampoo she used. These were all individual movements that were performed in the concert of her presence. There was no familiar concert now, only the sound of the rain tapping on the windows and tin covering the chimney.

He carried the amplifier up the stairs to the big walk-in closet in the spare bedroom in hopes of finding a place for it for the time being. The closet was very neatly packed with all the other exiled items. One item seemed to stick out like a sour thumb. A huge round poker table with folded legs standing on end once owned by Jake's dad's neighbor. It was a gift from the daughter of the old neighbor when she and her husband moved out of state. Jake had sold their home and they didn't want to throw the "heirloom" out. Since Jake's dad spent many hours playing poker with her father at that table, she thought Jake should have it. He stared at the collection of junk and saw that if he moved a few things around, he could make the amplifier fit. He rolled the table out first. As he did he saw a familiar item stored next to the wall behind the table—his old Epiphone guitar case.

Extensive packing and moving had scarred its gray hard shell structure. During the band years there were the rides in the station wagon almost every weekend to the places the band played. Then, after that, the guitar followed Jake to college where it stayed under his bed for four years, only to be handled each time he changed dorm rooms or came home for summer break. And after college, ten more moves. Even with his resolve to put things away, he couldn't resist just one peek at the old instrument. He rolled the table into the bedroom and leaned it gently against the wall. He pulled out his guitar case and unlatched the five chrome clasps that secured the lid. When the lid was open he saw a well-used but well cared for instrument. The last polish job he gave it just before he left for college had held up well. He picked it up and as he examined it, he noticed each scratch and remembered how they were inflicted. During the process he glanced at his reflection in the high gloss finish. He saw an aging figure with more wrinkles and less hair than he liked to admit, staring at his still youthful vibrant friend the Epiphone. It was like seeing an old friend at a high school reunion that looked thinner, younger and had more hair. *"Boy, you look great, you haven't changed one bit in thirty five years,"* he thought as he held the guitar carefully in his hands. The Epiphone didn't reply.

He strummed the guitar softly and heard a vibrating and clanking sound. He thought there was something seriously wrong until he noticed a guitar pick woven between the old strings. Jake had always kept a pick handy there so that he wouldn't have to fish for one in the little box built into the case that doubled as a support for the neck. He retrieved the pick and continued to strum. It was only slightly out of tune. After some trial and error as to which frets to use in tuning, he managed to improve the sound somewhat. And though the strings hurt his fingers as they fumbled to make a chord, he was surprised at how well he remembered what to do. It wasn't long before the high 'E' string broke. So, he decided to see if he remembered how to replace it. He laid the guitar down on the carpet and opened the little box built into the guitar case to see if there were any spare strings. There were none. But there was something in there that caught his eye. It was a silver chain attached to an old buffalo head nickel. The nickel was painted blue and had a quarter inch hole in it's center. It didn't take him long to remember its significance. It had been a gift from Lizzie Turner. He thought back to that day when he met her.

The Phogg had just finished setting up at the Music Box in Prudenville. It was about seven p.m., August 1966. The rest of the band went to a burger joint to get some take out for dinner before the Music Box opened for business that evening. Jake was sitting at a picnic table by the stage writing down a list of songs to be played in the first set while he waited for the guys to bring him something to eat. He also had been assigned the duty of guarding Darryl's new guitar. A double neck Mosrite his father picked up for him the night before as a birthday present.

Darryl's father, without checking with Darryl first, took Darryl's Fender Jaguar guitar and traded it in for the double neck Mosrite. Darryl, knowing nothing of the switch, had been hysterical while loading the trailer for the Prudenville trip. His Fender Jaguar was nowhere to be found. Jake and Darryl had been looking frantically for the guitar for at least twenty minutes when Darryl's father came out to the trailer with the new Mosrite in its case and said, "Happy Birthday Son," and handed him the new ax. Prudenville would be its baptism.

The place was empty except for the janitor who was putting the finishing touches on the hard wood dance floor. Jake sensed a presence. He didn't see or hear anyone come in, but he knew there was something or someone near him in the room. The tension was heightened by his sense of obligation to guard the new guitar. He looked up from his papers and didn't see anyone. So he turned around and was startled to see a tall figure standing not two feet from him looking over his shoulder at his song list. "Oh shhhit. You scared me," came out before he could find his manners.

Jake couldn't have conjured up a more strikingly beautiful prototype for his most outrageous teen-age fantasy than what was now standing smiling before him. She was slender and tall with long shiny straight jet-black hair parted in the middle. Her eyes must have been brown but they looked much darker and over-powered any other feature on her face except perhaps her full, deep vermilion lips. She wore all black. Black hip hugger bellbottom style slacks, wide black belt and a black knit top that exposed her midriff and left very little else to the imagination. There on her chest against her tan skin was the blue buffalo head nickel with the hole in the center attached to the silver chain around her neck. "I'm sorry, I didn't mean to scare you. I'm Lizzie," she said as she extended a slender hand with long painted fingernails.

Jake didn't immediately respond because he wasn't sure if she was real. He just stared with his mouth slightly ajar. As if being used to this sort of reaction, she just repeated her name in an effort to awaken Jake from his trance. "Lizzie Turner," she said again with a little laugh.

Jake suddenly came to his senses and said, "Oh, I'm Jake," as he reached for her hand. It was soft. Real soft, warm and dry as opposed to his hand that had gone cold and clammy on him the minute he saw her. He continued to stare. It was a little rude of him but he couldn't help it. She was so beautiful and some-how strangely familiar to him.

She said, "I know your name. I just came over to see if you would sign my photo album."

It was no surprise he hadn't noticed the black leather album in her left hand when there was so much else about her for his eyes to explore. "Photo album?" he asked with a puzzled look.

"Yeah, I've been collecting photos of certain bands that I like and I hoped you would sign your picture for me."

"OK," Jake said, with the same puzzled look on his face. She sat down next to him at the table and began turning the pages of the album to find the picture she was looking for. Jake could see that the photos weren't photos at all. They were pictures on promotional flyers, advertising each group. Some were of bands that he'd seen before. Some were of groups he knew personally. Only a few of them were signed. The ones that were signed were only signed by one band member. As she came upon 'The Phogg's flyer, Jake recognized it as one that Rick had taken. It was a flyer advertising one of their previous dates in Detroit about a year back. She carefully pulled it from the protective plastic page of the album and picked up his pen that was lying on the picnic table. "Would you like me just to sign my name?" he asked.

"I'd rather you'd say, 'To Lizzie with love,'" she confessed, while her lips thinly disguised a flirtatious smile. And moved in closer to offer up the pen.

"It's getting hot in here," he thought as he took the pen making sure their hands touched again. He signed the picture 'To Lizzie with love' as she rested her body against his arm. He signed the autograph as slowly as he could, hoping it wasn't so slow that she would pick up on the fact that he didn't want the moment to end. Once finished, he handed her the paper and said, "If you'd like, I can get the rest of the band to sign it when they come back."

Lizzie moved in closer, looked him straight in the eye not more than two inches from his face and spoke in a sleepy whisper, "I don't want anyone else to sign it, Jake."

He had heard his name a million times since birth, but never did he hear it spoken the way Lizzie just did. He didn't know if it was her silky tone or the hint of the delta in her accent that made it sound so warm and personal. It was as if she'd spoken his name, gift-wrapped it herself and airmailed it special delivery. At that moment the only thing on his mind was, *"I need to kiss her now,"* so he inched closer to her. She tilted her head slightly as if to submit to this minuscule advance. The kiss appeared to be inevitable when they heard the big steel front door of the building slam.

"Hey, Jake, it's burger time," Dan hollered. Lizzie and Jake simultaneously turned in the direction of Dan's voice to see the rest of the band standing in a line all holding bags of takeout food and marveling at the scene at the picnic table. Both Jake and Lizzie stood up.

"Would you like something to eat?" Jake offered.

"No thanks, I have to be on my way for now, but I'll see you tonight though if it's all right with you."

"Sure," he said with a smile he couldn't contain.

"OK then, I'll see you later. And as she spoke she leaned over and kissed him quickly and left out the back without being introduced to the group, who were still frozen in the same position by the front door.

"Who was that?" they all asked as they brought their dinner to the picnic table.

"Her name is Lizzie Turner," Jake answered, still a little dazed and breathless from her kiss.

"Was she fine or the kind that gets uglier the closer you get?" Darryl asked, hoping the answer wouldn't make him green with envy.

"Unless I'm blind, she was fine," Jake said, not comprehending he was speaking in rhyme.

"Man, she musta been a foot taller than you," Dan said. "How'd you get her to kiss you? Did ya threaten her or anything?"

"No. She just came in and wanted me to sign her album. She's collecting flyers of groups and wanted me to sign one of ours. The one from that place we played on McNichols in Detroit last year. She says she's coming back to see me tonight."

After listening to the account, Tom surmised, "Well Jake, it looks like ya might have your own personal groupie there, bud."

Under normal circumstances Jake didn't mind the term 'groupie' but in this case and in his newly infatuated state of mind, he took offense and said, "Come on Tom, she just seems like a nice girl who happens to like me. I don't think you have to rush to put a label on her."

Trying to keep a lid on the situation Tom said, "OK man…don't get so up tight about it. I'm sorry about the groupie thing. Just don't let her get in the way. OK?"

"There won't be any problem, Tom," Jake promised.

"What do you bet she doesn't even show? I mean, a woman like that's got better things to do than hang around you Jake," Doug injected. "I got a buck that says she's a no show."

Nobody took the bet. Not even Jake, because even though he felt the chemistry he couldn't be sure that she did. So every one in the band kept one eye on the front door to see if she would show up. The band was half way through their first set when Lizzie walked into the building. As she wove her way through the packed house she left a wide wake of turned heads. She didn't stand up near the stage like you might think a groupie would do when she made it up to the front. She just winked at Jake and took a seat at the picnic table where they met. Lizzie showed little if any excitement about being there. She didn't pay any attention to the band at all and really seemed apathetic about the whole thing. This didn't go unnoticed by any of the band members. Jake was troubled enough about it that he missed a few cues for his backup singing parts which aggravated the rest of the band.

After the set was over, Tom walked over to Jake as he was switching his amplifier to standby and asked, "Are ya OK? You messed up pretty bad there, bud."

Jake was listening to Tom but looking in the direction of Lizzie. His only comment was, "Sorry, Tom, I guess I was a little distracted. Hey, did you see? She showed up." Tom shook his head and walked away knowing this was going to be trouble.

Jake didn't use the stairs to get off the stage. He jumped the set of four steps and jogged over to meet Lizzie at the picnic table. She greeted him with a kiss and said, "Can we go somewhere less crowded?"

"Sure," Jake agreed. "Where would you like to go?"

"How about my truck?" Lizzie offered as she dangled the keys to her old Chevy pickup in front of his face.

"Great, I've got about twenty minutes before the next set. Let me tell the guys where I'll be." Jake was afraid that if he left her, she would disappear forever so he said, "Don't go anywhere. I'll be right back." He ran to the first band member he could find and said, "I'm goin' to the parking lot with Lizzie. We'll be in her pickup. See ya." When he ran back he was surprised and thankful to find her standing where he left her. She held his hand and led him out the front door to the parking lot where her black 1961 Chevy truck was waiting. Somehow he hadn't pictured Lizzie driving a truck, much less one in such terrible condition as this. The paint on the hood had been dulled from the heat of the sun and probably the heat from the motor. He figured it for at least one-hundred thousand miles. The rocker panels were almost completely rusted through and the weather stripping from the passenger door was loose and hanging down almost touching the ground. As they got in, Jake noticed a diamond ring on her left hand and once they were settled in, he inquired. "Lizzie, are you married?"

Lizzie glanced at her left hand and said, "I was. My divorce was final two weeks ago. I still wear the ring because it keeps guys from bugging me. I really don't like being out there, if you know what I mean."

"Yeah," Jake acknowledged, too naive to have a clue what she was saying, but at the same time, being relieved to know she wasn't spoken for. "How long were you married?"

"Almost two years to the day."

"What happened to you two?"

That question triggered something in her that caused her to vent almost more information than Jake could comprehend. "Getting married was a stupid mistake on my part. Neither of us really knew what we were getting into. My father told me Frank was no good. Boy, was he right. Thank God there aren't any children. He left me about six months ago for someone else and moved out of town," she explained. "You know, my father was devastated. I hurt him pretty bad. I'll probably be spending the rest of my life making it up to him." She didn't even stop to take a breath. Once her catharsis was complete she became much more relaxed, paused for a moment then continued. "I'm sorry for venting Jake, but I guess I just really needed to get that out of my system." As he looked on, she slowly removed the wedding ring, placed it in the ashtray, and put her arms around him.

It wasn't long before he lost track of all time. Then he heard a tapping on the foggy windshield. Jake listlessly broke away from Lizzie's embrace to see that it was Darryl standing by the car whispering, "Come on Jake we're late for our set and Tom's not happy."

"Oh no," he cried. "Lizzie, I got to go." He hurried out of the rust bucket. The passenger door made a loud groaning sound as it closed, as if it were calling out for the grease and oil it needed so badly. He looked in to apologize to Lizzie for the abrupt ending to their "little talk" but she had already fired up the engine to make her own exit.

"Bye, Jake," was all she said as she sped away leaving him and Darryl standing there.

"Man, I didn't even get her phone number," Jake blurted out as he grabbed his head in anguish. He looked pretty foolish standing there with his hair going in every direction, face flush and his shirttail hanging out.

"Come on, man. Get it together. We got a set to do," Darryl prodded nervously. "The guys are pretty pissed. Tuck in your shirt and comb your hair and let's go."

Jake followed his orders and did the best he could. Luckily for Jake nobody had any time to say anything to him until after the set was over. As they were packing up to leave after closing, the guys were very quiet and Jake was waiting for someone to say something just to get the pending reprimand over with. So Jake decided to force the issue and said, "Look guys, I know I screwed up tonight. I'm a jerk. I won't let it happen again. Honest. But, can you blame me? You saw what a babe she was. Any one of you would have done the same thing. Wouldn't you?"

Darryl spoke out to Tom's displeasure and said, "Man, I know I woulda done the same thing."

"I guess I woulda too," they all agreed—all except Tom. Tom had a different mind set than the rest of them. He was the most serious when it came to the band and he was the only one that realized that with this kind of distraction the band couldn't survive.

"Jake, please. I'm beggin' ya. Don't let that chick get in the way of this band. OK?" Tom pleaded, but pleaded with the authority necessary to convey to all in earshot that he *would not* be let down like this again.

"OK, Tom. I probably won't be seeing her again anyway. She took off pretty fast and I didn't get her number, I don't know where she works or where she lives. Hell, I'm not sure she's even from this planet."

"You got a point there, bud," Tom agreed. "She sure didn't look like any of the girls I know—way too high class and experienced. I figure her for about twenty to twenty-two years old. She's way out of your league man."

It was 12:30 a.m. when they finished loading the station wagon's trailer and headed down the road for their two and a half hour drive home. Jake was silent most of the way. He knew the guys were talking but he was distracted by the memory of those moments with Lizzie. He had crushes on other girls before—lots of them. And at his age, it would manifest itself as a kind of pain—but a good pain—that would develop in his heart and go hand in hand with the infatuation. It was sort of a longing that he couldn't control. It would steal his appetite, sleep and concentration. Jake was amply familiar with that. But the feeling that had overcome him when he met Lizzie was not your garden-variety crush. It was probably 11.3 on the Richter scale of crushes. Under the influence of a crush, he could do silly things that might take a day or two to live down. But he was afraid to think about to what lengths he might go, under the control of this strange dominating force. He tried not thinking about her, but that didn't work. He tried to get some sleep but he had never been able to sleep in a car, moving or otherwise. So he gave in to the fantasy of what might be if she came around again.

The band's next dates to play were Friday and Saturday night at the Elizabeth Lake Estates Pavilion in their hometown of Waterford. It was situated on the beach at the center of and within walking distance to, the huge subdivision of the same name. Bands from all over the lower half of Michigan would play there, but when 'The Phogg' rolled in, it was like old home week. Everyone went to school with the guys in the band. Everyone would spend the afternoon on the beach and pack the pavilion to overflowing around dusk. Without question, this was the band's preferred venue.

On Friday night the place was going wild near the end of their last set. During the last song, two girls jumped up on the stage and pretended to be go-go girls. They had come in from an evening swim, long wet hair and all. Shedding their over-the-swimsuit garments revealed their tiny two-piece suits and a lot of tanned flesh. Before the bouncers could drag them off, they shimmied and shook till they were completely dry. The crowd was screaming uncontrollably as the band quit for the evening. The guys were all glowing over the performance and the welcome they had received. Dan tapped Jake on the shoulder and nodded toward the front door of the pavilion. Jake turned to see Lizzie making her way to the stage. As Tom turned to speak to Jake, he noticed her too. Tom put his arm around Jake's shoulder, stuck his face right up next to Jake's ear and said, "Remember what I said to ya last week?"

Jake answered after a deep breath, "I do, Tom. You don't have to worry about me."

"Oh, but I do, Jake," Tom rebutted. As Jake turned to give Tom a look of reassurance, he could feel his knees buckling beneath him.

Leaving Tom there, he stepped down from the stage tentatively toward Lizzie, not knowing if or when his knees would give out. As she approached him, his face guided her bearing as if he were the lighthouse and she, the ship returning home. He couldn't interpret the expression she wore and therefore had no idea of what form of greeting to expect. As far as he was concerned, virtually any emotion she expressed toward him, whether positive or negative, would be better than not having her there. When they converged, she took the initiative and put her arms around him and planted a big kiss on his lips. "Did you miss me?" she asked as she studied his face for the answer.

"I haven't stopped thinking about you all week, Lizzie," he said breathlessly, as his knees sent a second signal of pending collapse to his brain.

She smiled and grabbed his hand as she did at the Music Box and led him outside. They were headed for her truck again when he pointed toward the beach. They found an old gazebo with a porch style swing and sat down. The moon and the stars cast their reflection on the lake rendering an idyllic glow to the night. *"Is this real or am I cooking up another fantasy?"* Jake wondered.

As she held his hand she said, "I didn't know if I was going to come, but I had to see you again. There's something inside me telling me I need to be with you."

"Now I'm sure I'm dreaming," he thought as he took her in his arms and kissed her. "You know I want to be with you too, Lizzie, but I want you to know that I've made a commitment to the guys in the band and I've gotta respect that."

"What do you mean?" she asked, unable to hide the concern.

"It's just that…you know, the guys were upset that I was late getting back to do the set last week. We were in the parking lot and everything…you know? It's just that I can get a little carried away with you and forget about everything else."

"I understand," was all she said in response. So he took that as a confirmation that she not only understood but also agreed with him.

That night they talked mainly about Jake, his relationship with all the guys in the band, his father's college plans for him, his songwriting and every detail about the band's plans to advance in the business. She acted as if she was so interested that when he made an effort to get to know her, she would respond with another question about him. It was almost dawn when she looked at her watch and said, "I don't want to go but I've got lots to do tomorrow. Can I come see you tomorrow night?"

"Sure."

"I want you to have something from me," she said. "I want you to wear it and never take it off. I don't want you to forget about me and start looking at those half naked dancing girls you had on stage tonight." She took the silver chain with the blue buffalo head nickel from around her neck and made him put it on. "Now I have to go, but I'll see you tomorrow." They got up from the swing and he walked her to her truck. She turned to him and gently fondled the nickel on the chain she had given him and said, "My father would approve of *you*." And she drove off again. He immediately stuffed the chain with the nickel down the inside of his shirt. *"Not a good idea to wear this on the outside around the guys in the band. Just fuel for the fire,"* he thought. And he never did.

He vowed never to take it off but always kept it hidden under his shirt. He turned around to find his mother's car and remembered he had come with Darryl. The parking lot was empty. The sun was coming up. Jake had only one option. It was a long walk home. He dragged himself up the driveway about 5:00 a.m., retrieved the morning's newspaper from the front lawn and laid it on the kitchen table for his dad. He didn't notice the headline, "Popular Blues Bar Owner Battered and Robbed."

Jake heard the garage door opening. Joyce was back from the Sunday grocery shopping and he needed to get downstairs to help her put the groceries away. He carefully put the silver chain with the buffalo head nickel back into the compartment of his guitar case, fit the amplifier, guitar and poker table all back into the walk in closet and came down to greet her.

CHAPTER 16

▼

The week went by quickly. Jake heard that Tom had to leave town to continue his tour. Jake felt bad that he didn't call before he left. *"Maybe I'm being a little too thin skinned about the whole thing,"* Jake justified.

By Friday Jake was ready to leave town to see his friend Brian MacLeod. Brian was born in Scotland and came to the States when he was seven. He moved from Walled Lake with his parents and six brothers and sisters to Waterford in his junior year of high school. He and Jake struck up a friendship and decided to room together in college. After college Brian got married to Graciela and entered U of M to become a doctor—then more school to become a psychiatrist. During the process he became a father. Upon graduation he and Graciela and their daughter Stephanie moved to Maryland where he was offered a position. They had been there for close to thirty years but always stayed in touch with Jake and Joyce. They'd been wanting to get together for a weekend at the MacLeod's for years and finally the arrangements were made.

The plane trip there was uneventful and Brian and Graciela both met Jake and Joyce at the airport. The usual hugs were exchanged and in no time they were on the road. It was dinnertime, so Brian suggested they stop and get something to eat. During dinner they talked about the plans that they had for the weekend—a movie tonight—a walk around the lake in the nearby park early tomorrow morning. Then a trip on the train to Washington DC to tour the Capitol, an early Sunday brunch and a few hours to catch their breath before they boarded a plane home. It all sounded great to Joyce and Jake.

Over dinner the conversation drifted from their daughter Stephanie's progress in law school, to Brian's practice, to Graciela's battle with a rabbit that ate her prize flowers, to Joyce's job. Then Brian asked, "How's the real estate business these days?"

Joyce and Jake glanced at each other wondering if they really wanted to start up with that subject. But Jake decided it wouldn't hurt to bounce it off his friend the psychiatrist. "Well Brian, lately I've been thinking about getting out of the business."

Now Brian and Graciela glanced at each other in surprise. "Why?" Brian asked in disbelief.

"Where do I start?" Jake moaned.

"We're all friends here and we've got nothing but time, so why don't you start at the beginning?" Brian suggested.

"You asked for it," Jake warned and began a Readers Digest version of his dilemma. "I like the real estate business for the most part. I've been at it over thirty years now. But there are things about it that I have a hard time tolerating as I get older. And lately the bad things are outweighing the good. And when 9/11 happened, I'm sure I wasn't the only one who got to thinking about how finite our lives are. We only have so much time on this planet, you know? Then I thought about the futility of continuing a career where the satisfaction level keeps dropping for me and decided I need to look for something else to do for the next 30 years. Something less stressful and more creative than what I'm doing now."

Brian saw an opportunity to jump in when Jake took a breath. "You got any ideas?"

Joyce reported next. "His brother Rick thought he should take a break from the business for a while and write songs."

"Oh yeah," Brian recalled. "I remember you doing that in high school when you were in the band. You know, I bet Tom Tyler could give you a hand with that. He probably knows a ton of people who could help you out. Do you two stay in touch?"

"As it turns out, Tom was in town last week end. He played at Meadowbrook and we all got a chance to visit with him. I told him what I'm telling you and he said that Rick's right. He also gave me all my unfinished songs that I wrote in school. He stopped to see his mom and found them stuck in the back of an old amplifier he loaned me way back. When I left for college, I gave him back the amplifier. I guess I forgot the songs were there."

"Well, it sounds like you have a plan then," Graciela reasoned.

"I wish it were that easy for me. But it isn't. I guess my concern is, what if I find out I can't write after all? When I was in high school, I was just playing around with songwriting. It was fun—not work. I never worked hard at it and I wasn't a success at it either. I found out what hard work was when I went to school and later, when I started in business. In business, most of the time, if you work your tail off you'll succeed. And I think I did that, for the most part. But songwriting is an art. It's not the same as the jobs we regular people do. There are thousands of talented, hard-working musicians, artists and songwriters out there who are starving. The odds of success aren't good and the level of success doesn't seem to be a function of how hard you work. So, I guess I'm concerned about it being a big waste of my time."

"Well, I see your point. You got any other ideas for the next thirty years?" Brian asked.

"Not yet," he confessed.

"Interesting," he replied in typical psychiatrist's fashion. "Well, I wouldn't toss that idea out the window right away. It might be worth a little more consideration," he warned.

"I'm trying to keep an open mind," Jake answered. "What movie are we gonna to see tonight?"

Joyce had picked up a newspaper at the airport and brought the movie section with her into the restaurant and they all participated in the decision-making.

It was an early Saturday morning ritual for Brian and Graciela to drive to the nearby park and walk twice around the small lake there. It gave them a chance to communicate with each other in peaceful surroundings uninterrupted by the outside world. So that morning it would be the four of them. Joyce and Graciela wanted to do their catching up and announced that they would walk together. Brian and Jake decided to run together around the pond and do some catching up on their own.

One lap of running was enough for the two men. Not much talking took place because it was difficult for them to talk. They needed their mouths and noses full time to gasp for air. After the first lap they decided that the girls' idea to walk was the wise choice. Unable to take another step, the two would-be athletes sat on the bench and waited for their wives to catch up. Once they caught their breath, Brian said, "You know Jake, I've been thinking about what you said at dinner last night. I went to bed thinking about it and woke up about two this morning with it on my mind."

"Really?"

"Yeah. And I've got some input to offer you, for what it's worth."

Jake had a lot of respect for Brian and after all he was a well-respected psychiatrist. What could it hurt to get a little free advice? Jake started to lie down on the bench and said, "Hey, your couch isn't too comfortable, Doc."

Brian gave Jake a look that indicated his words shouldn't be taken quite that lightly. Seeing that his joke bombed, Jake sat back up. "I'm really interested in what your thoughts are, Brian, otherwise I wouldn't have bothered you with it last night. Go ahead…please."

"OK. The reason you're hesitating to try the songwriting seems to be out of fear that you won't be successful."

"Right," Jake agreed, to indicate he was with him so far.

"If you write some songs and fail to publish and sell them, you will have failed."

"That's right."

"So you measure success by how much money you earn."

"True. I'm still with you," Jake assured Brian.

"Here's a concept I want you to try and get your arms around. Let's say you take a year off just to write. You learn a lot about songwriting. You learn a lot about the business. You have fun because you're doing something creative. And you spend the year completely away from all the negativity of your real estate job. Are you with me so far?"

"So far," he answered wearing a curious look.

"The way I see it—if you take a year off to try your hand at songwriting and no songs get published or sold, that's not failure, if doing it makes you happy. Don't you see? You're measuring your success in dollars and cents. I think you've used that philosophy long enough and it's not working for you anymore. You should be considering what makes you happy at this stage of your life. I know that you aren't going to starve if you take one year out of your life to do this."

To show Brian he understood the concept he was trying to convey, Jake recited the title to Tom's one hit song. "So you're saying, it's not about the money."

"It's not about the money," Brian confirmed.

"I honestly never looked at it like that before. Ya know I think you're right. You're *absolutely* right."

Brian elaborated. "When you started the business, survival was your goal or standard for success. To survive, you needed money. So money became your standard for success and you forgot about the other things in life that can be interpreted as success—like general well being, happiness and stuff like that. These are things that can't be measured in dollars and cents."

Brian's words gave Jake a whole new perspective on the subject. He didn't have to go do something that would make him money. It was as if he had been given permission from a higher authority to go do something that would make him happy. Soon a smile came over his face. No matter how hard he tried, he couldn't wipe it away. "Brian, I want you to know that I appreciate that you were concerned enough to figure this out for me. Thanks a lot."

"Glad I could help you Jake. You know I can't always help all my patients," he answered.

"There is one more thing though," Jake interjected. "How are you with interpreting dreams?"

At that point the girls walked up and scolded them for sitting down during their exercise period. "I thought you two were running today," Graciela teased.

"This looks more like sitting than running," Joyce pointed out.

The guys rose from the bench and joined them on the second loop around the lake. After the exercise, they drove back to the house to get ready for their trip to Washington, DC. Everybody showered and changed in record time and soon the four found themselves on the train headed for DC. Jake and Joyce sat together on the hard plastic pre-formed seats facing Brian and Graciela. The conversation was lively and plans were made to take a short tour passing by the Capitol Building, the White House, and the Lincoln Memorial among others. But Jake was distracted from the conversation by the ever-changing scenery as the train sped on its way to their destination. Farms, fields, little towns and buildings that must have been over two-hundred years old streamed by as the train rocked with a hypnotic rhythm that overtook him.

As he stared out the window he thought about his conversation, or more aptly put, 'session' with Brian that morning. It felt good to think about taking a sabbatical from the business. Now he had to plan the logistics of such a project. There was the office. Who would run it? Would he sell it? How much time would he plan to take in order to give himself sufficient time to try his hand at writing? Would one year, as Brian suggested, be the right amount of time? He remembered that when he started the real estate business, he told himself that he'd work as hard as he could for six months before he'd even consider giving up. *"Don't let yourself get caught up in the minutia of trying to work all this out right now,"* he told himself and rejoined the conversation.

The train station in Washington, DC was a mammoth structure. Jake and Joyce both found themselves looking up at the unbelievable beauty of the domed area. They had to be led around by their hosts so they wouldn't bump into others as they passed by. Upon finding their way out of the huge entrance they all boarded a red steel and wooden vehicle that resembled an old time trolley. They were driven all around DC to all the sites they had planned to see and more. The trip took a turn southwest across the Potomac River on Washington Boulevard into Arlington, Virginia. As they rode along, they could see the west side of the Pentagon being restored. The driver said that the Pentagon had been attacked sixty years to the day that they first began construction on September 11, 1941. The passengers could see the scaffolding that rose up against the five floors of the westerly outer ring where the airliner had penetrated this fortress. Now, even on Saturday, the workers were busily laying the limestone facade to match the original construction material used those sixty years ago. Jake noticed a big electronic sign that had been erected next to where the men were working. According to their driver its function was to count down the days to the one-year anniversary of the attack. The goal of the workers was to complete the restoration of the outer ring by September 11, 2002—the one-year anniversary of the tragedy. He went on to explain that the workers were so dedicated to the task that the estimated eight-month job of removing the debris was completed in one month and one day. This effort to reconstruct the Pentagon was called the Phoenix Project.

The driver said that the Phoenix bird was a mythical creature from Greek and Egyptian mythology that sang to the sun god every day. According to the myth there could only be one Phoenix at a time. Every five hundred years or so the bird would build a fire, be consumed by it and the new Phoenix would emerge from its ashes. The Phoenix was the symbol of resurrection and life after death, because it was the only creature that had the power of self-reincarnation. The Phoenix project was a fitting name. After they passed by the Pentagon, the four looked at each other to see there were no dry eyes among them. Joyce reached in her purse for tissues and handed them out.

That ended the tour and after dinner in DC they took the train back to Maryland. By the time they hit the door they all were so tired that there was little ceremony involved in getting ready for bed. Sunday mid morning found everyone still sleeping and by the time everyone was awake there was only time to shower, pack and have a late lunch on the way back to the airport. Brian and Graciela accompanied Joyce and Jake to the terminal to see them off. Hugs were exchanged and promises were made to get together on a more regular basis. After the last goodbye hug, Jake and Joyce headed for their gate to catch their plane back home. It was a good weekend.

CHAPTER 17

▼

Driving home from the airport Jake and Joyce talked about the trip and what a good time they had. It had been good to see Brian and Graciela. "You know, Brian gave me some advice yesterday morning about what I might do instead of real estate?" Jake said.

"Really? What did he say?"

"He said that my problem was that I've been measuring success in dollars and cents. And he thought *that's* what might be keeping me from trying songwriting. He said if I took off a year from the business and my only accomplishment was to learn about songwriting, I would have been successful, if I was happy doing it. It wouldn't matter if I sold a song or not."

"Brian is a wise man, but I could have told you that. I hope he didn't charge you for that little bit of advice."

"So you think it's OK for me to just take the time and do this?"

"Like I said before. It's time you started thinking about doing what'll make you happy."

Once they were home and unpacked Joyce decided to do the laundry before making dinner and Jake was on his own to contemplate a songwriting career. It was as if a whole new Jake was being born today. He'd spend the next year with the project of writing songs and he thought, *"Why not call it The Phoenix project?"*

The first order of business was to go to the closet upstairs and have a look at what he'd written all those years ago. He opened the closet door, rolled away the poker table and pulled out the amplifier and his old Epiphone. There he sat in the middle of the bedroom floor with his open guitar case to his right and the amplifier to his left. In his lap lay the envelopes filled with the unfinished scribblings of a scatterbrained seventeen year old. He pulled out the thick stack of lined paper, noticing that each sheet was dried out, brittle and exhibited a yellowish patina. The song at the top of the stack was *Suburban Blues*. As he began to read the lyrics he was transported back to that night at the 'Silverbell Hideout'.

It was the night before his eighteenth birthday. The band had just finished setting up and many of the kids were lining up to get into the building. The line that wove around the building was at least the length of a football field. That's when Lizzie walked in. The guys attending the door all recognized Lizzie so there was no waiting in line for her. They knew she was with the band. Jake and Lizzie had been seeing each other for about six months now to the dismay of Tom and now some of the other band members. Their routine was a simple one. If the band played a gig she would show up. Lizzie and Jake would spend each break together in some dark corner of the room or out in the parking lot in her truck. This left little time for the band members to get together between sets to consult about how they were performing and if changes needed to be made. For the last three months of the 'relationship' Lizzie had been encouraging Jake to quit the band so that they could be together and go out on dates like a regular couple. She thought that he should get a real job, so that he could buy his own car. She even tried to get him to quit by dancing with other guys on the dance floor while he was playing. She'd say, "If you can't fully commit to me, I'm not going to be committed to you." That made Jake crazy with jealousy and caused his performance to suffer noticeably. She'd left him so emotionally drained that songwriting was the furthest thing from his mind.

Jake hoped that tonight would be different. He already explained that the band meant a lot to him and he couldn't let his friends down by quitting. The last time they were together he'd been reduced to the point of tearfully begging her to reconsider her demands. She told him that she'd think it over and let him know what she was going to do the next time she saw him. Tonight was the night.

He was sitting alone in the snack bar having a Coke—his stomach in his throat with worry about what Lizzie would decide. He was worried about what he would decide if she still wanted him to quit. He loved the band. And up until Lizzie, he thought he loved it more than anything. She came up from behind him and put her cold hands on his face as she swung around the booth and sat across from him. She smiled and held his hands so that he could warm them up for her. While he was rubbing her hands, his stomach began to settle. *"At least she showed up. Maybe that's a good sign,"* he hoped. "I'm glad you came tonight. I've missed ya," he said as his lip quivered involuntarily in anticipation of her reaction. "Can I get you a Coke?"

"No thanks, I've missed you too," she said as she smiled and took a sip of his Coke.

They sat staring at each other without a word and slowly he saw her expression change as she prepared to speak. Just behind those dark eyes Jake could see an idea was brewing. *"She's been thinking about us and she's come up with a solution to our problems and now we can stay together and stop all the fighting,"* he hoped.

Then she broke the stillness. "I've decided what we should do."

"You have?" he asked with more than moderate anticipation.

"Yes," she affirmed with authority and an engaging smile. "You know you'll be eighteen on Sunday and well, being eighteen, you can make more decisions for yourself without permission from anyone and there's one decision I want you to make tonight for me. I want to marry you. And I think we should get married."

"Married?" Jake asked just in case he hadn't heard her correctly. "You want to marry *me*?"

"Yes, silly," she affirmed with a laugh. "Yes, I want to marry *you*."

It wasn't something he hadn't thought about. In fact one of his major fantasies was that they would get married some day. But he never thought Lizzie would be the one to suggest it. He thought she would be the kind who would take years of convincing. "OK!" he agreed. He had no friends who were married. A few couples he knew were hoping some day to be married. And that's what he thought Lizzie was proposing—merely suggesting a future plan so that each of them knew there was a strong and binding commitment between them.

"So you'll tell the guys in the band?" she asked.

"Sure, I guess they'd like to know," he replied with a little hesitation. Jake was having a little trouble understanding why the first thing she would think of was to tell the guys in the band.

"Good. Let's go do it now," she said in a tone that was somewhere between a suggestion and a demand. She rose from the booth and took both his hands in hers to pull him up from his seat.

"OK Lizzie. But I don't see why we have to be in such a hurry. I mean, it's not like were gonna get married tomorrow," he said as he tugged on her hands, reluctant to be pulled up.

"No silly—tomorrow's Sunday. The courthouse isn't open on Sunday." She attempted to pull him up again. "I've scheduled us for ten-thirty Monday morning."

"You what?" he laughed when he surmised this all was a joke. "OK, you got me Lizzie—pretty funny. For a minute there I thought you were serious."

Lizzie let go of Jake and he fell back into his seat. She opened her purse and withdrew some paperwork that looked pretty official and waved it in his face. It looked like a marriage license. "I'm not joking, Jake. I just got a great job offer in California. I'll be earning more than enough for the both of us. You can finish school and go to college if you want to. This is a real chance for us to finally be together. I knew you wouldn't go on just a whim, so I wanted us to be married first. The thing is, I have to be out there by next Friday or they'll give the job to someone else." She paused with the most tempting and seductive look Jake had ever seen. "So what's it gonna be. Do we go together or will you make me leave without you?"

He was facing a life choice that was more monumental than any he had ever encountered. This was clearly a life altering decision between pure ecstasy with Lizzie on the one hand and absolute agony without her on the other. And he knew he just didn't have the mental or emotional capacity to process it. He put his head down on the table and cried. She could barely understand him with his face hidden in his hands. "Lizzie, I want to be with you forever. But I just can't go with you now. I've got my parents to consider, I've got six months till graduation, and the band is counting on me to finish the songs and…"

Lizzie lost her patience and must not have been too impressed with his agenda. "Songs, Jake? Those aren't songs. They're just some rhymes you haven't had the time or inclination to finish. If you think for one second that you have what it takes to be a songwriter…" She leaned down to where he was crying and hissed into his ear, "think again." She turned and left. And Jake never saw her again.

Jake's trip to the past was interrupted by Joyce calling up to him. "Dinner in 15 Minutes."

"*Thank God for Joyce,*" he thought, "*If I had married Lizzie, I woulda never met Joyce. So apparently I was actually capable of making good decisions back then. I wonder if Lizzie can cook. Nobody cooks like Joyce.*" At that moment, he got an idea. He couldn't tell if he was just feeling the need to get motivated and get his creative juices flowing, or if he was inspired by vengeance. Nevertheless he began to write a practice song. The rules were simple. Write a song before dinner. Fifteen minutes. "*I can't write a song in fifteen minutes. This has failure written all over it,*" he whined to himself. Then he quickly recalled Brian's words to stave off the pessimism, "*Remember, it's not failing if you learned something and had fun doing it.*" He had no time to think of a subject so he thought of the last thing on his mind—dinner. "*I'll write about Joyce's cooking. I'll call it 'Joyce's Cookin'.*" So he quickly picked up his guitar with only five good strings. The only thing he could remember were the chords to a song that Paul Newman sang in the movie *Cool Hand Luke*. He lifted those chords and the melody. In the next ten minutes he penciled out a song.

> If you wanna make me happy
> It'll take more than your crappy
> Beans and franks and pizza that you make
> All I want is Joyce's cookin'
> She's the one that's so good lookin'
> Over in the kitchen by the cake.

> She always has my dinner ready
> Since I asked her to go steady
> Even if I get home pretty late.
> She never asks me where I've been.
> Just smiles and lets me come on in
> Says honey let me warm you up a plate.

> Biscuits gravy and fried chicken
> She can make 'em finger lickin'
> Swear I've seen her do it all the time
> I always get a real good dinner
> Otherwise I'd be much thinner
> And I thank my lucky stars she's mine.

"Dinner's ready," Joyce called.

Jake took his guitar with him down stairs and walked into the kitchen playing and singing the new song. His fingers stumbled badly over the strings and had to stop to read the words from time to time, but it was a good effort for fifteen minutes. Joyce placed the dinner plates down on the table and took her seat to listen to Jake struggle through it. When he finished, she applauded and said, "That's good, Jake. I like it. You should write a chorus for it—then it would be a finished song."

He smiled and said, "Well, it *was* just a practice song to get me started. But, I guess I could." He remembered that one of his biggest problems with finishing songs was writing the chorus or bridge. That part had always been a stumbling block.

CHAPTER 18

▼

Jake woke before the alarm clock went off Monday morning. It was 5:47a.m. The sun was still hiding but its rays were tinting the sky with morning's light. He wanted to get an early start so that he could plan his sabbatical. At 6:30 he was in his vehicle and ready to turn the key when he stopped, got out of the car, went back into the house and retrieved his guitar and the envelope of songs. He wasn't sure why he did it. It just felt right to have the tools of his new trade with him.

He walked into the empty office building, leaving the guitar and songs in the SUV. He wasn't ready to tip anyone off to his plan because it still sounded pretty silly, even to him. Most of the day was filled with the normal duties of a real estate broker. All his paperwork had kept him from planning the escape. It was frustrating. During the day he couldn't get an image out of his mind. It was an image of himself, slowly digging a tunnel from the basement of the office out to the street with a spoon. *"It may take me that long to get free from this place,"* he thought.

The key to a successful sabbatical would be to put the right person in charge while he was gone. He knew that person was Jenny, but getting her to agree would be a whole project in itself. There were two or three others that might work out but he wanted Jenny. She knew the everyday workings of the company and could keep the system intact while he was gone. The biggest issue he'd have to deal with would be her self-confidence.

As the day dragged on a few salespeople drifted into the office and then back out, as if being controlled by the tide. It was four o'clock and, except for Jenny at the front desk, he was alone. Jake picked up the phone and buzzed her.

"What!" she demanded. As if he was keeping her from something important. Jake knew better. Except for a few scattered deals here and there, business was slow.

"Are you busy with anything right now?" he asked.

"Well, I have two more chapters in my novel to read if that's what you mean," she reported.

He contemplated asking her to fill in for him right then and there but lost his nerve. *"I had better prepare for this first,"* he thought.

"Why don't you take a break from all that work and leave early for a change?"

"OK. Thanks." She hung up the phone, gathered up her things and hollered a goodnight to him as she fled.

After she left, Jake poked his head around the corner of the hallway to make sure no one else was in the building. He quietly walked to the front door, cracked it open and cautiously looked left then right as if he were leaving the scene of a crime. Seeing no one, he went to the SUV and brought the guitar and the envelope of songs back to the office. Locking his office door behind him, he began to read each song he wrote from those teenage years. The phone rang. He was so involved in his review of the songs that he didn't hear it. He pulled his guitar out and tried to play what was written and ran into two problems. He didn't remember how to play the notes to the chord progressions that were written. All he could remember how to play was 'C', 'F', and 'G'. The high 'E' string was the other problem. It was broken. Undaunted by the complications he packed up the songs and the guitar and set out for Guitar City to pick up a chord chart and some new strings for the Epiphone.

Jake had dressed relatively casual for work—light tan corduroys, dark brown dress shirt and tie—a step up from the usual Levi's and sweatshirt. He'd seldom feel out of place clothed in this manner. However, when he arrived at Guitar City he saw a striking contrast between himself and the patrons of this store. Enough so that he felt a twinge of fear for his safety. As he entered, he saw no merchandise. It was there in plain view, but his eyes were drawn to the body jewelry, reckless yet colorful hairstyles, and the tattoos. Well, not really tattoos—more like murals inked in colorful designs on many of the shoppers as well as the help. He was as out of place as a geek in a biker bar.

He timidly began to look around at the great selection of guitars, amplifiers and just about anything a band would need. He was floundering around the songbooks, just as the fear was wearing off, looking for a chord chart when someone from behind him said, "Hey, man, can I help you find something?" He sounded friendly enough so Jake turned to see a tall skinny kid about twenty years old with scraggly blond hair covering most of his bearded face and running down to the middle of his back. He wore a dark blue tank top that had an unrepeatable slogan printed on the front and a nametag that read 'Warren'. His arms were both fully tattooed even down to his fingers. His assignment for the moment was to stock the songbook bins while helping customers find what they needed.

"Yep, I'm looking for a guitar chord chart and some guitar strings."

He laid a small stack of song books aside and walked over to a bookrack. "Well, the charts are over here. I think this would be the most comprehensive and easy to read one we have, but we have some cheaper charts that aren't as complete."

"I'll take that first one…Thanks."

"Now the strings are over here. Do you know what kind of strings you want?" Warren asked as he led him to another part of the store.

"Not really," Jake answered as he followed Warren past the rows of new and used guitars hanging on ether side of the aisle.

"Well what kind of guitar are the strings for and what kind of music will you be playing?"

"It's an old electric thin hollow body Epiphone. And I guess I'll be using it for rock and roll or blues after I relearn how to play it," he admitted doing a poor job of concealing his embarrassment.

Warren, without hesitation reached for and selected a pack of strings. "These should be good to get you started. They're not too expensive and they should sound great on that Epiphone. They're what I use," Warren said as he handed him the strings and the chord chart. "Is there anything else you need today?"

"Well, that should do it for now. Thanks for your help, Warren," he said, then turned to find the cashier.

As Jake turned away, Warren asked, "How long has it been since you played, man?"

He turned back toward Warren. Jake couldn't tell if he was genuinely interested in what he was up to or if he just didn't want to go back to filing songbooks. "Thirty five years or so."

"Wooah, that's a while, man. What makes you want to get back into the guitar after so long?" Jake wasn't used to getting personal questions asked by anyone he didn't know, much less a store clerk. He didn't realize that this store wasn't like big box stores where the customer is avoided like the plague. Guitar City was where patrons went to talk music to anyone who would listen. And the staff not only listened, they wanted to know.

"Well, I'm kind of thinking of getting back into writing some songs. I used to do a little writing back in high school and it's something I've missed doing over the years," he reported as they walked together up to the cashier.

"Well I wish you luck man," Warren said with a smile.

"You can call me Jake."

"Did you know about the American Songwriting Contest?" Warren asked.

"No but I'm not ready to enter any song in any contest. I'm just getting started with this."

"You might want to read up on it just in case. I think the deadline to enter isn't for about a month or two," Warren said as he took a brochure from the counter and handed it to Jake.

"Thanks, Warren. You've been a great help," Jake said as he took the brochure.

"Any time, man," Warren said as he turned to resume his filing of songbooks.

The line to the cashier was long enough that Jake had time to read the brochure. Apparently this was an annual contest that offered prizes for the winners, which included a contract with a recording company. There were several categories—one being Rhythm and Blues. Still in line, he began to read the small print that listed the sponsors and the judges. None of the names were familiar to him except one. He recognized the name Maurie Best on the list of judges. He knew the name only because he was the most famous band manager since Brian Epstein of 'The Beatles'.

Finally it was his turn to be cashed out. He stuffed the brochure into his pocket, paid for his items and was out the door. On the way home he turned the satellite radio to his favorite station. As he drove he thought about the songwriting contest and began to estimate if he had time to enter. *The brochure said that the deadline was June 28, 2002. That gives me thirty-nine days to finish a song and get it on a CD. Well, it is possible,"* he thought. Goal setting was one of the first things he learned in order to survive in the real estate business, so right then and there he set a goal. The goal was to have a song ready to enter into the song contest by the deadline. He pulled into the driveway and as the garage door opened, he could see that Joyce hadn't gotten home yet. That was OK with him today because he was anxious to start working right away.

He figured the den was the best spot in the house for songwriting. The room was lit by an old wooden bridge lamp that cast a warm and inviting glow. He felt comfortable in there with his hutch style desk and big green leather and wood recliner. When he closed the door, the boundaries of his world were those four walls. There were no distractions and time didn't exist. He brought the stack of songs, strings and chord chart in and placed them on the desk.

Re-stringing the guitar was the next order of business. He wasn't sure if he remembered how. His mind strained and failed to recall even one instance when he re-strung his guitar. He knew that he had done it many times but the act must have been so second nature that his mind hadn't registered it. It would have been like remembering balancing your checkbook thirty years ago. So he studied the way the old strings looked, which way they were wound on the tuning posts and in what direction the tuning pegs turned to tighten the strings. He began by removing one string and replacing it. Then moving to the next string using the old strings as a template. The most difficult part of the process was holding the string in place at the tuning post in order to keep it winding around the post and not overlapping on itself. After forty-five minutes he had replaced all the strings. He found a pitch pipe in his guitar case for tuning and, to his surprise, he caught on to that rather quickly. He strummed the guitar and it sounded pretty good. But it looked pretty bad. The excess of each of the six new strings protruding from their respective tuning posts made the head stock of the guitar resemble a steel porcupine. *"I'll take care of that later,"* he thought as he opened the chord chart to look up the chords to *Suburban Blues*.

After a few minutes practicing the chord changes he had made some progress but his fingers hurt bad enough to force an intermission. During the respite Jake decided to study some of the words to the song to see if he could come up with any new ideas for the verses. He was concerned mainly about the style of the song. It was just a basic three-chord blues progression. Even though blues was his favorite, this type of song fit neatly into a category that only those interested in blues would listen to. Jake didn't want to write a song that appealed to only one group. He wanted to write a song with broader influence. But a blues song that would cross over to other listeners was the exception rather than the rule. As he turned one page, he noticed that on the back there was a list of ten song titles scratched out. It was a set list for a performance at one of the many places 'The Phogg' had played. As he read down the list, he came upon a title that was out of the ordinary for the band. But it was a song that Tom lobbied for. Jake remembered the day Tom got his way.

It was the beginning of their senior year at Waterford Kettering High School. An assembly for the entire student body had been called. The Kettering Glee Club, which had received countless awards for their performances, had been corresponding with an out-of-town traveling orchestra who just happened to be appearing that weekend in Detroit. With the school's blessing, the Glee Club had invited the orchestra to join them in a performance for the students and teachers in the auditorium.

Tom and Jake were making their way to the auditorium and debating about whether to include a new song in the set for the weekend gig. Tom and Jake liked all music and weren't tied to any particular style when it came to considering a song to perform. Tom loved the Righteous Brothers and had wanted the band to do *Georgia On My Mind*. Although he had been overruled several times, he would make a case for it whenever the opportunity arose. Today was one of those occasions. As they walked into the auditorium, Jake was explaining that he felt that the crowd wouldn't accept the song. The crowd they catered to was mainly frat who generally didn't like soul or rhythm and blues. Jake and the rest of the band felt that they should play it safe. Tom's argument was that any song, whether it be blues, soul or rock and roll would be liked by anyone no matter if they were frat or grease as long as the song was good and was performed well enough.

The debate went on as they walked through the tall steel double doors into the auditorium and across the hardwood floor to a row of vacant folding chairs. As they took their seats, the debate took an awkward turn at least for Jake. Tom said, "Are you tryin' to tell me that there are people out there who don't like this song? Just listen to this." He began to sing. "Georgia oh Georgia." Jake, forgetting for a moment, where he was, listened to Tom sing. His voice was so well trained that each note and nuance of the song was performed perfectly even at the low volume. More kids and teachers filed in for the assembly and stared at Tom and Jake as they took their seats. Jake became uncomfortable, not necessarily with Tom, but the appearance of being serenaded by another guy while others watched—others who he feared would not appreciate the context from which this exchange had sprung. Jake tried to get Tom to stop but he wouldn't. Pretty soon everyone had taken their seats and the principal was on stage for the introduction of the Glee Club and the traveling orchestra. The principal noticed that there was some sort of disturbance in the audience and could see Tom in what appeared to be a discussion with Jake.

The principal began by saying, "May I please have your attention?" He was flanked on one side by the Glee Club and on the other by the orchestra. Tom kept singing. The kids in the row next to Tom were turned toward Tom, listening to him sing. They were all hypnotized by his voice. He was singing soft enough that anyone further than the row immediately next to him couldn't hear. The principal said again, "May I please have your attention?" Now he had everyone's attention except about four people. But Tom, so intent on showing Jake how this song could sound just kept singing. From the principal's vantage point he couldn't hear Tom. He could only see what he thought was a student discussion going on when they should be paying attention to him. He didn't get to be principal by letting kids disobey him. So he called out, "Mr. Tyler, could you please come up here to the front?" Tom kept singing until Jake slapped him on the shoulder and pointed to the stage. Tom turned to look. He turned back to Jake with the most amazed and horrified look on his face. The auditorium was as quiet as a morgue when the principal repeated, "Mr. Tyler, could you please join me up here?" Tom started to sweat as he rose from his folding chair making a clanging sound that echoed loudly in the otherwise hushed room. Jake could feel his embarrassment as Tom brushed past him and the twelve other students who had to stand up to let him out.

The long walk to the stage must have been brutal for him. As he slowly walked, heads turned toward Tom as if they were watching a condemned man taking his final walk toward that ultimate punishment. He made it to the foot of the stage and paused for a moment hoping that this was as far as he was required to go. It was the start of a brand new year at Waterford Kettering High School and letting an incident such as this go unpunished could leave the floodgates open for a very unruly year. Deciding that an example had to be made of Tom, the principal called him up on stage with his finger. Tom slowly climbed the steps as every eye in the audience, Glee Club and orchestra were on him. He moved up next to the principal who handed him the microphone. When Tom accepted it, the principal said, "Could you please repeat, to the whole student body exactly, to the word, what was so important that you had to disrupt today's assembly?"

"I don't think it'd be a good idea to do it exactly…"

The principal interrupted Tom. "Exactly, Mr. Tyler…and without any further delay, please."

So Tom, who was normally pretty comfortable with a microphone in his hand, nervously started to sing a perfect imitation of the Righteous Brothers version of *Georgia On My Mind* to scattered giggles. The principal at first was pleased to see that he had embarrassed Tom and was about to let him off the hook when the Glee Club, who happened to know the song, chimed in with the back up parts. Tom was a little startled, but with other voices singing back up for him, his embarrassment disappeared and he instinctively switched to entertainment mode. The orchestra, thinking that this was a planned stunt, faked it and played along too. Tom could see that his audience stopped giggling and began enjoying themselves. They'd expected a boring medley of folk songs like *Michael*

Row the Boat Ashore. Instead they got the Righteous Brothers. When the song was over everyone in the audience, student and teacher, frat and grease, were all on their feet applauding and screaming.

Tom didn't take a bow. He simply walked over to the very frustrated principal and handed him the microphone. The principal was now faced with an interesting dilemma. He could have Tom hauled off to his office to await further punishment, which would surely qualify him for the most hated principal of all time award. Or, because the number had turned out so well, he could act as if the whole thing was planned, therefore saving face while still sending the message that unruliness would not go unnoticed. He chose the latter and started smiling and applauding along with everyone else. Tom was off the hook for now and free to go back to his seat. The walk back to his chair was more like a victory lap. Everyone within an arm's length mobbed him. The frats, the greasers, the nerds (including the entire chess club), the jocks, the brown-nosers and even the faculty were all waiting to congratulate Tom. He wasn't half way back to his seat when they started chanting, "We want Tyler. We want Tyler," as if this would inspire an encore. They hadn't stopped when Tom found his seat next to Jake. Tom leaned over to Jake and shouted into his ear in a struggle to be heard. "Look at who's applaudin'."

Jake yelled back, "Everybody is applauding."

"My point exactly," Tom replied as he finally sat down.

"OK Tom. *Georgia On My Mind* is in as far as I'm concerned."

Jake went back to working on *Suburban Blues*. Taking only a short break for dinner, he kept at it. It was 2:30 a.m. when he had crafted all the verses the way he thought they should be. The only thing missing was the last line of the bridge. This was the most important part of the song, the heart of the song that gets the point across. It's the thread that ties together what your verses have in common in order to solidify the message. He had made progress, but still hadn't broken down that barrier remaining firmly in his way. All he had for the chorus was, "I've got the blues, the lowdown suburban blues. And you know I can't escape them DA DADA DAA DA DA." Barely able to keep his eyes open, he dragged himself off to bed.

The first three hours in the horizontal position were used planning what to do when and if he could finish the song. Thirty-eight days left till the contest deadline and he didn't have all the words yet. He couldn't play guitar well enough to participate in the recording of any song. He didn't know the first thing about recording. He didn't know how to get help. All these problems were solvable but the sheer magnitude of the task threatened to render him sleepless trying to sort it all out. Finally with one hour till morning he fell asleep.

It was an eerie morning—darker than usual for this time of day. The clouds were a mixture of dirty yellow and gray as if a bad storm was brewing. Each one, as they moved along, seemed to hold an unrecognizable yet somehow familiar shape against the glowing firmament. The satellite radio was playing *Tarantula* by the Tarantulas, a haunting electric guitar instrumental from the early 1960's. "That same dream again," he cried, as he suddenly sat up in bed. "That damn dream!" Undaunted by the lack of sleep but a little shaken by the dream he dragged himself out of bed determined to figure out a way to get that song finished and recorded.

The shower is a good place to think. It really would be a lost opportunity if you didn't think and plan things while in the shower, he thought. So Jake thought and planned as he rinsed off his sleepless night and soaped off the residue of that recurring dream. After showering he had a plan for the day. First on the schedule was to convince Jenny that she had what it takes to oversee the business during his absence. Then he'd be free to work on the song.

CHAPTER 19

▼

Jenny heard the front door open and close but she didn't look up. She rarely did this early in the morning. Most of the people coming in would be agents making their way to their offices in so much of a hurry they seldom said hello, so neither did she. If they did speak to greet her she would respond. But she never went out of her way to do so. *"I'm not the Wal-Mart greeter. If you want a greeter go hire one,"* she would say. Because she didn't look up she didn't see Jake standing in front of her holding his guitar case. But neither did she hear the continuation of footsteps connected with the sound of the door, so she knew someone was standing at her desk. She didn't have to look up to know it was Jake. They often would play this game. He'd wait as long as it took. She'd go as long as she could ignoring him until she couldn't stand it, and then look up with the mock-evil stare and say, "What?"

Usually Jake would say, "Nothing," and walk away just to get her goat, but this time he said, "Hey, Jenny, could you please come with me? I want to talk to you about something."

"OK," she agreed and they went into his office.

As he closed the door behind him she said, "What's up with that case there? Is that a guitar? What are you doing with a guitar, Jake?" She knew nothing of his high school days. She had no idea that he used to play the guitar much less be in a rock and roll band.

"That's part of what I want to talk to you about."

"First you want me to get my real estate license and now you want me to learn to play the guitar? I think this is getting a little strange, don't you?" she joked.

"Well no, I don't want you to learn the guitar unless you think it will help you run Strong Realtors while I'm gone."

"Gone? Where are you going?"

"I'm gonna take some time off—maybe up to a year. And I want you to oversee things for me while I'm away."

"What's wrong? Are you sick? I knew it. I just knew that something was wrong with you the way you've been acting lately. Is it bad? I hope it's not bad," she inquired as she put her hand over her mouth in fear of his answer.

"No. I'm not sick," he assured her.

"Thank God," she said in relief. "So if you're not sick, then why are you doing this?"

"I guess it's no secret that I've been losing patience with clients and starting to slip up a little on my follow up. And to tell you the truth, I'm not so sure I want to be in the real estate business anymore. I just need some time away from it in order to sort that out."

"Well, I'd like to help you Jake but I can't. I can't run this office. I told you before, I don't have the experience."

"How do you think one gets experience?" Jake asked. "By doing." He answered his own question for her.

"Well, I can't argue with that. But I'd never forgive myself if I made a decision or did something or forgot to do it, and it got us sued or something. I mean, you put your trust in me to do a good job and then I mess something up. I don't want to be in a position to screw up like that."

Again, he remembered his discussion about songwriting with Brian who told him that if he tried and had fun and learned something he would not have failed. "Well Jenny, the only way you'll fail, is that after the year's up you haven't become more comfortable with responsibility. If you do that, and learn something along the way, you wouldn't have failed, no matter what happens. I'll tell you what. I'll take this week to go over everything I think you should be doing and we'll meet every Wednesday morning to go over any questions or problems you might have until you're comfortable."

"Can't you get one of the salespeople to do this?"

Jake needed to close hard on her so his response was confident and forceful. "Yeah, I probably could. But out of everybody in this office, you know and I know that you could do the best job. You wouldn't be distracted with having to sell real estate like they would. You're already doing most of my job now and you'd get the most benefit out of taking the position. So what do ya say? Let's notify the crew and tell them you're getting a promotion."

"Why'd you bring a guitar into the office? I didn't know you played the guitar," she said, hoping that changing the subject would buy her some time, before she had to answer.

"I don't. And don't change the subject." Jake scribbled a number representing her new salary on a piece of paper and slid it across the desk. "So what's it gonna be? Can I count on you to help me out?"

Jenny paused in thought, slowly nodded her head and said, "OK. But if I screw up and we all go to prison it'll be on your conscience."

"Great!" he cheered. "Let's sit down and draw up an outline of the job description and I'll call a meeting to make the announcement. Who do you think would be best to turn my clients over to?"

"Jerry," she said without hesitation. Jerry was the agent most like Jake in business style and Jake would have chosen him too.

"That's who I would have picked. See—you just made a great decision." As they sat down to hammer out the details he said, "This really means a lot to me Jenny. Thanks." She knew what it meant to him, she knew he needed the time off and she knew that she needed to do this for herself too.

After the announcement was made and the questions were all answered, Jake was comforted by the support both he and Jenny received from the sales staff. Not one of them felt that the company was in any jeopardy because they didn't interpret the event as a crisis—just a change.

It was noon and most of the office emptied out for lunch. Jake was glad that with all the excitement of the new job, Jenny never followed up on the question about why he was toting a guitar case around. He went back to his office, locked the door and sat down with his guitar and began to work on the bridge to *Suburban Blues*. An hour had gone by and he was still stuck with, "I've got the blues, the lowdown suburban blues. And you know I can't escape them DA DADA DA DAA DA DA." His satellite radio was playing songs from the seventies—an era that was not his favorite. He was willing to try any little thing to get inspired. But with the restless night he had just experienced, all it did was lull him to sleep. As he slept, that eerie dream came creeping back. Speeding around the corners of the treacherous road while writing 'Pay the dues' on the file folder. But this time the dream was just a little different. He was on the cell phone with the title company and he could hear himself saying "What do you mean, the dues aren't paid? I thought I paid them myself."

And just before he smashed through the guardrail, the voice from the phone said, "You haven't yet paid the dues." Jake's office phone buzzed, waking him out of the dream. Still shaken and groggy he reached for the phone but paused to

A friend loves at all times.
 - Proverbs 17:17

11:30 PM   Fri Nite

notice that the song on the radio was Ringo Starr singing *It Don't Come Easy*. The part he heard was the chorus or bridge to the song. "If you want to sing the blues, you gotta pay your dues and you know it don't come easy." He picked up the phone and it was Jenny.

"The Board of Realtors is on the phone about your board dues. They're saying you haven't yet paid your dues, but I sent them a check. Jake told her to stop payment on the check she sent, and send them another one.

At the same time Jake spoke, Jenny said, "How about if I stop payment on the check I sent them, and send them another one?" They both hung up in unison.

Then Ringo sang the verse again. "If you want to sing the blues, you gotta pay your dues and you know it don't come easy."

Finally the light went on in Jake's head. "I haven't yet paid my dues. I haven't yet paid my dues. DA DA DA DA DAA DA DA. I haven't yet paid my dues. That's it. Those words fit the song perfectly. I've got the blues, the lowdown suburban blues. And you know I can't escape them 'cause I haven't yet paid my dues." He hurried to write the words down as if to capture them before they flew out of his mind. He sat there and read over the lyrics twice looking for flaws. No—everything was in order. He had finally finished a song. He thought, "*Well, it really wasn't finished, exactly. There's the arranging left to do. What instruments would be right for this song? Will there be backup singing? I've still got to invent the guitar parts.*" He used the word invent instead of write because to write the parts, he would have to put the notes on paper and he had long forgotten how to do that. He would have to make all the parts up by trial and error on his guitar. That meant that he would have to practice the guitar to regain some of the proficiency he once had in order to facilitate the inventing.

It must have been 6:30 p.m. or so when Jake decided to pack it in. He fumbled around with the guitar, trying to come up with a good rhythm part for the song, but he just didn't have it in him. Then it came to him that he used to pick up on how to play tunes by listening to the recording over and over. "*I need to get a CD player and some earphones,*" he thought. Then he thought some more. "*And I need to try and learn how to read music again. I need to take guitar lessons.*" With those thoughts fresh in mind, he packed up the guitar and the songs and headed for Guitar City. During the drive, he decided that he needed to set up a schedule that included time for practicing guitar by ear, practicing reading music, guitar lessons and time for forced creativity. As he parked the car in Guitar City's parking lot he could see Warren through the front window filing songbooks.

"Hello Jake," he heard as he walked through the front door. It was comforting and not totally unexpected to learn that Warren remembered not only him but his name as well.

"Hey Warren," Jake said as they shook hands.

"How's that Epiphone sound with the new strings, man?" Warren asked as he pointed to the guitar case Jake was holding.

"Great, Warren. But it would sound better if I knew how to play it. It's been hard starting up again."

"We've got Mel Bay if you want to learn from scratch," Warren announced.

"The last time I saw a Mel Bay book, I think I was thirteen."

"They're still great instructional books. If you don't know how to read music you'd want to start with the *Mel Bay Modern Guitar Book Grade 1*."

"Well, it *is* as if I never knew how. So that sounds right for me."

Warren remembered that Jake wanted to play blues and suggested he take *The Mel Bay Complete Blues Guitar Book and CD* too. As he paged through the guitar primers the true magnitude of his task began to reveal itself between the lines of unrecognizable hieroglyphics. *"I can't believe I used to know this stuff,"* he thought. But, after all, it had been more than half his life ago.

Warren sensed that discouragement was brewing and said, "Why don't you tell me just exactly what it is you want to accomplish, and I'll see if I can help you get to your goal."

"Don't laugh. OK?" Jake requested.

"OK, I promise," he pledged as he outlined a cross on his chest with his right index finger.

"Well, I got to looking at that songwriting contest brochure and decided that I wanted to try and submit an entry."

"Cool," Warren responded.

"So I just finished the lyrics to a song that I started to write back in high school and now I need to invent the parts for the instruments. The problem is that I want to do this myself and I'm so rusty on the guitar that I don't think there's enough time to get good enough to ad lib some riffs for the song," Jake admitted.

"Can you pick up tunes by listening to them?" Warren asked.

"I used to be able to. In fact I was going to buy a CD player and earphones today."

"Well, that's the easiest way to get your proficiency up. I'd try that and if you want guitar lessons maybe we could get you hooked up with Luther. Luther teaches mostly blues and some jazz. He caters to guys that don't read music. Want to meet him?"

"Sure," Jake confirmed.

"Follow me," Warren called as he led Jake and his guitar through the bass guitar section, around the percussion room and down three steps to a small waiting room occupied by what appeared to be budding musicians whose ages ranged from six to probably fourteen, all accompanied by their parents and each of whom was at least ten years younger than Jake. They continued down a dark narrow hall lined on each side with doors. Jake could hear tiny bits of guitar, violin, and piano music played at varying levels of skill and volume emanating from each door. They finally came to an open door at the end of the hall. Warren greeted the man in the room and began to introduce Jake as a potential student. From where Jake was standing he couldn't see the man, he could only hear the rattle and scraping of a metal stool as the man rose from his sitting position and peered around the door casing. Jake, expecting to eventually see a face, had his eyes fixed at an elevation where he thought eye contact would be made. When Luther materialized, Jake found himself looking at the pocket of the huge man's tent-like shirt. The dim light that had previously illuminated the doorway was all but blocked, not unlike an eclipse of the sun. His colossal frame cast a shadow over Jake's head and down the hall, up the sides of the walls and on down to the waiting room. Luther looked at Jake and turned back to Warren wearing a confused smile and then back again toward his new student. He was in his mid fifties and had been teaching guitar for thirty some years but couldn't remember the last time he had a student over the age of 14. He reached out with his right hand and Jake followed suit. Luther's mammoth hand was endowed with fat stubby fingers, the size of 'D' cell batteries and it swallowed Jake's hand whole—the customary interlocking thumbs notwithstanding. "I'm Luther. Nice to meet you," he said in a soothing but higher than expected pitch coming from a three hundred pound blues guitar player.

"Likewise—I'm Jake."

Luther had been playing guitar since he was seven years old. His uncle gave him his first guitar. It was an old hollow body Harmony acoustic. He learned to play listening to recordings of all the old blues guitarists like Robert Johnson, Son House and even B.B. King. He got in a blues band at age thirteen and had been playing and singing ever since. Over the years he'd been summoned by many local Detroit recording artists to do session work in the recording studio. Also he'd been playing lead guitar in a blues/rock band in Detroit on the weekends between recording sessions and teaching.

"You got an old Gibson there?" Luther asked as he pointed one of his 'D' cells at Jake's guitar case.

"Epiphone—want to take a look?"

"I sure do."

Jake laid the case on the floor, opened it and handed the guitar to Luther for inspection. The only complaint that Jake ever had about the guitar was that the body style was really too big for him. But when Luther strapped it on, it looked like a miniature. He started to play. How those massive fingers could navigate the neck of that guitar with such speed and grace was a true wonder. Of all the guitars that exist in the world there can't be many that have ever had the pleasure of being played that well. Warren glanced toward Jake with a smile, knowing that Luther would be the right man to help his new customer. "That's sure a fine ol' guitar, Jake. They just don't make 'em like that any more."

"Thanks, Luther. That's sure some fine pickin' too."

It wasn't long before they made the arrangements and set a schedule for lessons. With the help of Luther and Warren, Jake put together a daily regimen of study and practice that he hoped would produce results. He pledged to himself that every morning he'd do two hours of playing by ear to his favorite blues guitarist CD's—then two hours of book study with the Mel Bay primers and then two hours of practicing riffs and other essentials Luther would show him during the two lessons per week. Then finally he'd try two hours of inventing pieces of music to go with his song. "You've got to do your time in the woodshed," Luther explained. The term woodshed was a new one to Jake. To Luther it meant practice, work, rehearse, study, and sweat it out. To Jake it just meant 'pay your dues'—and that's exactly what he intended to do.

CHAPTER 20

▼

As promised, Jake met with Jenny at 8:00 a.m. on Wednesday to go over any problems or questions she had so far in her new role at the office. Over coffee they talked about a list of issues that hadn't been considered in the hasty transfer of power. Jake was pleased to hear that Jenny had been up late the night before formulating procedures to handle each of the concerns on her list. He too had spent the better part of last night "woodsheddin' it" to the point where the finger-tips of his left hand were sore and close to blistering. He had made great progress and judging from Jenny's input for the morning, so had she. The list was very organized and well thought out and with only a few added suggestions, he agreed with everything she proposed. "You've just had your first success at policy making," he complimented. And seeing that there was nothing else for now, he headed out for his guitar lesson.

"Oh Jake, I've been handling your messages here. But how do you want me to handle the personal ones? For instance, Dan called you yesterday and I haven't called him back yet," she asked.

"I'll get hold of Dan, Rick, David and whoever I can think of and let them know what's going on and tell them they won't find me at the office for a while. Hopefully that should work. I guess we'll kind of play it by ear." That reminded Jake that he had to pick up a portable CD player and earphones after his lesson so that he could practice playing by ear again.

On the way to Guitar City, Jake put in a call to Dan. "Hey Dan, I got a message you called. What's happening?"

"Well, I wanted to let you know that Rick and I had a great idea. We're gonna make a Tom Tyler room in my basement where the bar and pool table are."

"Tom Tyler room?" Jake questioned. "What's a Tom Tyler room?"

"Well, you know all the pictures Rick took when we were in the band? He's probably got a couple hundred. We got to talking and come to find out, he still has all the negatives. And I've got a bunch of memorabilia that Tom has sent me over the years. So, Rick and I are gettin' together to sort out the photos and the stuff Tom sent me, and we want you to give us a hand tonight at my place."

"OK," Jake agreed. "Sounds like fun."

"Hey…by the way, how come you took so long getting back to me? Are you gettin' busy at the office again?"

"No—actually I've set things up so I don't have to be in the office for a while. From now on, when you need me, just try my cell phone. I'm actually doing it, Dan. I'm trying to take some time off to finish some of those old songs I wrote in high school."

"No kiddin'? You actually pulled the trigger?"

"Yep, in fact, I'm on my way to my guitar lesson at Guitar City. And you probably won't believe this, but I finished the words to one of my songs already."

"Unbelievable. Is this a permanent retirement from real estate or are you plannin' to go back?"

"I'm not sure at this point. I'm just gonna work on this and see how it goes. My first goal is to get one song ready for this song contest, so I have to work on all the parts and get it recorded to send in by August twenty-eighth. I'm so rusty that I'm taking guitar lessons to try and get my skill level to come back. By the way…do you remember when Darryl and I used to record our songs on that big old four track reel-to-reel tape recorder?"

"Yep, I remember how cool I thought it was that just you and Darryl performed and recorded all four parts by yourself."

"Yeah, I'd play your bass and sing while Darryl would play drums and sing. After that was recorded we'd wind the tape back and record the lead and rhythm guitar parts over the bass and drums. We had to wear earphones so that we could hear the first track while we played the guitar parts on the second track," Jake recalled.

"Yeah, and we used those recordings to play for the crowd while we were on break. That was a great idea. Whose idea was that anyway?" Dan asked.

"I'm sure it was yours. Your brain was the only one that worked that way in high school," Jake admitted.

"You are correct, my friend," Dan boasted.

"Dan, do you know where I can get me one of those big reel-to-reel tape recorders?"

"What for?" Dan asked.

"I need it for two reasons. I want to be able to record the riffs I invent and keep them on tape so that I can remember 'em. And, I have to send in a recording of the song for the contest. I figured that I could do it with one of those reel-to-reels."

"You're kidding me, right?" Dan snorted. He broke into an uncontrollable laugh that Jake found particularly obnoxious because he had to hold his cell phone away from his head to preserve his hearing.

Once the laughter died down, Jake asked, "What's so funny?"

As he tried to catch his breath, Dan started to tell Jake about that handy invention—the computer. "You don't need to go lookin' for an antique reel-to-reel, Jake. You have a computer at home. So buy a recording program for your computer. You can get one at any of the electronics or computer stores."

"Dan, I'm sorry, but I don't follow you. Are you saying that I can load a program on my computer that'll do all that the reel-to-reel will do? How can that be?"

"Jake, it'll do way more than that reel-to-reel could ever do and the quality'll be as good or better. You can add effects and if you make mistakes there's no rewindin' time wasted. It really is a beautiful thing."

"But how do I get the sound into the computer? Do I plug my guitar into the computer or do I plug in a microphone and have it pick up the sound that way?"

"You may need an adapter or a new sound card for your computer, but it can be done. And you can record at least eight tracks, man. I'm tellin' you, it's great."

"Dan, how do you know so much about this stuff anyway?"

"I've got a program on my computer and I use it to record my harmonica," Dan revealed. But Dan could tell that Jake still didn't have his mind around the concept of a computer doing the job of a piece of equipment that was made especially for recording. "When you come over tonight, I'll show you what I'm talking about. Don't go wastin' your money on some dumpy reel-to-reel. All you need to do is get one of these programs, a microphone and a mixer and you'll be amazed. Rick's gettin' there around seven-thirty. So, how's seven o'clock sound?"

"I'll be there, but I'm still pretty fuzzy on the concept," Jake said skeptically.

"Just be there and you'll see. Bye."

Jake was still driving, holding the cell phone to his ear. No one was on the line. He was just staring down the road driving by instinct and thinking about what Dan had just told him. If Dan were even half right about the recording program, it would go a long way to help him with his mission. He pulled into Guitar City's parking lot, grabbed his guitar and went inside.

As he made his way to the back where the lesson rooms were, he thought that he would ask Luther about recording on computer. He got to the waiting area and found a seat. The place was empty and silent. Being a Wednesday morning, all the music students were in school. That was fine with Jake. It would be a little uncomfortable sitting in the waiting area alongside other students who weren't old enough to walk across the street by themselves. As he waited, he tried to imagine what the lessons would be like. In the quiet he could almost hear the fingers on his left hand throbbing from his practice session the night before. They hadn't felt that bad since he first started learning the guitar in junior high school. But it felt bad in a good way. The pain reminded him of what the weight lifters say. No pain, no gain. He didn't remember how long it took for his fingers to form the proper calluses, but he did remember the blisters on his fingers that formed first. Now he could see that his fingers weren't just a little swollen, three of them had small bulges in the skin at the tips. "*Blisters,*" he thought as he touched one then the other with his thumb. "*It won't be long now. I should have calluses next.*"

He could tell Luther was approaching because a large shadow appeared on the floor next to him. Jake turned to see Luther smiling down on him. "Hey Jake…how *are* you man?" He emphasized *are* which gave him away as the sincere type who cared about everybody, even a fifty-three year old music student.

"I'm good Luther, how are you?"

"I'm fine, just fine. Come on back and let's get started."

Luther opened the door to the five-by-seven foot practice room and walked in. He had to go in first and take his seat on the metal stool closest to the back corner of the room; otherwise there was no comfortable way a student could navigate around him. The tiny room seemed even smaller once the two were seated among the music stand, two small amplifiers, CD player and Luther's inexpensive knock-off of a Fender guitar perched on its stand. Jake sat there with his guitar case in his lap and proceeded to open it. Once he had the guitar in hand and case closed he couldn't see where to store the case. Luther observed his dilemma, took the guitar case off his lap and hung it by its handle on a big wooden dowel rod sticking out of the top of the back wall. The music store must have added the lesson rooms as an afterthought because there didn't seem to be any air conditioning. Jake casually looked around for vents and didn't notice any. The room didn't take long at all to heat up and they both began to sweat before the lesson started.

Soon Jake forgot about how uncomfortable he was and focused on Luther's instruction. Luther's lessons were usually prescribed in half hour doses, but given Jake's deficiency and timetable, the prescription needed to be strengthened to two one-hour sessions per week. After his first hour with Luther he was drenched in sweat and all three of his blisters broke. But that was OK because he learned things in that first session that would have taken him months to learn on his own. Knowing that retention of the material is key, Luther had taken the time to chart out some guitar riffs and the pentatonic blues scale in a code that those who don't read music can pick up easily. A chart consisted of six horizontal lines with numbers placed in various locations on the lines. The lines represented the six strings of the guitar and the numbers represented the fret location on the guitar neck. It looked complicated, but as Luther continued to instruct, its simplicity soon was revealed. Luther explained that there was much more to learn about the charts. "For example," he said, "there are symbols for bendin' strings and slidin' from one note to the other and so on, but you ain't gonna learn it all in one lesson."

He and Luther shook hands at the door to the tiny lesson room and Jake turned to go. He remembered his conversation with Dan about recording by computer and he spun around and said to Luther, "If you were going to record your music, what would you use?"

"*Cakewalk, Pro Tools*, or *Q Base*," he said as he gave Jake that big friendly smile. "You know, you'll be needin' one of them pretty soon, Jake."

"Thanks, Luther," Jake said as he turned and walked down the hall. He had no idea what Luther was talking about.

CHAPTER 21

▼

After a stop at the electronics store to pick up a portable CD player and some earphones, Jake went home to perform his daily regimen of study and practice. He couldn't wait to practice the charts that Luther had written down for him and get used to reading them fluently. When it came time to listen to a CD and play along, he plugged in the earphones to the CD player and dropped in B.B. King. He could hear the recording great but with the earphones on he couldn't hear his guitar. The whole idea of having the earphones on the CD player was so that he wouldn't disturb Joyce. But how could he hear himself play guitar and listen to the CD at the same time? *"There has got to be some trick to it,"* he thought. So he abandoned the earphones and went into the living room to use the CD player in the entertainment center that was connected to speakers and played his guitar along with B.B. until his fingers could take it no longer.

Just as he stopped, Joyce came home from work. They exchanged accounts of their respective days and he told her of Dan and Rick's plans to build the Tyler room in Dan's basement. Joyce asked Jake to play *Suburban Blues* for her now that he had finished the lyrics. Even though all the parts weren't formulated he did have the basic rhythm and notes to the vocal part memorized. So he played a rhythm part that Luther showed him that morning and sang the song for her. "That's great, Jake," she said when he finished. "By the way, I marked the calendar for you. You have thirty seven days left to get the song submitted to the contest." She was keeping track, too. It was reassuring to know that she was in this with him.

After dinner Jake drove over to Dan's house to take a look at the computer program he said would take the place of the reel-to-reel recorder. As he came up the walk and looked into Dan's office window he could see that Dan had his computer on and there were colored horizontal lines stretching across the screen. Dan saw Jake through the window and waved him in. As he kicked off his shoes, Jake could hear the sound of Dan's harmonica coming from the office. More specifically it was coming from his computer speakers. Jake watched the computer screen that displayed what looked like a picture of several sound waves and a vertical line speeding across the sound waves keeping track of where it was in the song. He noticed at the left of the screen, each horizontal section was labeled. Number one was drums. Number two was harmonica. Number three was vocal. Dan said nothing and let Jake soak up what he saw while he went to the kitchen to grab a couple beers. Jake's eyes floated down to the table next to the computer's keyboard and saw a device he remembered to be a mixer. This he knew was a device that allowed the user to plug in a number of instruments, adjust their individual volume, bass, mid range, and treble then send each instrument to a main "out". The "out" could be earphones or a recording device and in this case the recording device was the computer. By the time Dan came back with the beer, Jake had begun to see what Dan had been talking about. Dan nudged Jake's shoulder from behind with his right hand holding a cold beer. Jake turned, accepted the beer, took a sip and went back to his survey of the set up. He could see that Dan had his harmonica microphone and a small five-by-ten inch black box both plugged into the mixer. "What's that?" Jake asked as he pointed to the unfamiliar black box.

"It's a drum machine," Dan answered. "The drumbeat you're hearin' is a drumbeat I programmed on that machine."

"I see you connected the mixer to this 1/4 inch input in the front of the computer. My computer doesn't have any inputs like that," Jake pointed out.

"Right, I did upgrade the sound card on my computer. I'm sure you'll have to do the same. Just make sure you get one that is *full duplex*. That'll allow you to record while you listen to playback of a previously recorded track."

For the next half hour Jake asked questions and Dan explained and demonstrated the computer recording system. After the lesson was done Jake was convinced that this was what he needed, so Dan brought out the box that his program came in and showed it to him so that he could find it in the store. *Cakewalk Guitar Studio* was the title he needed to look for. Jake remembered that Luther had mentioned *Cakewalk* when he asked about recording. *"So that's what Luther meant."*

There was a knock on the door. Rick usually would have just opened the door and walked in, but tonight he needed help with his entry because he carried a huge cardboard box containing hundreds of unsorted photos in varying sizes from the band days. Fortunately all the negatives were filed safely away in their white paper sleeves in a big brown carrying case that he left in the car. Dan and Jake ended their tutorial on the computer and came to Rick's aid. After getting Rick his customary beer, they all proceeded to the basement where the Tyler shrine would be assembled.

First Dan illustrated, in great detail, the finished design of the room now under construction. He was proudly pointing and gesturing with his hands to complement the verbal description—a showcase here, a framework there and a gallery from here to there. The photo gallery was first on their agenda so the big box of photos was emptied onto the poker table. The goal was to eliminate the photos where Tom didn't appear. Once all the photos of Tom were found, the judging would commence. But first they would have another beer.

As they surveyed a sea of black and white photographs piled high on the poker table, they began to identify the pieces of their history and attempted to assemble them as if it were life's jigsaw puzzle. Each picture was its own mystery and seemed to hold clues that might lead to a clearer understanding of that time so deep in their past. Perhaps if they completed this puzzle, it would hold meaning not just for them but also for anyone who cared to look. As the night wore on and the empty beer bottles mounted, the three made good progress. Finally they had what they called the top forty. It was really fifty photos, but they couldn't identify where ten of them had been taken. Now, if they could arrange them properly, it would be 'The Phogg' anthology, from first practice session to the final gig. Some of the selected photos were nearly rejected due to their small size, but Rick guaranteed that they could be blown up to reveal even the smallest detail. The camera angle and composition of each chosen photo was superb. Jake especially liked the photos taken from behind the band showing the back of the band as if they were shadows with the focus on the faces in the crowd.

Next came the Tom Tyler memorabilia that Tom had sent Dan over the years. Tom Tyler 'T' shirts, Tom Tyler hats from ball caps to sombreros, a Tom Tyler watch, a Tom Tyler ring, a miniature Tom Tyler Grammy for a charm bracelet and on and on. Finally Dan reached into the bottom of a box he had purposely hidden away till last and drew out an old cheap-looking microphone that was readily recognized by all. This was the first microphone Tom had ever used. It was a microphone made for a cassette recorder—by no means sufficient for their purpose. They all remembered when Tom contributed it to the community stack of band gear and laughed just like they did back then as if it were yesterday.

The beer began to speak when Rick initiated what he thought was a comedy routine. "Ya know, Tom woulda never been anything without us," knowing that more likely, Tom was who he was in spite of them, didn't matter. They were drunk and thought they were hilarious.

"Thaz right, Rick man," Dan slurred. "Where would he be today, if we hadn't been 'round to wipe his whining little nose all the time?" He pointed randomly at the air with his index finger as he struggled to keep his balance.

"Yeah," Jake agreed, almost missing his mouth with the beer bottle. "We made Tom Tyler. We taught him every—*burp*—thing he knows. You know we should be the rock stars, not him."

"We *haare* the rock stars," Rick confirmed as he weaved around, looking for a place to sit or fall down. "And we could bring him down with one little phone call. Get me my agent. Get me the President. And another thing…" By the time they were done, they were all laying on the cold uncarpeted basement floor laughing uncontrollably. And that's where they found themselves the next morning.

"My head," Dan cried, breaking the morning silence. "What the… Hey Jake, Rick, wake up. I can't believe we spent the night on this floor. Coffee, I need coffee," he said as he lumbered up the basement stairs unceremoniously scratching his butt. Jake and Rick slowly came to life, wondering for a moment where they were. They looked around in a blurry daze past a pile of empty beer bottles only to be assaulted by the sunlight.

"I don't feel so good," Rick said as they both followed Dan for coffee. It was 7:00 a.m. Fortunately for them, no one was late for work yet. On the kitchen counter was a note from Patty who had taken calls from Joyce and Carolyn the night before just about the time the boys had passed out.

"Jake, call Joyce. Rick, call Carolyn. I told them you were spending the night."

"I can't believe we sat there and got drunk like that on a school night," Jake said as he rubbed and scratched his chest and yawned, contorting his face into an unrecognizable blob. The bouquet of the coffee bean began to fill the room, silently consuming their attention. The afflicted stood mute as they patiently watched the coffee maker preparing their antidote.

The coffee was poured and the three sat at the kitchen table talking about the progress they made last night. Rick told them how the photographs could be blown up to poster size without losing detail and proposed that they go around the whole room with them. The four-week time frame required to process the photos appeared to coincide with the completion of construction, so a party was planned for next month.

"So far so good," Jenny reported to her mom.

"See. You really had no reason to be afraid."

"Mom, it's only been two days," Jenny warned with a noticeable level of apprehension. "Look, I got to go. I've got a closing package to proof and I want to finish it before the phone starts ringing."

"OK hon. Do good."

Jenny began to review the paperwork. She couldn't find anything wrong with the file and was about to sign off on it when she remembered that she hadn't checked the legal description on the purchase agreement against the title work and new deed to see if they were the same as the original deed granted to the seller. Jake usually did this for her when the legal descriptions were long and involved. As she compared the lengthy meets and bounds legal descriptions, she could see that the legal description on the new deed, to be conveyed to the purchaser at closing, was clearly not the legal description on the purchase agreement. The purchase agreement's legal matched the legal of the original deed but the title company had completed the entire closing package using the neighbor's property description. The closing was that afternoon and the paperwork wasn't right. She began to pick up the phone to call Jake for advice but hesitated for a moment. She realized that calling Jake would have been out of habit. She really knew what to do. So she did what needed to be done. She called the title company and informed them of the error and instructed them to immediately revise the documents and fax the revised documents as soon as possible. She called the listing agent and the buyer's real estate company to advise them of the revision and to make sure their clients knew the error was being corrected. It was really a small problem. But she had uncovered an error that, up till now, only Jake would have found. Then she took control of the situation and solved the problem on her own. With a hint of a smile, a dauntless smile of confidence, she went to the next task.

"Well boys, I got to get back to the songwriting grind," Jake announced as he got up from Dan's kitchen table and found his car keys. "See ya later."

CHAPTER 22

▼

The next two weeks were packed with serious study, practice, and lessons from Luther. Jake gained proficiency reading and writing the chart system he had learned from Luther. His ad lib blues riffs seemed to be improving rapidly which allowed him to invent and chart parts for all the instruments in *Suburban Blues* except for the drums. The drums would be handled by a drum machine that he soon would own. In order for Jake to get his song submitted, he needed to somehow end up with a performance of his song on a CD. Thanks to Dan he now knew the technology was available and as close as the corner computer and music stores. And after researching the individual pieces of equipment needed, he was ready to commence a buying spree.

He spent the whole day buying equipment and piling it into the SUV. That evening he and Joyce unloaded the vehicle and piled everything up in the hall next to his home office. It didn't look like it, but once assembled he would have his own little digital recording studio. There was no time to waste. He had only three more weeks before the deadline so he dug right in and began to set everything up. The most time consuming part of the job was the assembly of the recording desk. This would accommodate most of the other equipment. It was as frustrating as putting together toys on Christmas Eve. There were parts of every shape and size that had to be identified. There were instructions—complicated instructions, but he suffered through it.

He bought a new faster computer that could record and create CD's. He bought the *Cakewalk* recording program. He bought microphones. He bought a mixer. He bought the right sound card. He bought a drum machine. And instead of buying a closet full of instruments he bought a workstation. This piece of equipment looked like a piano keyboard but was capable of, among other things, reproducing the sound of a huge list of instruments. The assembly was complete about 3:00 a.m. Jake had everything up and running. It was running, but it wasn't pretty. There were wires of all sizes and colors snaking along the carpet and in behind and draped over the recording desk. It took two multi-plug power strips to power all the devices. Jake's comfortable little home office with the big green leather chair was transformed into the electronic laboratory of a mad rock scientist.

After the assembly he didn't feel tired. The sheer excitement of the project must have been propelling him on. So he worked through half of the tutorial sessions in the *Cakewalk* manual, and then made his first CD recording. It was just a few simple and crude guitar riffs with simulated Hammond B3 organ back up played with the workstation, but it was an actual recording he made himself. Tomorrow he would begin to rehearse the parts one by one and lay down some tracks. "*Wait a minute, it's 5:00 a.m.,*" he thought. "*It's already tomorrow.*"

As he walked into the bedroom Joyce was just getting up. "You didn't come to bed last night?" she asked.

"No, but I've got the recording equipment all hooked up and running. I actually made a CD with it. It really works."

Jake's excitement was a little too much for her this early in the morning. Mustering only an occasional nod she patiently listened and finally said, "Try and get some sleep now. I've got to get ready for work. OK?"

"OK," Jake agreed and prepared to crash.

A few hours later he was up and at it again. Laying down the drumbeat first seemed logical. Once the drums were recorded that would set the tempo for everything else. The manual began easily enough but as he read further the complexity of this little black box became painfully evident. Three hours later he was ready to program a drumbeat for *Suburban Blues* and three hours after that he had it recorded on track one. For the next hour he experimented with some of the other features of the drum machine and found that he could put half of the drums on one track and the rest of the drums on another track, thereby achieving more control of how the drums sounded.

Next he would add the rhythm guitar part. He plugged his old Epiphone into the amplifier Tom had given him, then made sure it was properly tuned. He painstakingly adjusted the tone and volume knobs on the guitar along with the controls of the amplifier until he had the sound he was looking for. He jotted notes in a three ring binder regarding each setting so that he could go back to that sound easily, expecting the need to arise. Then he placed a microphone close to the face of the amplifier and plugged it in to the mixer. He recorded a few chords and played it back to see how it sounded. He adjusted the bass, midrange, treble, and EQ on the mixer, and the volume on the computer sound card input, recorded more chords and played it back again. He kept it up until the recorded sound was what he wanted. Then more notes were made in the binder and finally he was ready to record the rhythm guitar part.

He donned the earphones so that he could hear the drum beat and began to play the rhythm part to the song. The song lasted approximately four minutes. That was a long time for Jake to play the guitar without a mistake. So he kept playing the part, stopping when he made a mistake and starting over. Sometimes he'd only go twenty seconds before he screwed up. That was bad. But several times he had gone over three minutes without a mistake only to err in the final remaining seconds. That was the worst. This went on for hours until he was finally satisfied with the track.

He continued with the bass part. That was played on the keyboard of the workstation. This took even longer to get right because he had less experience with keyboards than guitars. But he plowed through it and finally got it recorded. Tomorrow he would record the lead guitar part and the vocal to finish the project. As he shut down the equipment, he began to think about the progress he'd made. Three weeks ago he was selling real estate and hadn't even looked at his guitar in years. By the end of the day tomorrow he will have re-learned the guitar, finished writing a song for the first time in his life, orchestrated and performed each part, and produced a CD of the whole thing. The fact that he had three weeks to spare on the contest deadline was just icing on the cake.

It was the ability to focus on a project gained from the conditioning provided by his career in real estate that saw him through to this point. He certainly didn't have the focus in high school. That isn't something you can get from a book or a lecture. You learn it when your survival depends on it. You learn it by paying your dues.

Just as he was finishing up, Joyce peeked in. She had worked late again at the office and wanted to go out and get something to eat. Jake, deciding a celebration was in order, suggested their favorite steak house. Without hesitation Joyce instructed Jake to get ready while she called ahead to the restaurant. They liked this restaurant because diners could call ahead to be put on the waiting list. That way they didn't have to wait so long in the lobby to be seated. In no time they were on the road and looking forward to some time together.

The Longhorn Steak House lobby was teeming with hungry patrons holding their square black plastic flashers. The devices were equipped with red lights that light up when it's the customer's turn to be seated. After being issued their flasher, Joyce and Jake waited at the bar. It was a rare and cherished moment for them to relax and talk over a glass of wine. Too soon the little red lights of their flasher put an end to the moment. They both looked at the flasher and then back at each other. "Next time we won't call ahead," Joyce said as they picked up their drinks and proceeded to the lobby to be seated.

The hostess led them past many tables of patrons enjoying the company of friends and family. Halfway to their non-smoking booth, Jake noticed a man in his early thirties look up at him as they passed by. He was sitting at a table with his wife and two children. Jake smiled politely, like one would do when a stranger catches you looking their way, and continued on to the booth. After they were seated, handed menus, and got the speech regarding the specials, they were able to pick up where they left off at the bar. In the middle of their one-on-one Joyce's eyes left Jake's and looked up to see someone standing behind him. Sensing there was something or someone behind him, he turned to see the young man he had passed, standing before him.

"I apologize for interrupting but, are you by chance, Mr. Strong, the real estate broker?" he asked.

Given another look at the young man, Jake noticed something vaguely famil-iar about him. "Yes, I am," Jake replied as he extended his hand to the young man.

The young man shook his hand and said, "I'm Ray Davies. You won't remem-ber me but..."

"Well, yes I do Ray. Weren't you about three years old when I sold your dad and mom the house on Signet Street?"

"That's what they told me just yesterday," Ray said in total shock that Jake could recall one home sale so long ago. But, it wasn't that Jake had such a remarkable memory at all. Jim Davies, Ray's father, had been referring customers to Jake ever since the Signet Street deal. Jake had met a lot of appreciative clients like Jim Davies over the years. They were the main reason for Jake's longevity in the real estate business. It turned out that most people who dealt with Jake would recommend him to their friends. "I recognized you from your picture on the magnetic calendar you send my parents every year. It's been on their refrigerator ever since I can remember."

"Your parents are good people, Jake remarked. "This is my wife, Joyce."

"Nice to meet you," Ray said. "Well, Mr. Strong, my wife and I have been saving up for a down payment on a house and my dad told me that it was time I got you involved. Would you be willing to help us find a house?"

When Jake made the decision to take time off from real estate, he hadn't thought about the people who appreciated and depended on him. They represented the good and rewarding side of the job. They were the people he enjoyed helping. The people that made his job seem worthwhile. The people like young Ray standing before him waiting for his answer. "Well, I'm sorry Ray, but as fate would have it, I've just begun an extended leave from the company. But there is an agent in my office that I've selected to take care of all my clients. Would you like me to have him call you?"

"That'd be great," Ray said as he handed over his business card. "He can call me at any of those numbers." As they shook hands again, he said, "My dad will be sorry it won't be *you* helping me, but I'm sure I'll be in good hands."

"You will, Ray. Say hello to your dad for me."

Jake turned back to Joyce and he saw in her eyes the reflection of his sense of loss. "That's the part of the business you're gonna miss, isn't it?"

"I sure will," he confirmed.

"I noticed you didn't tell him why you were taking time off," Joyce observed.

"I know," Jake responded. "I guess it's a little embarrassing for me to actually say I'm taking time off to write songs—sounds a little weird when I hear it come out of my mouth."

Joyce replied, "I know what you mean. I haven't discussed it with anyone outside of Carolyn and Patty. I haven't even told mom and dad and I talk to them almost every day. I guess I don't wanna have to explain it to anyone and have them think we're crazy. So if anyone asks, you're taking a well-deserved extended leave of absence for some R & R. How's that sound?"

"Perfect," Jake agreed. "I was even toying with the idea of turning in my contest entry with a pen name instead of my own."

Joyce laughed and said, "I don't think anyone would laugh if they knew you were entering a songwriting contest. I think they *would* laugh if they knew you quit your job to do it without having written a song in over thirty years. That's what's funny."

"Yeah, but I still think a pen name would be fun. This whole experiment is supposed to be fun. So why not make it a little more fun?"

"You got any name ideas?" Joyce asked.

"No. Not yet. Why don't we try and think of some names and make a list or something? Jake suggested.

They raised their wine glasses and vowed to come up with some names to choose from.

Jake got an early start on the recording project Saturday morning. What he thought he could finish in three hours took him twelve. But he did finish and had a CD to prove it. He played it back and although it was definitely not a professional job, he hoped it would give the judges enough to prove the songwriting was good.

CHAPTER 23

▼

When Jake walked into the office for their weekly meeting, Jenny greeted him wearing a dress and directed him into the conference room where they had coffee in brand new mugs with his company logo. She led him on a tour of the office. The entire office had been thoroughly cleaned; there were workers repairing, painting and assembling things everywhere. It was as if she had breathed new life into something unrevivable. "Wow! This place looks great. You look great. Did I authorize all this in my sleep?" Jake asked.

"Nope—I authorized it," she said immediately and with authority. "I've started a recruiting program for new agents and in order to attract them we've got to look our best. How do you like the coffee mugs?" Jenny asked.

"Can we afford all this?" he asked.

"I don't think we can afford *not* to, Jake. I've been reading a book on management and the theory is that if you don't grow, you die. And we're not going to die on my watch. Anyway, we'll need at least two good agents to make up for what the company doesn't have, now that you're not around."

He knew she was right about the growing versus dying theory but he also knew she was blowing smoke up his butt about having to hire two agents to take his place. But everything she was doing was what should be done. The things he should have done but was too burnt out to find the initiative. There was a noticeable increase in her energy level. It looked like someone had breathed new life into her too. "I think you're right. Keep it up. You're doing a good job here. Any problems that we need to discuss today?"

"Not this week," she replied with a smile that Jake had never seen before. *"Responsibility becomes her,"* he thought as he said his goodbyes and headed for his guitar lesson.

Luther and Jake had gotten to know each other pretty well during the lessons and Jake wanted to get Luther's opinion of his recording for the songwriting contest. Luther was excited for him and wanted to support him any way he could. Jake sat quietly as Luther patiently listened to the four-minute, one-man performance of *Suburban Blues* on the CD player in the practice room. After it was over Luther pressed the stop button, forced a smile and said, "Well Jake, the song's good. I think it's real good. But, man, you can't enter it like that in the contest."

"Why not?" Jake asked. "What's wrong with it?"

"Well Jake, I'll tell ya. Just about everythin' is wrong with it. I know it's you playin' all those parts and I'm impressed with your progress. You've come a long way, but you're really not qualified yet as a musician to play this song or even sing it for that matter. This CD was worthwhile and it'll be a nice keepsake for ya but it's not the quality that those judges are expectin'. Jake, you'll be competin' with lots of real talented folks and I think your song is fantastic, but it should be shown in a much better light than what you have here, man."

With each word that Luther spoke a little more air escaped from Jake's ego balloon until finally it vanished completely. He knew Luther was being honest—brutally honest. But Luther wouldn't be helping Jake with false compliments. Jake needed good advice. "What do I do now? There's less than two weeks left to the deadline and now I've got nothing."

"You set up a real recordin' session with musicians and vocalists and do it right," Luther advised.

"Sounds complicated," Jake remarked. "Can you help me get something like that together in time? Maybe your band could do it for me. I've been meaning to go down and see you guys play."

"I know I can. I think my band would even like to be able to add your song to our song list. It's that good. My band has everything you need in the way of musicians and vocalists and Warren knows a guy who just built a recordin' studio nearby that could use some work."

Warren and Luther spent Jake's lesson time making calls to arrange for the recording session. Once Warren had called his friend who owned the recording studio and Luther contacted all the members of the band, they sat down with Jake to go over the game plan.

Luther began, "I've contacted everyone in the band. I explained that we're friends and I'd like to help you out with the recordin' and they're all excited to help you, too. They need to hear this CD and individually practice the song. If you don't mind, I'm gonna' make copies of your CD and give 'em each one tonight. This way they can get used to it, so that they can play it together once or twice at the rehearsal we have this Friday afternoon. You can come and watch if ya like. Then we should be ready for the recordin' session. And by the way, I'd like to play your guitar in the recordin' session if you'd let me."

"Sure you can. I'd be honored," Jake said with a smile.

"OK then, you put these strings on it today so they'll be stretched good enough for Sunday."

"What do you mean, stretched good enough for Sunday?" Jake asked.

Luther explained, "Well, new strings take a little playin' before they'll hold their tunin'. They need to stretch a little. So if you put them on today and do your normal 'woodsheddin', then they'll be ready for Sunday and I won't be wastin' recordin' time tryin' to keep the guitar in tune."

Then Warren added, "Next Sunday the sixteenth we have the recording studio and their engineer from eight to five. That should give us enough time to get the job done with some time to spare. Luther's drummer will be using the studio drums. They should already be tuned and ready to go. This'll save the time of him setting up his own gear. This recording will be a demo so we won't spend extra time doing a master. First the drummer will be recorded. Then each of the instruments will be recorded one at a time. Once we get an acceptable take from the first instrument, we set up and do the next one on a separate track. After the instruments then the vocals will be recorded. After the recording is done, the engineer will spend time mixing the tracks to where he thinks the sound is optimal. This hopefully will take place on Sunday too, but he couldn't promise anything. Hopefully that'll only take one to two hours. Once that's done we'll have a chance to listen to the recording on monitor speakers and earphones and suggest changes to the mix. If we don't have any changes, he'll make some CD's and we'll be done. You'll get to keep the tapes and computer files just in case you want duplicates or want to pursue mastering.

Luther added, "The band will do this for four-hundred dollars if you let us use the song when we play out. We'll give you the proper credit when we do."

"The recording session will be thirty-five an hour including the engineer," Warren said. "They're cutting us a pretty good deal here. I grew up with the owner and the engineer and told them about you. They were pretty intrigued with the story. Do you have any questions?"

Not having understood half of what they were talking about but not wanting to sound ignorant, Jake said, "No, I don't think so. I say let's do it."

To be this close to a deadline and feel as untroubled by it was refreshing for Jake. In the past, a deadline would create a buildup of tension that would manifest itself in his neck and shoulders. This was probably the result of knowing that the customers and clients he had to satisfy in the real estate business relied on Jake alone to meet the important deadlines. But Luther and Warren showed Jake a whole different attitude than he was used to by arranging a solution to his problem in less than an hour. "You really want to put my song in your lineup, Luther?"

"Well, it's not entirely up to me, but I know my band and I'm pretty sure how they'll react to *this* song, man."

"Well, it's OK with me. I'd be thrilled to hear it. Where are you guys playing?"

"It's called 'Eddie's Place' on McNichols in Detroit, not far from the Detroit City Airport. I'll get you directions. Try and be there about six-thirty or so. We should be startin' the rehearsal about then. Our first set is at nine."

"*'Eddie's Place' on McNichols? Now why does that sound familiar?*" Jake thought.

On the way home, Jake made calls to Dan, Rick, and Joyce to tell them about Luther's band, the Friday night rehearsal and the recording session on Sunday morning. Dan and Rick were up for going to 'Eddie's Place' on Friday but weren't happy that he was going to miss golf on Sunday. Joyce wanted to go but knew she wouldn't be able to handle the smoke those places generate. So it was settled that Friday would be a "boys night out" for Dan, Rick and Jake.

The bars that these three were used to all had televisions hanging from the ceiling in almost every corner. Pool tables, video poker and air hockey were all expected staples of the trade. Although you wouldn't find them there past lunch hour, they assumed that there was entertainment provided in the evenings— probably Karaoke. But this knowledge didn't prepare them for their visit to 'Eddie's Place'.

After passing it three times Jake finally pointed to an old red brick building where he saw Luther's rusty blue van pulling into its empty gravel parking lot. Dan wheeled the car around and as they got closer they saw a small sign that said 'Eddie's Place' painted on the glass on the front door. The brickwork on the old building was concealed in spots with a chalky white residue that betrayed its age. The entrance in the center consisted of an old wooden nine-foot double door adorned by an arched top transom. Although there were no windows now, you could see by the brick pattern where they once had been. The doorframe had recently been painted a gray blue over a previously red unprepared surface. The wooden front steps creaked a little as they opened the door to a dark but open room. They stood there in the quiet of the foyer as the door closed behind them, afraid to step further until their eyes adjusted to the murkiness. Soon images of an unmanned bar area to the right and vacant tables and chairs to the left began to materialize. Just as they began to make out a small stage at the far end of the room their noses picked up the distinctive essence of stale beer, wet cigarette ashes, and mildew. The three slowly proceeded toward the bar where a faint rustling and then clanking sound could be heard. As they each took a stool, a short lean gentleman suddenly popped up from behind the bar holding a big red monkey wrench. His dark-skinned face bore the deep crevices of age and his short gray hair formed a horseshoe band around the back of his head that thinned out just above his ears. He smiled at the three men sitting before him after the surprise of the unexpected guests had left his expression. "Sorry gentlemen, I didn't know ya'll were sittin' there. I was tightenin' up the drainpipe in the sink. It's always sumpthin' 'round here. If it ain't the roof it's the sink and if it ain't the sink it's the cooler. Seems I'm always fixin' sumpthin'. 'Round here, I'm either a-fixin' sumpthin', or I'm a-fixin' to fix it. Can I get you boys sumpthin' to drink?"

Dan spoke up and said, "Three drafts.

The old man slowly filled the order. With shaky but skillful hands he placed a clean beer glass underneath the tapper and pulled down on the handle. One after another he placed each of the three glasses of beer in front of Dan. Then he looked at Rick and said, "What can I get ya sonny?" Rick was at a loss for words when the old man smiled as if he'd pulled this joke a thousand times. Jake paid the bartender as Dan distributed the beers.

"We're supposed to meet Luther Washington here. Is he around?" Jake asked.

The old man answered as he pointed a wobbly finger in the direction of a curtain-clad stage. "Yep. I just heard him come in. He's probably over there a-settin' up for the rehearsal."

Sensing that introductions were in order, Jake began, "I'm Jake and this is Dan and my brother Rick."

"Pleased to make your acquaintance—I'm Eddie," the old man said as he smiled and nodded in their direction.

"So you're the proprietor of this establishment," Rick said hoping to strike up a conversation. "Has it always been a blues bar?"

"Yep—blues, soul, and rock and roll for nigh on fifty-five years now. I've seen lots of great ones here at Eddie's—Jimmy Reed, Junior Wells, John Lee Hooker, Buddy Guy, Bob Seger, Wilson Pickett and many unknown groups—some who got big—some who didn't. The list goes on and on. Heck, we've even had some of the boys in 'It's About Time' play here. They were in other bands back then but you coulda seen 'em here first. Heck, we, had 'em play here as young as thirteen and as old as ninety two—some great and some...well, not so great." He pointed toward the opposite wall behind the table and chairs. "That wall yonder has photos of pretty much everyone that's played here. If you're a blues or rock and roll fan it makes for some interestin' browsin'."

The three took their beers and walked over to the wall of photographs. "Maybe we can get some ideas for the Tyler room," Dan hoped aloud.

Just as they began to get interested in the display, they heard some voices behind the curtain on the stage. It was Luther greeting the rest of the band who had just arrived through the back door and were gathering on stage. Jake walked over and peeked behind the curtain and said hello to Luther. "Hey Jake, come and meet the band. Hey everybody, this is Jake, my student who wrote the song we're gonna rehearse tonight. This is Paul, Leon, Bobby, Ruth and Janie."

As they all greeted him with warm smiles and compliments about the song, Jake could tell that this group was more than just a band being held together by economics and aspirations. There was something stronger at work here. After the pleasantries were done Jake excused himself to let them rehearse and went back to Dan and Rick who had resumed browsing the wall of fame.

"Hey, Jake, 'The Phogg' is up here on this wall," Rick said in amazement.

"No!" Jake responded in disbelief.

"Take a look," Dan commanded as he pointed to an old 'Phogg' flyer.

"I'll be," Jake said as he remembered. "You know, we did play a place on McNichols once. I remember that Rick made this flyer from one of the photos he'd taken. See, that's us at Mt. Holly. I guess we *did* play here but I'll be darned if I can remember. I guess a lot can change in thirty-five years or so."

Eddie came up from behind with three more beers and overheard the conversation. "If that flyer was from '66' or before, well, you fellas played at the old Eddie's, about two blocks down. It was a mite bigger and newer place than this. It's a carpet store now," Eddie said with a sigh. "We lost our lease in sixty six after the robbery and had to move down here."

"Robbery?" Jake asked.

"Yep...it was a Friday night—August of sixty six. I was hit over the head and robbed as I was puttin' some cash into the safe just before the first show. When I came to, the safe was empty and my head was split open. Took ten or twelve thousand from me. Couldn't pay the rent. Took me a year before I could start up here."

"Did they ever catch the guys who did it?" Rick asked with an anguished frown.

"Nope…the cops took a report but didn't really make an effort, near as I could tell. You know, I don't think the cops believed me about that money. I don't think they thought a man like me could put together that kinda bread." He set the beers down on the table and slowly shuffled back to his place behind the bar.

"Bummer," Dan said as he turned to see Jake and Rick temporarily paralyzed by Eddie's story.

"Well that explains it. This isn't the 'Eddie's Place' that we played," Dan surmised. "Wow, poor Eddie."

"Yeah," Jake agreed with a perplexed look as he thought, *"That flyer was just like the one he had signed for Lizzie Turner on the day they met."* Jake took a closer look at the flyer. At the bottom he noticed some writing in faded ink. He could barely make it out. 'To Lizzie with love' "That's the one I signed for her," he confirmed, pointing to his signature.

"Signed for who," Dan asked.

"Lizzie, Lizzie Turner."

"You sure?"

"Yep. See here?" Jake said as his finger directed Dan's attention to the inscription.

Then they browsed the wall with more interest. Scattered throughout the wall were four more band posters with half faded 'To Lizzie with love' inscriptions. They couldn't make out the names of the people who signed them. The names of the groups were only vaguely familiar to Jake; 'Blues Train', 'Crossroads', 'White Powder' and 'Ghosts'. All of a sudden he questioned the relationship he had had with Lizzie. He thought that Tom might have been right all along. She really may have been a groupie. *"But how did this part of her photo collection get on this wall?"* It was a mystery for sure, but Jake's concentration on the matter was interrupted by a loud rim shot from the drummer that was followed by Luther's band rehearsing his song.

Dan and Rick abruptly ended their browsing to listen to the music. The three took seats so that they all were facing the stage whose curtain had now opened. The last live music they heard together was at Meadowbrook among the beautiful affluent suburbanites listening to a Grammy-winning artist. This afternoon they were sitting in a building that could collapse around them at any moment being serenaded by a group that had seen no rewards of fame to speak of. Their much-battered instruments and old rusty microphones represented the lowest common denominator in musical hardware. They looked liked they shopped for clothes at the corner second hand store. But together they created a sound that you could tell had grown thick, rich and pure, nurtured by nothing more than their unconditional love for the blues. And the way they made Jake's song sound! Well, he heard the words and they were the words he wrote. He heard the music and it was the tune he invented. But a synergy was born, in the performance of those words and those notes that was beyond all comprehension. Rick and Dan turned toward Jake in disbelief and yelled in his ear, "You wrote that? That tune is amazing." Jake smiled at them, knowing that if they had first heard the CD he made, they would have said, "Man, that *band* is amazing. They can make something beautiful out of a mud fence."

Luther's band played the song two more times, making adjustments that were deemed appropriate to arrive at a final product that was, in Jake's estimation, a masterpiece. Following their rehearsal, Jake offered to buy dinner for everybody. They drove to a nearby diner and got to know each other over a hot meal. The compliments that shot back and forth across the dinner table were glorious, plentiful and lit up everyone's face just like fireworks on the fourth of July. The time was approaching for the band's first set so they all headed back to 'Eddie's'.

It was fifteen minutes till show time and there were only about ten other people in the whole place. "*What a rotten turnout for such a great band on a Friday night,*" Jake thought. "Eddie, is this the turnout you normally get on a Friday night?"

"For this time of night it's about right—most of 'em get here round twelve for the second set," Eddie answered.

About 9:20PM the band jumped on stage and after a brief introduction by Luther, they began to play. For two straight hours Luther's band played one spectacular song after another. They were tight. Not one note was off in timing or tone. Each lead guitar part had to have been improvised on the spot. Nobody could have played that soulfully and intricately the same any two times out of a million tries. Halfway through the set, one of the backup girls pulled out a saxophone. The other one played harmonica. Each song was a classic gem. With about ten minutes to go Luther came up to the microphone and said, "This next tune was written by a good friend of ours. He started writin' it over thirty years ago and just finished it. He's lettin' us try it out on you tonight. Hope you like it."

The drummer held up his drumsticks and with four solid whacks, set the beat. Then the room was instantly filled from wall to wall and from leaky ceiling to dusty floor with the product of Jake's creative side and the talent of this band that converged to form, in Jake's most biased opinion, one hell of a tune. When it was over all thirteen people in the place were on their feet clapping and whistling. If he never got anywhere with the songwriting after that night, Jake would have been satisfied being partially responsible for that thirteen-person standing 'O'. There could be nothing that would ever wipe the memory of this night from his mind.

Sunday morning came quickly and everyone was on time for the recording session. Jake brought his guitar as asked. *"My guitar…actually being used in a live recording session."* Until now Jake had only imagined what the inside of a recording studio would be like and he was looking forward to the learning experience. He had already resigned himself to the fact that his input was not necessary and, although it would be counter to his personality, he would speak only when spoken to. As far as he was concerned Luther was in charge here today.

The studio was located in a large and masterfully converted barn on the studio owner's farm. The interior consisted of a lounge/bar area just off the entrance, a control room, performance space with a drum booth and a vocal booth. Jake and Luther's band were all seated in the lounge area waiting for Gil, the engineer, to come in and discuss goals and expectations for the session. The lounge was strictly built for comfort. There were two brown leather sectional couches on thick plush carpeting flanked by four end tables stocked with magazines. There was a full bar with refrigerator, coffee maker and television. The television had a sign on it that read, 'This television will automatically mute during all recording sessions.'

Gil arrived and explained how he wanted the session to go and asked Luther for his input on procedure and the sequence of events. Although he didn't understand most of what they said, it was clear to Jake that they were of one mind. Gil then directed the drummer to set up and get used to the drums, while he led Luther into the control room for more briefing. Jake could see the contents of the control room through the window in the hall. There, perched on a beautiful wooden custom counter, was a huge mixing board with a limitless number of dials, sliders, switches and buttons that lit up when they were pushed. There were several complicated looking electronic devices all neatly encased in one long low wooden cabinet. There were at least eight monitor speakers stacked strategically around the mixing board. There were two flat panel computer screens affixed to their respective moveable boom style arms that were positioned directly over the mixing board for quick and convenient reference. This place was well laid out and resembled the bridge of the Star Ship Enterprise.

The performance space had a big window into the control room and three large windows overlooking a tranquil fenced pasture dotted with multicolored wild flowers and the occasional cow. The ceiling, which was nine to eighteen feet up depending on where you stood, had recessed lighting, wooden beams and metal channels from which hung several microphone cords. There were more microphones attached to several boom stands accompanied by music stands, chairs and bulky floor-type monitor speakers. Upon completing his tour, Jake went back to camp out in the lounge, grabbed an iced tea, a magazine and settled in for the long day.

The band worked hard for three hours. Jake hadn't been alone during the wait. Since there wasn't any one time when all the band members were required at once, Jake had been surrounded by different members of the band all day. It was great to get to know them all better and learn about each other's history. Soon Luther came toward him with a piece of paper in his hand. "*He wants me to come and hear what they've done so far. Or maybe he needs my input on something. How cool is this?*" Jake thought.

"Hey Jake."

"Yeah?"

"Hey man, we're all hungry. Can you run to the Burger King and get us somethin' to eat? I got a list here."

"Sure," Jake said as he stood up, yawned and stretched. "How's it going in there?"

"Fine, fine, fine Jake. It's gonna turn out real nice," Luther assured him. "Don't forget the ketchup."

"OK, Luther," he said as he headed out to his car.

At four o'clock the recording session was just winding up. The tracks were finished but the job of mixing was yet to be done. Luther explained to Jake that Gil would do his best to have a mix for them by Monday night and that he and Jake would come back to listen to the mix and hopefully give the final approval to make the CD.

CHAPTER 24

▼

Tom Tyler had just finished a performance in Albuquerque, New Mexico, the last in a disappointing string of low gate crowds and was on the bus headed back home to California when he got a call on his cell phone from his tour manager. Tom slouched in his seat; tired from the long road trip, barely keeping his eyes open as he listened. "The investors have decided to sell their share in the tour to Marlboro. They're going to make some cost-cutting changes in order to minimize the loss and push some smokes at the same time. If you want to stay on board, you're looking at a twenty percent pay cut. I'm sorry, man, there's nothing I can do about it."

Tom was too weary to argue and just hung up the phone and fell asleep.

Monday night came and Luther and Jake met at the recording studio to listen to Gil's mix of *Suburban Blues*. Both Jake and Luther were delighted with Gil's work and thanked him for the experience. Jake had instructed Gill that he wanted the song copied to the CD with no indication of who wrote or performed the song so that he could send it into the contest with a pen name. They went to the lounge to wait for Gill to make some CD copies of the song and to download the digital files of the tracks. "Didn't it sound great?" Jake asked Luther, knowing what the answer would be but nevertheless wanting to hear someone agree once more.

"It sounded great. Now your entry will make 'em stand up and take notice," Luther reassured.

"Thanks again," Jake said to Gil and Luther as they walked out of the studio.

Jake turned off the satellite radio in his car to pop in one of the CD's that Gil had cut for him and listened to it all the way home. He couldn't wait to play it for Joyce. As he walked into the kitchen he found her making dinner. "How was your day?" he asked mainly so that she would respond and quickly return the same question to him. She began detailing the intricacies of her day minute by minute. This was not supposed to go this way. It seemed like it was going to be a while before she was going to ask him. So as they discussed her day at work, Jake slipped over to the CD player and popped in the disk that Gill had made for him. She continued without reference to the music that was playing and suddenly, in mid sentence, she said, "I really like that group. Who is it? Did you just get that at the record store on the way home? Wait a minute. Is that your song? It *is* your song. They finished the recording? Honey, that's excellent."

"Thanks. I can't believe how great it turned out. I'm sending it in tonight," Jake announced.

"Well, we haven't come up with a pen name. Let's do that tonight," she suggested.

After dinner they settled down at the kitchen table and made a list. They started to consider the idea of putting together a name from names of other famous rock and roll or blues artists. This way anyone that heard the name should get the feeling they had heard the name before. For instance, Jimi Hendricks and Joe Cocker could be Joe Hendricks or Jimi Cocker. This process went on for hours until they settled on Sonny Dixon, a cross between Sonny Terry and Willie Dixon, both legendary for their contributions to blues music. Jake finished the application, and signed it, 'Sonny Dixon'.

Joyce reminded him that he hadn't picked up the mail, so he set out down the street to the mailbox to pick up the day's mail and put the entry in the box. As he walked toward the bank of mailboxes the sound of the neighborhood children laughing and playing made him smile. He was sure he had heard them before, but he couldn't honestly remember enjoying that sound like he was at the moment. The smell of the freshly-cut grass and the newly-spread mulch freshened the air. People say that you have to stop and smell the roses once in a while. He had never really gotten that concept until now. He gathered up the mail and dropped the entry in the outgoing slot. The application prepared him to expect that no results of the contest would come until December. On the way back he was leafing through the bills and magazines when he came to a small square cardboard envelope. The return address read 'New Horizon Publications'. He opened it as he walked into his garage. It was the CD he had ordered back in May for depression. Without giving it another thought, he dropped it into the garbage can and went inside.

A week went by before he got a call from Dan. The 'Tyler Room' was done and ready for viewing. So the christening party was set for Friday. Dan and Patty enjoyed throwing parties now that their kids were grown and the remodeling of the basement was designed to serve that end. Jake and Joyce arrived a little late with their standard bottle of wine as a gift to their host. Patty greeted them at the door and escorted them down to where the guests were gathered. Their basement had become a lower level. Jake told Patty, "When you finish off a basement this nice, you can't call it a basement, not even a finished basement. It must be referred to as the 'lower level'."

They had really gone all out. The bar area was redone with a new granite counter top. The new carpeting was thick and lush. The built-in lighted show-cases made from cherry wood and glass around the perimeter made you feel as if you were in an upscale art museum. Each showcase was filled with enlargements of Rick's photos and assorted memorabilia from the band days and Tom's ongoing career.

As they arrived, Dan led each guest on a tour of the museum while delivering a narrative of the life and times of 'The Phogg' and the famous Tom Tyler—pointing out the photos and memorabilia to his guests while adding interesting anecdotes and stories to make the history come to life. Patty was busy greeting guests and hadn't gotten a chance to enjoy Dan's narrative, so when Jake and Joyce arrived she was anxious to take the tour with them. Dan's dynamic delivery was exceeded only by his remarkable grasp of 'Phogg' history and chronology. As the tour proceeded, they came upon an enlarged photograph of 'The Phogg' on stage at Mt. Holly, which had been blown up to four times its original size. The detail was very good. Dan pointed to the photo and began his delivery when Patty pointed to a girl pictured in the crowd and said, "She looks familiar to me."

Dan said, "Well, that was Jake's girlfriend, Lizzie Turner."

"Lizzie Turner," Jake repeated with some trepidation. Joyce knew nothing of Jake's girlfriends from high school. They had never talked about ancient history when it came to the opposite sex.

"Well, you might have seen her around somewhere but the last time I saw Lizzie was that night the 'Silverbell' got snowed in. And that's the night I met you. But I'm pretty sure Lizzie left before you showed up," Dan recalled.

"Lizzie Turner. Hum," Joyce said with a sly, semi jealous tone. "She's very pretty. Look at that long straight black hair. She looks much more mature than the rest of the girls in these photos. How old was she anyway, Jake?" Joyce asked.

Not wanting to go into any detail at the moment, Jake said, "She might have been older. It was a long time ago. Hey, Dan, look at you there with the long hair and that shirt. A little fruity by today's standards, don't you think?" Jake said to change the subject.

"Yeah, but those shirts were cool *then*," Dan replied.

To Jake, Dan's narrative became muted as he studied the photograph. Something about it wasn't quite right. He took another sip of wine and reexamined the photo. Then it came to him. Darryl, the lead guitar player, was playing his Fender Jaguar guitar in the picture. Darryl's father had traded in the Fender Jaguar for a double neck Mosrite guitar the day before Jake met Lizzie up in Prudenville. Since Darryl was playing the Fender, this photo was taken before Prudenville and therefore before he met Lizzie Turner. *"So, what was Lizzie doing at Mt. Holly?"* He took a closer look. There were two guys on either side of Lizzie that were dressed more like they'd be in a band than just there for the entertainment. Jake spoke, unaware that he was interrupting Dan's delivery. "Dan, do either of these guys look familiar to you?" he asked as he pointed at the guys on either side of Lizzie.

"They look like Ghosts," Dan replied.

"Funny, Dan. I'm just wondering if you recognize them," Jake insisted.

"Ghosts, Jake. They're Ghosts. Don't you remember the 'Ghosts'? We played opposite them from time to time. They probably had the main stage at Mt. Holly that night. Man, they were great. As a matter of fact, I think their lead guitar player is with 'It's About Time' now."

"Oh. OK. I remember 'em now," Jake said as he followed Dan, Patty, and Joyce to the next exhibit. He didn't want to bring up the fact that the last photo was out of sequence. He would choose a better time to explain to Dan that the photo was pre-Lizzie, evidenced by the guitar Darryl was playing. In addition he didn't want to sound so painfully precise in front of Joyce about the exact moment he and Lizzie met. Although he was sure she wouldn't be hurt by it, he didn't want to field all the questions that could arise on the subject. He just wanted to enjoy Dan and Patty's party and relax.

The evening was filled with conversation about the old band, funny stories about Tom and the days they practiced at his mom's house. David was happy to be getting an education about the history of his golf partners Dan, Jake and Rick. It was getting late when Rick dimmed the lights, set up an old eight millimeter movie projector, and showed a short piece of film of the Phogg practicing at Tom's house. Dan and Jake took their seats and watched the fledgling group (captured in black, white and shades of gray) hack away at their instruments. There was no audio. Dan and Jake knew that the way the group sounded back then was best left up to one's imagination.

CHAPTER 25

▼

The next morning Jake felt energized. With his first goal of entering the song contest out of the way, he was ready to start on the rest of the songs in that old stack of uncompleted compositions. He pulled out one at random, sat down at his desk and began to read. This one was strictly old time rock and roll. "*Good,*" he thought. "*I want to have a good blend of blues and rock and roll when I'm done. Maybe something that could represent the evolution of blues and show how rock and roll is really the child of the blues. Yeah.*"

The studying, lessons, practice and writing became more intense. He increased his hours of work and the results slowly but steadily became evident. His recording skills improved too. Each time he finished a song he recorded each part on his computer just as he did '*Suburban Blues*'. But, with each new song and each new attempt at recording he became more familiar with the features and capabilities of the equipment. By the middle of December, Jake had finished eleven more songs and written three completely new songs. All fifteen were now memorialized in digital form on his recording program and on CD, not to mention that he had David working on copyrights. That was a good four months of work.

The ice, snow and gray days that winter brought didn't slow him down or dull his spirits. In fact, not spending Sunday mornings at golf allowed him even more time for writing and more time with Joyce. His guitar lessons, although increasing in difficulty, grew steadily more meaningful. One cold Wednesday morning in December Jake showed up for his guitar lesson just as Luther hung up his cell phone and turned toward Jake with a look of disappointment. "What's wrong?" Jake asked.

"Man, Paul's got to fly down to Arkansas for a funeral and won't be back till Saturday. I gotta find me a rhythm guitar player to fill in at 'Eddie's Place' for Friday night."

"Luther, you must know a dozen guys that could fill in for Paul."

"I do but I just made my last call and everybody's either sick, booked or out of town for the holidays."

"Oh well, Luther, you guys can pull it off without him, can't you?" Jake asked as he waited for a reply. But no reply came. Soon Luther got a look in his eye and stood leering in Jake's direction as if he were a hungry bear and Jake was a fresh can of garbage.

"*You* could do it," he said. "Sure, why didn't I think of it before? You could do it, Jake."

"I don't think so, Luther. I don't know your songs. I've only had seven months of practice. I'm no professional musician. You said so yourself."

"I could teach you your parts. We've got three days to get you ready. And you've been doin' great on the recordin' lately. You're soundin' good enough to play with us, easy."

"Luther, there's a big difference between sounding good on a recording and playing out. When you're playing out you get one take to do it right. When you're recording, you get as many takes as it takes to get it right. I bet I've got three or four thousand takes invested in those songs I've recorded. It's not the same thing and you know it, Luther."

Luther ignored Jake's rebuttal and said, "Wha'd-ya-say man. It'll be fun. And if you make a mistake or two, that'll be my fault—not yours." Luther stood looking on, waiting for Jake's answer, displaying a half sad half desperate look that Jake couldn't deny. After all, Luther helped him get his first song recorded. It wouldn't be right not to at least try and help him.

"OK, you win. What do you want me to do?" Jake finally agreed.

Luther worked with Jake for the next three days, prepping him on the songs they were likely to play. Then Friday night about eight, Jake walked into an empty bar with his guitar in tow. Eddie called to Jake from behind the bar. Hey Jake, Luther told me you were a fillin' in for Paul. Good luck tonight."

"Thanks Eddie. I'm gonna need it."

"No you won't," Luther protested from behind the curtain. "You're ready. Now get over here and warm up with the rest of us."

Jake plugged into Paul's amplifier and Luther showed him how to work the effects pedals. After that they rehearsed as a group for about an hour. Jake was nervous but was getting the hang of it by the time rehearsal was over. After setting his guitar on the stand he turned around to see his guitar case right where he left it, in the middle of the stage. Thinking it was latched, Jake picked it up to move it out of the way. The lid flew open and all its contents found their way to the stage floor. There were packages of spare strings, a capo, about twenty guitar picks and the blue buffalo head nickel with its silver chain that Lizzie had given him. Bobby stepped over to help Jake pick everything up and Luther joined them. The silver chain was the last item to be replaced and Luther had it in his hand. "Jake, where did you get this?" he asked as if it were something he had lost.

"It's a long story, Luther. But the short version is that it was given to me by a girl I met way back when I was in the band in high school. I found it in my guitar case in May when I started playing again. It had been sitting in that case since 1966 or so."

Luther held the chain for a moment to examine it further. His fist closed around it as if he was planning to keep it. "So you knew Lizzie Turner too?" Luther asked.

Jake put his hand out for the necklace. Luther paused before he dropped it into his open palm. Jake asked, "How do you know her?"

"There was a time." He paused, struggling to keep strong emotion from surfacing. "There was a time that I thought she was my girl," he said as they walked toward a table and sat down. "But she hurt me bad, Jake. I was in a pretty good blues band, 'Crossroads'. We were ridin' pretty high in those days. Then Lizzie Turner showed up one night and we hit it off. She always wore that buffalo head nickel necklace. Nobody in the band understood what she saw in me. She was beautiful and I…well I was almost as big then as I am now. But there was somethin'. At least I kept telling myself there was somethin' she saw in me. She asked me to quit the band so she and I could be together."

"Don't tell me you quit the band, Luther," Jake pleaded, as he paid the waitress for two beers.

"Yep…I quit the band and waited for her at the bus station with my bags packed. She never showed. It took me weeks to get over the embarrassment of bein' played like that. By the time I was fixin' to crawl back to the band, they were already split up." Luther took a long drink from the bottle as if to drown out her memory.

Jake was shocked at what he'd just heard. It appeared that Lizzie Turner conned Luther into giving up the band for her with no intention of continuing a relationship. "*But why would someone be that cruel?*" he thought. Then he thought about when Lizzie walked out on him. "*Was she trying to set me up too? No, I'm sure she really loved me. Didn't she?*"

Jake consoled Luther. "Man, Luther, I'm so sorry to hear about that. She dumped me too, ya know," he said in an effort to ease his pain while hoping that the 'misery loves company' theory would apply. "She gave me the same line. Although it practically killed me not to take her up on it, I didn't. She left and that was the last time I saw her."

Luther looked up from his beer and said. "When I first met you, I said to myself, 'This guy is as different from me as a guy can be.' But the more I get to know you the more I see how much we really do have in common." They clicked their beers together and downed the remainder as if to toast their common misfortune. "Come on, Jake, let's play some blues for this crowd." They left the table for the stage.

Jake picked up his guitar and switched on the amplifier. The curtain opened to reveal the same ten people in the audience he saw the night Luther's band previewed his song. Too soon the drummer clicked his drumsticks together four times, setting the beat for the first song of the set. The song sounded great—great mainly because Jake could hardly hear himself playing. When the song was over, Luther turned to Jake with a smile as if to say, *"We're gonna get through this all right."* After the set was over, Jake was drenched with sweat, not so much from the energy he expelled, but more from his nerves. He was a wreck and dreaded pressing his luck with another set. As he switched off the amplifier, he heard Luther say. "Hey Paul, you made it back." He told Luther he was able to get an earlier flight and came right over from the airport.

Jake walked up to Paul and put his arms around him and said, "Am I glad to see you. Let me buy you a beer."

Paul said, "Wait a minute. Did you fill in for *me* tonight?"

"Yeah, if you could call it that," he confessed.

Luther said with a laugh, "He did OK. But I'm really glad to see you, brother."

"OK, OK who wants a beer?" Jake asked.

Everyone but Paul was headed for the diner to get some dinner during the break. So Jake and Paul drank one together. As they relaxed at the table, Paul told Jake about the death of his uncle and how sad he was to lose him. They talked about the first set and what songs were played. Jake confessed that he was pretty scared as his sweaty shirt slowly dried off. "So how long have you known Luther?" Jake asked, making small talk.

"We've been playing together for as long as I can remember. We've been in three bands together over the last thirty-nine or forty years."

"I guess I know why he was bummed when he knew you couldn't play tonight. You guys probably know each other's every move."

"We really do. So don't you go getting any ideas about taking my place. You hear?" Paul laughed as he pointed his bony accusing finger in Jake's direction.

"Fair enough," Jake agreed.

"Luther tells me you were the rhythm guitar for 'The Phogg' back in the sixties.

"Yep."

"Dig this. We played some of the same places you guys did back then," Paul said.

"No kidding? Luther mentioned that he was in 'Crossroads' about the time 'The Phogg' was playing. Were you two in that one together?" Jake asked.

"Yeah," Paul answered. "We broke up after a few years and formed this group. Luther and I are the only members left from 'Crossroads'. The bass player got a regular job. He's got four kids now. Our sax man got drafted not long after the breakup. He was killed in Vietnam."

"I'm sorry to hear that," Jake consoled.

"Our drummer made the big time though. He's with 'It's About Time'."

"You don't say?" Jake responded. "How does one get a gig like that? Right place at the right time or what?"

"The way I remember it happened, was that the guy…that promoter. Oh you know who I mean. His first name was Maurie." Paul struggled to recall the name, closing his eyes and snapping his fingers to coax the name down from his brain to his tongue.

"Oh you're thinking of Maurie Best, the promoter or manager of 'It's About Time'. He's also a judge in the song contest I entered."

"Right—well, according to my memory, this Maurie dude tried to make a deal with Del, our drummer about two or three months before we broke up without any luck. Said he had a handpicked group lined up. Del wouldn't bite. The dude was driving an old rusted out 1960 Ford Falcon wagon and didn't give Del a good feeling, you dig? He didn't see any advantage to quitting 'Crossroads' 'cause we had it down man, if you know what I mean. But after we broke up, Del thought he'd better take him up on the offer. Lucky for him that he did."

"Sounds like Maurie Best's story is a real 'rags to riches' one," Jake said.

"Funny how life works out," Paul observed.

"Yep," Jake said as he finished his beer. "Well Paul, I should be getting on the road. I trust I'm leaving the rhythm guitar section in good hands."

"Thanks for filling in, Jake. It was a big help." Jake turned to leave, but before he got past the next table, Paul hollered out, "Hey man."

Jake turned to acknowledge him. "Yeah?"

"*Suburban Blues* man—I can dig it."

"Thanks, man," Jake said as he waved and pretty much floated on his own personal cloud to the parking lot.

CHAPTER 26

━━━━━━━━━ ▼ ━━━━━━━━━

"Dan? Dan? Are you awake, Dan? She was the girl who got into the Lincoln that slushed me," Patty insisted as she shook him awake at one in the morning.

"What? What are you talkin' about? Is everything OK?" Dan asked as he was pulled away from his dream of a come from behind win of the PGA championship.

"That girl in the photo—Lizzie. I did see her before. She was the girl that got into the big black Lincoln that slushed me at the 'Silverbell' the night we met."

"Lizzie was driving a Lincoln? No, I think she drove a pick up," Dan told her as he gathered his senses, yawned and scratched his chest.

"No, Dan. She was in the back seat of the Lincoln with some older balding guy with a black coat. Some other guy was driving. I think it was a chauffeur. I saw her get in with the older guy before I got splashed. I knew she looked familiar."

"And you had to wake me up for this?" Dan scolded.

"Yes. Otherwise I might have forgotten to tell you," she replied.

Dan shook his head, flopped back down on the bed and rolled over in a manner that revealed his disdain for her lack of consideration. "Good night, Patty," Dan admonished.

Patty remained sitting up in bed feeling a little silly that she had to wake Dan up out of his deep sleep, when she heard him mumble, "I bet the older guy was Maurie Best."

"Maurie Best? Who's he?" she asked.

Dan sat back up in bed and turned toward her as he explained, "One of the most influential people in rock and roll."

"What was he doing at the 'Silverbell Hideout'—and with Jake's girlfriend?" she asked.

"I know why he was at the 'Silverbell' but I don't have a clue what he was doin' with Lizzie. I know he was there to see Tom. I overheard him ask Tom to join a band he was puttin' together. 'It's About Time'."

"What? You've got to be kidding. Those guys are like the American version of 'The Beatles'," she said with her hands over her mouth. "What happened? Why didn't Tom jump at that?"

"Patty, I never let anyone know what I saw that night. Not even Tom. So this is between you and me. OK?"

"OK."

"First you have to remember that no one knew 'It's About Time' back then. They didn't exist really. Maurie Best was an unknown too. He told Tom he had acquired a song written by that songwriter. What's his name? Oh yeah. Chase Richardson. He wrote *What's the Point*—turned out to be their first song."

"Wow."

"Yeah—he said he had a band all put together and he wanted Tom to be the lead singer. So that's why Maurie was there, but why Lizzie was in his car is a mystery to me. But I gotta get my sleep, hon, we can think about this tomorrow."

"I'll do it. I really haven't got a choice in the matter. I gotta eat you know," Tom angrily replied to his tour manager's inquiry. "It's not like anyone is beatin' down the door to sign me." Tom made the decision to take the twenty percent pay cut in order to be included in the next tour to Florida. *At least it'll be warm,"* he thought.

"Well it's not a done deal yet. Apparently the Marlboro team is still studying the numbers. We should hear today if it's a go or not."

"OK. Let me know as soon as you hear," Tom urged.

"You got it," the tour manager assured.

It was early Saturday morning when Jake called Dan to tell him about his set with Luther's band. Jake didn't let a detail go un-recounted as he described the night down to the exact amount of sweat that exited each of his pores. Dan was jealous that he hadn't been a part of it, but proud that his buddy got the chance. Another interesting occurrence of the evening popped into Jake's head, "Hey, here's something I think will surprise you. Luther and I got to talking and come to find out he dated Lizzie Turner back when he was in a band called 'Cross-roads'."

"Get out man. I can't picture her with him. But then again I couldn't picture her with you, either," Dan quipped.

"Thanks, pal," Jake complained even though he knew Dan spoke the truth. "Anyway, she wanted him to quit the band and run off with her. So Luther did. He quit the band for her and she stood him up at the bus station. The band broke up because of it."

"You know, Jake, it looks like Tom was right."

"About what?"

"Lizzie Turner was a groupie."

"Maybe so. I guess I'm beginning to believe it myself," Jake admitted. "Did you know that their old drummer is in 'It's About Time'? He got scooped up by Maurie Best right after they broke up. And judging from the ride Paul said he had, Maurie must have been dirt poor—said he was driving some old rusted out Ford Falcon."

Jake felt a pause at the other end of the line. "Dan? You still with me?"

"Uh, yeah. I'm just thinking about something Patty said to me." On the one hand, Dan didn't feel it was right to tell Jake about Tom's passing up Maurie Best's offer. But on the other hand, he felt compelled to let Jake know there might be a connection between Maurie Best and Lizzie Turner.

"What did she say?" Jake inquired.

"Oh, nothing," Dan answered, confounded about what he should tell Jake if anything. If he told Jake that Patty saw Lizzie and Maurie leave together that night at the 'Silverbell', then Jake would want to know what Maurie was doing at the 'Silverbell'. Then Dan would have to lie to Jake or tell him something that Tom hadn't seen fit to repeat to anyone. He decided to let it go when Jake abruptly changed the subject.

"Hey, all this talk about Lizzie reminds me. I wanted to talk to you about that photo of her in your basement. That photo's out of sequence, Mr. Historian."

"What do you mean? The Historian Czar makes no mistakes. If I say it is so, it is so."

"When do you think that photo was taken?" Jake asked, setting his trap for Dan.

"Well, you met her in July or August of '66'. The photo was taken at Mt. Holly. We usually played there in the fall. I'd say fall of '66'."

"Oh great one, you are so full of it," Jake replied. "Take another look at that photo, my friend, and you'll see Darryl is clearly playing his Fender Jaguar."

"Yeah? So?" Dan returned, not grasping the significance of that detail.

"So. Darryl's dad traded in the Jaguar for the Mosrite double neck in August of 1966. Remember, his dad got him the Mosrite for his birthday, the day we left to play in Prudenville. He was frantic, trying to find his Jag when his dad came out with the Mosrite."

"How the heck did you remember that Jake?"

"Because I was guarding his new, fancy, double neck birthday present from his dad, stinking, Mosrite guitar while you guys went for food when we played Prudenville. You guys came back and there was Lizzie. So that photo has to be a pre-Lizzie photo."

"You're right," Dan finally agreed. But his mind was working overtime with the rush of all this new information.

"What a coincidence, having her in that picture," Jake remarked.

"Yeah—coincidence," Dan agreed. But he was thinking otherwise. *"It appears she may have been more than a groupie."*

"Well, I got to get back to the woodshed," Jake said. "So I'll catch you later."

Dan added up what he'd learned about Lizzie. *"She dated Luther and got him to quit 'Crossroads'. 'Crossroads' breaks up. Maurie Best signs the 'Crossroads' drummer. He's driving an old Ford Falcon. She's pictured at Mt. Holly surrounded by the 'Ghosts' band members. She dated Jake. She tried to get him to quit the band. Maurie Best appears, seemingly out of the blue, and tries to steal Tom away the night she dumps Jake. Maurie Best acquires the rights to a song written by a prominent songwriter. Lizzie and Maurie drive away in a big new Lincoln Continental driven by a chauffeur. Sounds like Lizzie and Maurie were collaborating. And how did they go from a rusty Ford Falcon and a Chevy pick up to a chauffeur-driven Lincoln?"*

Running on a well-fertilized curiosity, Dan decided to make a trip to the bookstore. He needed a cup of coffee anyway to compensate for the sleep his wife deprived him of. So he headed for Borders to do a little research on 'It's About Time'.

"It's hard not to like this bookstore." he thought. It had big high ceilings, soft colorful carpet and chairs everywhere. Not just your garden variety straight back wooden library chairs. They were leather. Plush overstuffed leather inviting customers to sit down and read the books they selected. The old bookstores, now extinct, had no chairs. Dan mused, *"If there were chairs, someone might read the book in the store and therefore eliminate the need to buy the book and therefore no books would be sold. If they didn't sell books, they'd be outa business. It musta been embarrassing for the traditional bookstores, when they finally realized that* chairs *had put them outa business. Chairs like the ones that Borders had."*

So Dan found the proper section with a large selection of books on 'It's About Time', gathered up what he thought might be the most promising works and searched for some history about the band and its promoter. It seemed odd to Dan that he couldn't find one bit of information on the band members prior to their joining the band. He reasoned, *"Almost any book about 'The Beatles' you pick up will tell you about the pre-'Beatle' life of John, Paul, George, Ringo and everyone who touched 'The Beatles' back then."* He walked up to the front desk and asked the clerk if there were any books published with more detail on the group's history. She punched a few keys on her computer and closely scanned the list of the books. "Have you seen all the books here on our shelves?"

"Yes, ma'am." Dan politely replied.

"All the books on this list that are still in print are currently in stock. There are a couple that are out of print that we don't have. If you want, you can try to find them on one of the web sites that deal in used books."

"Thanks, that's very helpful," Dan said as he turned and left. Then he remembered the flyers and photos on the wall at 'Eddie's'. There was one from 'Ghosts'. If he could just make out who signed the infamous 'To Lizzie with love' inscription, maybe he could find that person and ask if anyone from 'Ghosts' is in 'It's About Time'. Dan was a sucker for a mystery and he was trying not to let his imagination run away with him as he drove down to 'Eddie's'.

CHAPTER 27

▼

After his call to Dan, Jake's typical Saturday morning began. The standard full morning practice session reading music, then perfecting guitar riffs by ear. From there it was reading a book he picked up on music theory. By lunch time he was almost asleep in his big green chair. Writing songs was one thing. But reading about writing songs was brutal. Still he vowed to himself that he'd learn whatever the text had to offer. So he forced himself to stay awake and finish the first chapter. "Time for a break," he decreed out loud, though no one was around to hear it. He got up from the chair, stretched and went into the kitchen to fix lunch. Joyce had placed a container of her homemade soup on the counter for him before she left on a shopping trip to some mall somewhere.

With spoon in hand he stared out the window, thinking of absolutely nothing at all as if in a restful trance while the aroma of Joyce's soup curled around his nose. The sun's rays reflecting off the snow made it appear as if the yard was sprinkled with diamonds. His eyes were locked on the scene as he slowly came back to consciousness and took a spoonful of soup. *"Cold! How long have I been zoned out?"* he wondered. He looked at the clock. *"2:00 p.m. already. I think I've been working too hard at this lately. I think I'm gonna knock off for the rest of the day and veg out."* He popped the soup into the microwave, heated it up and finished it inside of five minutes.

Even when Jake goofed off, he didn't feel right unless he had a list of things to do. So he made a mental list. Go get the mail, come back, fix myself an iced tea, lay on the couch and watch a movie. It didn't take much for him to get over the initial guilt he felt about quitting. He figured he was entitled to take a break. After all he'd been at this non-stop now for seven months and had accomplished a lot. After cleaning up the kitchen he put on his coat and set out for the mailbox down the road. Some of the neighbors were out shoveling their driveways. He exchanged waves with all of them as he walked.

"One letter—hardly worth the trip," he mused as he walked back and looked at the return address. It was from the American Songwriting Contest people. *"Oh wow. I'm not opening this till I get home,"* he decided. He didn't want to be erratically jumping for joy or falling down in a heap in some snow bank crying uncontrollably while in plain view of the shoveling neighbors. It was best to wait for seclusion to read this letter. His trip from the mailbox was much quicker than the trip to the mailbox. He laid the envelope on the floor while he removed his shoes and hung up his coat. Now, taking time to gather up his composure, he reasoned with himself about the pending results. Sure he had worked hard on the song. Sure he thought it was good. He knew the performance on the CD was great because he wasn't involved. But he also knew that this was a national contest with a huge number of entries and it would be a million to one shot for him to win anything. He picked up the letter with shaky fingertips and felt a little dizzy as he sat at the breakfast nook table to open it. He tried to remain steady as he tore off the end of the envelope and blew inside to make it easier to extract the contents. That made him think of The Amazing Carnack. But unlike The Amazing Carnack, he couldn't predict what the letter said. He'd actually have to read it.

'Dear Mr. Dixon,' it began, 'Thank you for your entry in this year's American Songwriting Contest. Your entry was reviewed and considered by our entire staff of judges and we truly appreciate your being a part of our contest. However, unfortunately...Blah Blah Blah Blah. He tossed the letter up in the air without finishing it, and it floated down to the floor in a sort of circular zigzag pattern as if it were being flushed down an invisible toilet. He pushed himself away from the table and opened a bottle of red wine. *"Hey, you took a shot. There's no shame in that. You made an effort. It was a million to one shot anyway,"* he told himself, as he tasted a glass of his favorite wine. Although it tasted a little bitter, he knew the second and third glass would be much smoother.

He didn't feel much like a movie at the moment, so he carried the bottle and his glass into his office, closed the blinds, put on the earphones and turned on the 60's satellite radio station. These songs he knew. He knew how they started. He knew how they ended. It was predictable, no surprises, no disappointments. That's what he needed right now.

Tom liked to run. It was a cheap way to keep weight off. He'd tie his graying Jesus hair back in a ponytail and hit the paths in the park nearby. It was also a great escape for him. He didn't think much about his uncertain career while he ran. His mind stayed on positive things like his good health, the sunshine and the rush he got from a good workout. He'd just finished three miles in less than twenty-five minutes. *"Not bad for an old fart,"* he approved, as he turned the key in his apartment door. As he headed for the bathroom to take a shower, he noticed the light blinking on the phone recorder by his bed. He knew his tour manager had called him back. He was sure he had the verdict on the Florida tour. Tom decided that he needed a shower more than he needed to know if he had a job. So he took a long shower, extending his escape from reality.

After he dried off and got dressed, he wandered over to the message machine, pushed the appropriate button and heard, "Tom. It's not good. Marlboro decided to pass on picking up the tour. As of today we're canceled. There won't be any Florida tour, man. I'm sorry. You'll be getting a final check in the mail sometime next week. Call me." Beep—*end of final message.*

He knew all along this could happen at any time. When he was younger, this sort of thing happened constantly and it never fazed him. He didn't know back then that there was work just around the corner, but the uncertainty never bothered him. Now the uncertainty was the big elephant in the middle of the living room that everybody was afraid of, but nobody wanted to talk about. He sat down on the bed and shook uncontrollably as he tried to figure out what he was going to do now.

Jake was on his third glass of wine, still in the big green chair. The room was even darker now that the sun had slipped away for the night. Joyce could see his mouth miming the words to a song but heard no music as she stood in the doorway holding the letter she had picked up from the floor on her way in. So steeped in his disappointment, he didn't notice her there, so she opted to leave him alone while she made dinner.

Dan was happy to find his way back to 'Eddie's Place', having only been there once before. He walked into the empty place and looked for Eddie behind the bar. He saw no one and walked over to the wall of photos where he saw the flyers before. There they had remained, untouched since he last saw them and probably untouched for the last thirty-five years. He located the promotional flyer of the Ghosts near the top of the wall, so he stood on a nearby chair to get a closer look. There was a signature in black ink across the picture but it was too faded and its location on the black and white photo made it impossible to read. He moved to the other two flyers with inscriptions and was equally disappointed. While Dan was on the chair squinting at the documents, Eddie came out from behind the stage and said, "What the hell are you doin' up on that chair, son?"

Dan was startled and almost fell off the chair as he turned to see Eddie standing there with his hands on his hips, shaking his head. "Oh Eddie, I'm Dan. I was in here with Jake and Luther once and you showed us this wall. Remember, we found one of our flyers over there." Dan pointed to 'The Phogg' flyer. "And I was interested to see these other flyers that were signed. But I just can't make out the names."

"Oh yeah, I 'member you. That was one heck of a tune your friend wrote. You know he showed up 'round here and played with Luther's band last night," Eddie remarked. "Luther told me about him taking guitar lessons after all that time. I guess, once you got the blues in you, it's hard to shake it off."

"I feel the same way. I was in 'The Phogg' with him back in the sixties and all the memorabilia in this place blows me away. Eddie, how'd you get these flyers?"

"Well, lots of times when a band was fixin' to play here, they'd leave me flyers about a week or two ahead to let the crowd know. I'd always save one and put it on the wall," Eddie answered.

"But there's four that I can find signed, 'To Lizzie with love'. I don't see any of the rest with inscriptions," Dan pointed out.

Eddie scratched his head as he tried to answer Dan. "Seems to me after movin' into this place, I was unpackin' the boxes and came across a book full a them flyers. Nice book. Nice black leather. You'd think a body would miss sumpthin' like that. It didn't look familiar to me. I figured it mighta been part of our lost and found—had a little blood on the front too. I found those flyers in the book when I was a cleanin' it up, so I put 'em on the wall. I thought because they was signed by somebody, it made 'em look better'n the ones I'd put up before. So those went up and the unsigned ones came down."

Dan asked, "Do you remember a Lizzie Turner?"

"Who's she?"

"That's who the flyers are inscribed to."

"No, doesn't ring a bell with me," Eddie said.

Dan wondered about the blood on the album, then remembered why Eddie had to move, and hoped it wouldn't hurt to ask more about the robbery. "Do you remember anything from the night you were robbed?"

"Some. My memory ain't so good these days," he said as he rubbed his two-day-old beard. "I remember kneelin' down and openin' the safe in my office." Eddie struck a pose as if he were going to act out the episode blow by blow. "As I opened the safe, I heard a noise and turned to look toward the door. I couldn't lock the office door 'cuz the lock was jammed. I always locked it when I was openin' the safe. The door was still closed, but when I glanced back 'round, someone was standin' next to me. All I saw was a pair of legs in black pants. He musta been hiding by the filein' cabinets. I started to look up. He was wearing a black coat—in the middle of summer. Imagine that. I was this close to seein' a face, when I got whacked on the head. When I came to I was alone, my monkey wrench was a lying next to me and the money was G-O-N-E"

"Have you ever been robbed before, Eddie?" Dan asked.

"Never, not in all the time I've been in the bar business have I ever been robbed. I guess I wasn't careful enough that night," Eddie reasoned. "Can I get ya a beer?" Eddie offered.

"That sounds good. A cold draft would hit the spot."

Eddie brought two drafts over and sat down with Dan and they shared some stories about the sixties and had a few laughs. During their reflection on the past, no one else entered the bar. Then it was time for Dan to go. As Dan was walking to the front door and Eddie was returning to his post behind the bar, Eddie called out to Dan. "He was wearing a silver chain attached to a blue coin with a hole in the middle."

Dan stopped and turned around, not understanding Eddie's comment. Eddie clarified, "The robber—he was wearin' a silver chain attached to a coin with a hole in the middle, the size of a quarter or maybe a nickel."

"Do you remember tellin' that to the cops?" Dan asked.

"I didn't remember it at the time—just now come to me. Anyway, you done asked me more questions tonight than the police ever did."

"*That new bit of information mighta been helpful to the cops when it happened,*" he pondered. "Ain't nothin' wrong with *your* memory, Eddie. Take care now."

After dinner was made, Joyce peeked into Jake's office to see if he was hungry and found him sleeping in his big green chair. "Dinner," she announced as she touched his sleeve.

He came around slowly and lamented, "I didn't win, Joyce. You know, reason told me not to get my hopes up and I didn't for quite a while. But for some reason, as time went on and I got all that encouragement from everyone, I started believing there was a real possibility there. But I didn't win. And that's that."

"I know. I picked up the letter from the floor. It was a long shot anyway. You said so yourself. And look at all the songs you've written. You've completed an album's worth of songs, for crying out loud. And your recording skills have improved. And I know you're having fun with it, Jake. I see it in your face and the way you act every day. Come on now—let's have some dinner."

CHAPTER 28

▼

By Monday morning Jake had shaken off the bad news and had reconciled with his ego. He was back on track and in the woodshed inventing and practicing some blues riffs. He'd play randomly any blues progression that came into his head for about half an hour at a time while recording on the computer program. Then he'd sit back and listen to what he had done. When he came across a particularly catchy or intriguing segment, he'd isolate it on the computer, play it back and save it as a separate file. Then he'd practice and expand on each newly invented riff until it was second nature to him, hoping that someday soon he'd be able to play blues lead guitar and make it sound as if it were endless improvisation. He glanced at the clock. *"Noon already—and my fingers don't hurt."* In the middle of his listening he heard something ringing, and for a moment, thought there was something amiss with the computer program. He stopped the playback and still heard the sound. *"Damn."* It was the phone. *"Let it ring, the recorder will get it,"* he thought. *"No, it could be something important."* He begrudgingly put down his guitar and picked up the phone with a not so nice, "Hello."

"Uh, I'm sorry to bother you sir," apparently the voice of someone's timid secretary apologized. "May I speak with Sonny Dixon?"

"I'm sorry but you must have the wrong...." Jake stopped as he suddenly remembered who Sonny Dixon was. "Oh, Sonny...sorry it's a little early for me. Sonny can't come to the phone right now. Can I take a message for him?" Jake was looking for a pen and paper while he waited for the timid voice to respond.

"Oh sure," she said. "My name is Missy Thornton with MBP Incorporated in Beverly Hills, California. We are in the entertainment industry. Mr. Dixon was a participant in the American Songwriting Contest this year and our acquisitions arm reviewed his entry. They have made a recommendation to our corporate officers to discuss the acquisition of limited recording rights to his entry in the contest."

Jake sat down on the floor with the pen and paper in his hand trying desperately to locate his composure. "What does that mean?" was all he could manage to ask, and hoped his excitement was concealed.

Missy dumbed it down a little for him. "Well, we have an artist under contract that we think would like to perform Mr. Dixon's song on a future CD release. Could you please give him our phone number and ask him to give us a call?"

"Sure," Jake replied.

"Please have him call 310-555-6300 and ask for Mr. Henderson at extension 245."

"OK," Jake said as he hung up the phone and strapped himself in, because the emotional roller coaster just left the gate for the next ride. He decided to wait a while before he called back. After all, *Sonny couldn't come to the phone right now, could he?*" For an hour, Jake tried to busy himself. He went in the kitchen with the intention of making himself some lunch and decided he couldn't eat. He wanted to call Joyce, Rick, or Dan to tell them about the call. But he anticipated the questions that would follow and realized he had no answers, at least not yet. He settled on listening to his satellite radio for as long as he could stand it, then gave up and made the call. Busy. He tried again. Busy. He took another look at the number and realized, in his nervousness, he had dialed wrong. This time slowly punching in the numbers worked and it began to ring. "Good morning MBP. How may I direct your call?"

"Mr. Henderson, please," Jake answered.

"Henderson," a husky voice called out on the other end of the line.

"Yes, Mr. Henderson, this is Sonny Dixon. I got a message here to call ya."

"Yes. Mr. Dixon. Thank you for getting back to me so soon. Are you familiar with our company?"

"No. Can't say that I am," Jake responded, trying to sound (for no logical reason) how he thought Sonny Dixon would sound.

Mr. Henderson got right to the point. "We are a world renowned organization in the entertainment business and we like the song you wrote for the American Songwriting Contest this year. We would like to set up a meeting with you to discuss our acquiring limited rights to record your song. Are you interested?"

"I think so. I think it might be worth havin' a meetin'. Yeah," Jake said.

"OK. Great. I can arrange to have someone from our staff meet you this afternoon if you're free. We have some people in Detroit at the moment. Does that work for you?"

"Well, it's past one here in Michigan right now," Jake said, thinking Mr. Henderson didn't know what the time difference was.

"That's right, Mr. Dixon. I've got people ready to see you today at 4:00 p.m. *your time* if you can make it."

"OK. What's the address?" he asked.

"2211 Woodward Avenue. Do you need directions?"

"No, I can find it," Jake replied.

"Mr. Dixon, it would be helpful if you could bring down any other songs that you might have along the same lines. What we'd like to do is listen to them and give you one of our standard form contracts for your agent and attorney to review. During today's meeting we'll arrange another meeting to see if we can come to terms on *Suburban Blues* and others if any."

"Well yes, I can bring a few others with me."

"That's great. When you get there, go in the front entrance and up the elevator to room 300," Mr. Henderson instructed.

"OK, I'll be there at four," Jake said as the conversation ended.

"This isn't happening" he thought. Jake gathered up the CD's he planned to bring and a copy of the paperwork David had started, concerning the copyright to his work. He took a shower and, thinking he should try and make a good first impression, stood in his closet staring at his clothes all pressed and organized by color. It occurred to him that except for the occasional party, he hadn't put on anything but Levi's jeans and 'T' shirts since he started writing. All the clothes he used to wear to the office were hanging around like laid off workers in an unemployment line. He wished Joyce were there to tell him what might look good for such an occasion.

"Guy Rig's office," Joyce answered.

"Guess what?" Jake asked, knowing the sound of his voice didn't require the normal introduction.

"What?" she whispered. As if the answer to the question should be kept a secret.

"I'm going to Detroit to talk to some company about my song. They heard it somehow from the contest and they wanna discuss the right to record it."

Joyce started to laugh. "That's nice, Jake. Look, I'm kinda swamped today so what's up?"

"Really, Joyce—I'm not kiddin'. I got a call from them this morning. They asked for Sonny Dixon. I almost forgot that I'm Sonny Dixon. I'm getting ready for the meeting and don't know what I should wear. I thought you could tell me."

"Oh my God—that is fantastic. Put on your green striped shirt, the one with the orange thread in the buttons and your brown corduroys. Your brown sleeveless sweater will look nice with that, too. Did they say anything about why they wanted your song?"

"No. It wasn't a long conversation. I was too freaked out to think about any questions, and trying to impersonate Sonny Dixon and all. Oh, they still think I'm Sonny Dixon. I wonder when I should tell them that's my pen name. I guess I'll play it by ear."

Joyce was disappointed that she had no more time to relish the moment with him and said, "Gotta go, but I'll want a full report tonight. This is unbelievable."

He went back to the closet, selected and donned the items that Joyce had suggested. He glanced at the mirror as he passed it. "*I don't really think Sonny Dixon would look like this*," he speculated. "*I need to change.*" Back into his closet he went and came out with black Levi's, thin black sweater that looked like a designer 'T' shirt, black sport jacket and his prescription trifocal sunglasses. "*Oh man. Do I look ridiculous!*" he thought. Wasting no time, Sonny Dixon got rid of the black and went with what his wife had originally suggested.

After he grabbed a quick bite to eat, it was still too early to leave. He thought about packing his guitar along with the CD's and the copyright papers. "*Why would you need to bring your guitar?*" He thought. "*Can you think of a single reason that you'd need your guitar in a situation like this? Maybe it wouldn't be too totally illogical to assume that they'd request I play something for them.*" Although the odds weren't great that he'd need it, he took it with him anyway. It had become his companion again just as it had been many years ago. So, he packed it up, tossed it in the car and left for the appointment early. There could be traffic. He could get lost. A lot could happen to make him late and he didn't want to be late for this. On Woodward Avenue south of I-75 he began to look for addresses. On his right he saw the ten-story Fox Theater marquee overlooking Woodward Avenue. What an elegant landmark it was again after its restoration. He immediately thought of the Motown Review—a show that Motown Records used to put on for the ten day Christmas and New Year's break back in the sixties. He remembered when Tom brought him down to see Berry Gordy's Motown Review sometime in the mid 60's. He checked the address on the Fox to see how close he was to his destination. "*2211, that's it? My meeting's here at the Fox Theater?*"

He found a parking space. It was three-thirty. He had a half hour to kill so he did what he normally would do in cases like this. He listened to his satellite radio. The next song wasn't by Stevie Wonder; it was by Little Stevie Wonder. That's what he was called when he did *Fingertips (Part 2)*. He remembered seeing him perform that song in that very building maybe thirty-six, thirty-seven years ago.

It was snowing hard that winter night so Tom and Jake ran from their car to get in the ticket line sheltered by the Fox marquee. Both were excited to see some of their favorite artists. Although the band didn't play many Motown tunes, both Tom and Jake craved the style and it had become a big influence on the music they *did* play. Soon they got their tickets and headed inside the main lobby. Neither had seen a theater this spacious and ornate. As they were walking and gazing at the structure, Tom bumped into someone. After the apologies were mutually submitted, the stranger said, "Tom…Tom Tyler? I haven't seen you since Interlochen."

"Hey Jerome," Tom said unenthusiastically. "Jake, this is Jerome. Jerome, my sister and I did a summer together at Interlochen a few years ago."

"Yes, I think four or five years now. I thought you were going back the following summer. What happened?" Jerome inquired.

"I got in a rock and roll band and couldn't really schedule both. Listen, it's been nice talkin' to ya, we better get to our seats before the show starts," Tom responded. Jake could tell Tom was uncomfortable talking to Jerome for some reason.

But Jerome wasn't done talking. "You know, your sister told me you spent your tuition money on some guitar amplifier for a friend. What was that all about? You were all psyched up to learn from that voice coach coming in from Juilliard. You really blew it man."

At that Tom said, "Nice seein' ya Jerome. Come on Jake, lets go see if we can find these seats," hoping Jake would forget what Jerome had just said.

"So you gave up voice lessons at Interlochen to buy the amplifier—so I wouldn't get kicked out of the band? Is that how you got the money for the amplifier?"

"Don't sweat it, Jake. I didn't really wanna go to Interlochen. The band is more important. Right?" Tom answered as they both walked through the huge doors leading to the auditorium.

"Just one more forgotten sacrifice from Tom," Jake thought as he turned off the radio and went inside for his appointment, forgetting about his guitar in the back seat.

CHAPTER 29

▼

Entering the great lobby of the historic Fox Theater was an eye opener for Jake. He'd heard that it had fallen on hard times since his visit those years ago. Sure, he thought, it was a wonderful place when he and Tom took in the Motown Review, but nevertheless it was showing its age. It had been completely restored in 1988 and perfectly maintained since. The lighting was bright and clear, no longer afraid to reveal dingy walls. The paint was new. The gold leaf had to be new. The hand-stenciled canvas on the ceiling was new. The stained glass had been restored. Even the custom-made carpeting with the elephant pattern had been re-made. The Fox had been resurrected from the ashes of neglect and decay. *"Maybe they should call it the Phoenix Theater,"* he thought as he took the elevator to the third floor.

As he got off the elevator, a very well dressed man greeted him and asked who he was here to see. Mr. Henderson hadn't given him a name that he recalled, so Jake just said that he had an appointment with some people from MBP. He was shown to a suite with a big long conference table overlooking the main auditorium of the theater. He asked Jake to be seated and offered him coffee while he waited for a representative to appear. Soon a tall thin man who resembled Bob Marley with wild Afro hair and a three-day-old beard entered wearing a sharp black and gray pinstriped suit, patent leather shoes and dark glasses. *"There's no way I could have dressed right for this,"* Jake mulled as he noticed three more well dressed men, following close behind. One held a briefcase. Another held a huge boom box style CD player and the third man, the largest of the three, stood by the door with his arms folded.

"Hi, I'm Ken Darby and you must be Sonny Dixon," he said with an out-stretched hand that Jake shook as he nodded to affirm his counterfeit identity. "These are my associates, Kelly and Don. The guy by the door is Francis. My boss asked me to leave you with a standard form contract for what we are propos-ing." Kelly opened the briefcase and retrieved a twenty-page contract with the word 'Sample' written in red across the front. "In addition, we were told that you have other songs that we could hear."

"I have another fourteen songs on these CD's," Jake said as he slid the jewel cases toward Ken. He felt he should prepare Ken and friends that they weren't quite the quality of the contest entry. "Unlike *Suburban Blues*, that was profes-sionally done, these recordin's were done by me on my computer at home. So there'll be a big difference in quality…hope that's OK."

"Were used to that sort of thing, Mr. Dixon," Ken said as he took the jewel cases.

Jake hoped that there would eventually be a good opportunity to tell him his real name while he wondered if it really mattered. "Call me Sonny," he granted. "Are you plannin' on listenin' to these songs right now?" Jake asked as he nodded toward the big boom box.

"That's right," Ken replied. Jake leaned back in his chair and crossed his legs in a move to get comfortable figuring he'd be present for narration and/or ques-tions. "However, we need to listen to these tunes in private. You see, we have a process—a procedure, if you will—that we always follow. We'd like you to make yourself comfortable in the next suite while we listen and compile our opinions. If you need anything, just let Francis know," he explained as he led Jake to the next room.

Jake sat sipping coffee with his feet up on a rich leather ottoman in the next suite, reading the sample contract and occasionally taking in the view of the five-thousand seat, one-hundred-ten foot high auditorium from the glass picture window. For over an hour, through the wall between the suites, he could hear his tunes being played on the boom box and muffled voices as they offered their cri-tiques. Then there were no more voices and the boom box was silent. The con-necting door to the suite opened and Ken peeked in. "Sonny, could you please join us?" he said as he waved Jake back into their room.

"We enjoyed your songs. In fact I will be making a recommendation to MBP that they seek to acquire limited rights to all the songs that we listened to. Your songs intrigue me. They sound as if they were written years ago. They have the carefree flavor of Buddy Holly along with the unmistakable influence of delta blues and 1960's Motown soul. And when these songs are played in the order you have arranged, it's almost like a musical history of rock and roll and its evolution from the blues. This is an amazing collection of work, Sonny."

Jake was doing all he could to keep his composure. He wanted to jump out of his chair and traverse the big conference table to hug Ken for the unbelievable things he said, but a warm "Thank you," was all Jake would allow himself. After all this was a business meeting, not *Star Search*.

Ken continued, "The project we have in mind is a CD that represents a return to original rock and roll—my boss's idea, really. We own our own record label and we have a certain recording group under contract that has been around a long time. He wanted a selection of original songs that would represent a return to the roots of rock and roll for their next CD. When we heard *Suburban Blues,* we knew it fit the profile."

"Ken, I'm truly honored by your remarks and I'm looking forward to working with you on this contract," Jake replied, having completely shelved any attempt at sounding like a Sonny Dixon.

"Well, thank you Sonny, but you won't be working with me from here on out. Once I give my recommendation, my involvement will be over. What we need to do next is set up a meeting with the executives and the legal staff to hammer out a deal. And that's not my area. But I can have the revised contract faxed to your attorney tonight. And if this Friday works for you, I can set up a meeting right here about one."

"That works for me," Jake said without checking his schedule. There would be nothing short of death that would keep him from that meeting. After leaving David's fax and phone number, Jake stood up from the table, shook everyone's hand and put on his coat for the trip home. "Thanks again, gentlemen," he said as he stepped toward the door. "By the way, Ken, who's your boss?"

"Maurie Best," Ken replied with a smile. "Have you heard of him?"

"Oh yeah," Jake said as he calmly closed the door and walked toward the elevator.

Once safe within the elevator, Jake jumped around with hands fisted in the air like Rocky. He could almost hear the Rocky theme in his head. In mid dance, the elevator door opened to the lobby. A small group of people gathered nearby waiting for their trip up witnessed his celebration with fear, stepped away quickly and gave him a wide berth on his way out. Once he reached his car, he called David to let him know that he would be receiving a contract by fax for his songs and asked him if he could make the Friday meeting. David agreed and said he would look the contract over and go over the details with an associate who had experience in the entertainment field.

Dan picked up his cell phone to take a call. "Tom. How are ya, man?"

"I've been better. I wanted to let ya know that my tour was canceled and I'm plannin' to take a plane back home once I'm sure I've got my apartment sub-let," Tom replied with a hint of misery in his voice.

"Oh man, I'm sorry to hear it, Tom. Can't you get another gig goin'?" Dan asked.

"Well, I hope to get things going again someday soon but in the meantime I've got to cut my expenses. I figured I could live a lot cheaper in Waterford than I can in L. A. And my apartment will rent for a lot more than my lease agreement. So basically, I can bank or live off the difference...for a while anyway," Tom explained. "How are Rick and Jake doin'? I know I didn't leave on the best of terms with Jake."

"Oh, he's over that. Don't worry about Jake, he can take it," Dan replied. Dan normally would have been happy to tell Tom about the efforts that Jake had made since Tom was last in town. However, given Tom's bad news, Dan wasn't going to rub salt into his wounds by telling him that Jake finished writing a lot of those old songs and entered a songwriting contest. So he just added, "I know he and Rick'll be sorry to hear about the tour, but happy that you're comin' back to town. Hey, just let me know what the schedule is and I'll come get you at the airport. You can stay with Patty and me until you get situated."

"That sound's great, Dan. Believe me it won't take me long to get a place and I'll be outta your hair in no time."

"Don't worry about it. By the way, I've got a little surprise in my basement I want ya to see. So, I can't wait for ya to get here."

"Well OK, I got lots to do before I can fly outta here. So I'll talk to you soon. And thanks again, Dan. Tell Patty hi for me."

After Jake called Joyce to let her know the good news, he called Dan. "You're not gonna believe this," Jake said as Dan answered his phone.

"What exactly, am I not gonna believe?" Dan asked in an animated tone.

"I just walked out of a meeting with a company that wants to acquire the rights to record my songs," Jake yelled into the phone.

"No kiddin'. How'd that happen?"

"I got a call today from MBP, Inc. They're out of California. They have their own record label. They said that they heard my entry in the song contest and liked it. Then they asked me to come down here and bring all my songs so they could hear those too. They're faxing a contract to Dave tonight and we have a meeting on Friday."

"That's unbelievable, Jake. You're officially a successful songwriter. That makes up for the bad news I just got from Tom," Dan remarked, knowing Jake would ask what he meant.

"What bad news? Is he OK? Is his mom OK?" Jake asked anxiously.

"Nobody's sick. It's just that Tom's tour was canceled and he's comin' back here to live until he figures out what to do," Dan explained. "He's gonna stay with Patty and me until he gets a place of his own."

"Wow. That's not good news. But…you know. He's been in the business a long time. I'm sure he'll find another tour or something in no time," Jake responded. But even as the words were coming out of his mouth, he couldn't help but feel somehow guilty that he appeared to be on the verge of something big while Tom seemed to be headed in the opposite direction. "Maybe I can hook Tom up with the people I've been talking to."

"Maybe—anything is possible. I guess," Dan agreed. "What's the name of their record label?" Dan asked.

"I don't know," Jake replied.

"Well, do you know anything at all about these people?" Dan asked with a fair amount of skepticism.

"I really don't know much except that this guy named Ken told me that Maurie Best was his boss. You know, he owns 'It's About Time'. I'll know more when Dave gets the contract," Jake reported to ease Dan's concerns.

"Maurie Best. I don't believe it. This can't be happenin'," Dan whispered in bewilderment.

"What the heck are you talking about? Jake asked.

"Jake, where are you now?"

"I'm at the Fox Theater in Detroit. Why?"

Dan's voice grew stern. "I think it's time you and I sat down and had a drink. There's a few things you should know. How about we meet at 'Eddie's Place'? Say in forty five minutes or so?"

"OK," Jake agreed. "I'll let Joyce know I'll be a little late. See ya there."

At least Eddie's wasn't hard to find anymore for either Dan or Jake. Jake arrived first and took a stool at the bar. The place was deserted. Not a soul or sound, except the faint hum of the traffic outside accompanied by a steady dripping that seemed as if it were coming from the ceiling just above his head. Then he noticed that he needed to put his jacket back on. The place was cold. He got up to see if he could locate Eddie or maybe the thermostat when the light from outside momentarily beamed into the bar as the front door opened. The comforting darkness returned as the door closed behind Eddie. "Been here long?" Eddie asked as he came closer and slowly recognized his patron. "Oh Jake, you better watch out. You're starting to be a regular 'round here."

"Hey, Eddie. I'm meeting my buddy Dan here for a drink," Jake replied.

"He better watch out too. He's been here as much as you," Eddie observed. "He was here Saturday, a lookin' at those pictures on my wall of fame again. He's a kinda memorabilia nut, that one."

"*That seems odd,*" Jake thought, but didn't probe further.

"Want a beer, Jake?"

"Yeah I would and you know what else I'd like?" Jake ordered boldly.

"What's that?"

"Some heat. Eddie, It's really cold in here and something is dripping up in that ceiling right above that chair," Jake pointed to the suspect area.

"Well the heat should be comin' on pretty soon. That's where I was when you came in."

"Where?"

"Consumer's Power—payin' the heat bill. They cut me off this mornin' so I went down and gave 'em what I could. They told me they'd put it back on today," Eddie said with a little embarrassment.

"Has business been slow for you lately?" Jake asked with a look of concern.

"It's been like this for years, Jake." Eddie spoke as he pulled down on the tapper to get Jake a beer. "Pretty much hand to mouth. People don't like to come to a broken-down place like this. Only the die-hard blues fans come anymore. If I could afford to fix this ol' place up, I could get some of my old clientele back. But without the customers, hell I can't hardly afford the heat bill. It's a vicious circle I'm in here. A real catch twenty two is what I got for sure," he lamented as he slid the beer over.

Another blast of light from the front door and the black outline of Dan's frame appeared in the doorway against the illumination of the outside world. They both greeted him as he took a bar stool next to Jake, glanced briefly to the ceiling when he heard the dripping and said, "Man, its cold in here. Eddie, can't you turn up the heat?"

At that precise moment while Eddie was sliding Dan's beer to him, the unmistakable rumbling of Eddie's antiquated gas-forced air furnace filled the room, and the heat began to flow over the three men. Dan looked up toward the ceiling again but not to survey the roof leak. Eddie gave Dan a serious look and said, "How's that for service?" His serious look cracked and a big smile broke through as he shuffled to the other end of the bar to wash some glasses.

Dan picked up his beer and motioned for Jake to follow him. They took a seat at a table near Eddie's wall of fame. Jake broke the silence. "So tell me, Dan. What's up?"

"I've been thinkin' about how to say this to ya all the way down here. And I guess there's really no good way to do it. So, I'm just gonna tell ya." Dan took a breath and continued. "Remember that night at the 'Silverbell' when we got snowed in?" Dan asked.

"Of course, that was the night Lizzie and I broke up and you met Patty. Not an easy night to forget," he said with more than a little sarcasm in his voice.

"Well, there was a guy there that night who offered Tom a job with his band. Said he had just bought the rights to a song and just put a new band together and wanted Tom to be their lead singer."

"You're kidding," he said with surprise in his voice. "You mean Tom told you that and he didn't tell me?"

"Not exactly, Tom doesn't even know that I know it happened. I was walkin' up to 'em to tell 'em it was almost time to play, and I walked in on the two of 'em talkin'. I stood back at first not wantin' to interrupt, but as the conversation went on, I couldn't leave."

"So what happened?" Jake probed.

"He turned the guy down. He said that 'The Phogg' had its own songwriter and that he liked his chances with the band he was in, or somethin' along that line."

Feeling that guilt come creeping up through his stomach and into his throat, Jake said, "Boy, that's a test of loyalty I couldn't have passed. Why didn't you tell me about it?"

"Because Tom never mentioned it to me, so I figured he wanted to keep it to himself," Dan answered. "So I kept it to *myself.*"

"So why now? Why would you be telling me this now?"

"Well, that guy. The guy who offered Tom the job? When he left the place, he took Lizzie with him."

Jake was about to take a drink of beer when that piece of information registered in his brain and he froze for a moment with his mouth open and the beer glass just inches from his lips. "This guy took Lizzie with him?" he finally asked as if he didn't hear Dan the first time. "And you're just telling me this now?"

"I didn't know it happened until this Saturday mornin'. Patty woke me up in the middle of the night. Remember, when she saw that picture of Lizzie at the party, she said that she looked familiar. Well, she remembered that she saw her get into a big black Lincoln Continental with an older balding guy as she was headed in from the parkin' lot. That Lincoln was the car that splashed slush all over her that night. I guess that's why it stuck in her mind."

"OK Dan, all this stuff is interesting history, but why are ya telling me this now?" Jake asked.

"There's more. Remember, you told me that Luther got stood up by Lizzie and their band broke up?"

"Yep."

"Remember who you told me the drummer went with after the break up?"

"'It's About Time'," Jake replied.

"And who owns 'It's About Time'?" Dan asked.

"Maurie Best," Jake quickly answered.

Then Dan delivered the punch line. "The guy that offered Tom the lead singer job was Maurie Best. The song he said he'd acquired the rights to was *What's the Point.*

Jake sat speechless for a moment as he tried to comprehend all that Dan was saying. "It must have killed Tom later to find out that he could have been a part of that group. Wait a minute. Do you think Maurie Best and Lizzie were working together so that Maurie could hire away the band members for his group? She was dating me in order to break up 'The Phogg' and get to Tom? She dated Luther to get to the 'Crossroads' drummer?"

"I think so, Jake, but the point I wanted to make was that if you get a contract with Maurie Best, what's that gonna do to Tom when he finds out?"

"Yeah. You're right, he might be pretty upset," Jake agreed. "But Dan, it was a long time ago. I mean he's gotta be over it by now. Wouldn't ya think?"

"Maybe if his career was going great, but he's moving back to Waterford, man. Come on. It's gonna kill him. Well, at least think about what I said and remember it's just between you and me. OK?"

"OK," Jake agreed. "But this thing about Lizzie…man I can't believe it. You think she was really trying to break us up?"

"Yep, and I think she was doin' the same thing with the 'Ghosts' before you met her. But I couldn't find any information about that," Dan bemoaned. "I went to the bookstore and tried to read up on the early days of the band and not one book talks about where the members came from—just very sketchy family history. I came down here Saturday to take a look at those signed flyers to see if I could find out who signed the 'Ghost's' flyer to Lizzie and couldn't read the name. I thought if I could, I'd try to track down the guy who signed it and ask him about it."

Jake's curiosity exploded. "Where's the flyer? Maybe I can figure it out," he said impatiently, as Dan pointed to it on the wall.

"Eddie, do you mind if I take this flyer down for a minute so that I can have a closer look?" Jake asked.

"Now he's got you all up in my wall too. Oh well, go ahead, can't hurt nothin' I guess," Eddie grumbled from behind the bar.

Jake carefully pulled the staples from the corners of the flyer and brought it to the table. He pulled up his trifocal glasses and rested them on his head so that he could focus in on the signature. "It's written in black ink over the black and white photo."

"I know," Dan offered.

"I got it," Jake said as he picked up the flyer and turned it over. "Maybe we can read the name from the back. If the pen made any indentation we might get lucky."

Just then Eddie came over to see what the boys were up to. He trusted Dan and Jake but decided to supervise any dismantling of his wall of fame, just in case. Jake looked closely at the back of the flyer as Dan and Eddie looked on. "Can I borrow your pencil?" Jake asked Eddie. Eddie pulled a slightly chewed up No. 2 from behind his ear and handed it over as he rolled his eyes. Jake gently rubbed the edge of the graphite from the pencil over the signature area of the reverse side of the flyer. This made the indentation of the signature stand out so that it could be read. The signature was clear but hard to read in reverse, so Jake held the back side of the flyer up to the Budweiser mirror nearby and the name was clear. Todd Logan. Excited about their newly discovered detective skills, they tried the same thing with the rest of the signed flyers—'White Powder' and 'Blues Train' with equal success. Now they had three more names.

Eddie asked, "What are you two trying to find out with all this research?"

Dan spoke up proudly and said, "Eddie we think that 'Blues Train', 'Cross-roads', 'White Powder', and 'Ghosts' all have somethin' in common."

Instead of asking what they had in common, Eddie said, "Well, I know two things they have in common. They all played at my bar at one time or another." And before Dan or Jake could speak he said, "And each of those old bands had a member who's now playin' with 'It's About Time'. These ain't just pictures up on the wall, boys. This wall, in a way, represents a big part a my life. So, I've always tried to follow theses groups as best I can. You know, I could write a book just from the pictures up on that wall. All the jumpin' around the musicians did, from band to band back then. It's all right up here in my head. Lucky for me I didn't lose any of it when I got whacked back in '66'. Now you boys put those flyers back up where you found 'em."

Dan and Jake immediately did what Eddie told them to do and ordered another beer. As they sat at the table Jake thought that it all fit together now. Lizzie definitely had her own agenda. Although his heart wasn't convinced, he was pretty let down to have it virtually confirmed that Lizzie was not interested in him. It seemed clear her goal was only to help Maurie Best put together a dream team. Jake was a little depressed and staring into his beer when Dan mentioned Eddie's robbery. "You know, I think it's possible that Maurie Best might have been the one that robbed Eddie."

"What? Why would you think that?" Jake asked.

"Well, you told me that when he got the drummer from Crossroads, he was drivin' an old rusty Falcon. Next thing we know, Eddie is robbed and Maurie's acquired the rights to that song which had to cost money, and he's got a chauffeur drivin' him around in a Lincoln Continental. It just seemed to fit, you know. I mean, if he knew all these bands he must have known about 'Eddie's Place'. He coulda done it. Oh yeah, Eddie said that he found all the signed flyers in a leather thing, like a photo album and it had blood on it too, man. If Maurie and Lizzie are connected, he coulda had the album on him at the time of the robbery. I mean, I suppose it's possible. If I just could think of a way to find out if he used to wear a chain with a blue coin attached."

Jake slowly looked up from his beer and asked, "What did you just say?"

"I said, if I could find out if Maurie wore a chain, a silver chain with a coin attached, I might be able to connect 'em to the robbery."

Jake stood up from the table and said, "Wait right here. Don't go anywhere. I'll be right back." And he ran out the front door, went to his car, opened his guitar case and withdrew the silver chain with the blue nickel attached. He hurried back in, sat down at the table with Dan, and held out his hand displaying the chain. "I wonder if it looked like this."

"Where did you get this?" Dan asked as he held it up to get a better look.

"It was Lizzie's. She wore it all the time, until she gave it to me back in the summer of '66'. I remember it was late on a Friday night because she showed up after our last set at the Elizabeth Lake Estates dance."

"I remember that night too. Those girls got up on the stage dancin' in their bikinis. That was one fun night," Dan recalled. "Hey, Eddie," he called. "Can you come here? I want you to see somethin'."

Eddie walked over and Dan showed him the silver chain and said. "Could this have been the chain you saw the night you were robbed?"

Eddie's eyes opened wide and said, "That's it—the chain with the blue coin. What're you doin' with it?" Dan could see the rage building up from within him and he was about to explode. "Which one a ya two robbed me?" he yelled as he stepped back and picked up a chair expecting the need to defend himself. With the chair held high over his right shoulder he was locked and loaded. Eddie's eyes grew even wider, moving his suspicious glare from Dan then to Jake and back to Dan in panicked hysteria. Jake and Dan simultaneously put both hands out to fend off the expected incoming chair and leaped up from their table, sending their chairs careening into the wall behind them. Then Eddie wound up and flung the chair at the two. The large projectile came tumbling end over end through the air, whooshing past their heads, bouncing off their table, wiping out the two glasses of draft beer like a bowling ball picking up a spare, then crashed into Eddie's wall of fame, sending B. B. King's photo from its place of honor straight to the floor in a broken heap of wood, paper and shards of glass.

As Eddie scrambled to hoist another chair over his head, Dan yelled, "Eddie, Eddie, look. If we robbed ya, why the hell would we come in here and show ya this chain, man? Wouldn't that be the dumbest thing a crook could do?"

"We'd sure be wasting our time in here if we were crooks," Jake added. "The best we could do here would be to get some free beer and a Consumers Power receipt."

Eddie, breathing hard and sweating, was too exhausted to contest their logic. He released the chair and it fell on the floor behind him. Feeling unsteady, he hung his head and caught his breath. As he wiped the sweat from his forehead he said, "I'm sorry, boys." Dan and Jake helped him to a seat at a clean table. They all sat silently, each gathering his composure and thoughts about what just took place. Eddie broke the silence and said, "I take it you know whose chain that is." Dan and Jake filled Eddie in on their findings that led up to the recent chair throwing.

"I got robbed by a girl?" Eddie asked with astonishment.

"Sure seems that way," Jake responded. "But I don't see a way to prove it by just this chain."

"So even if we found her we couldn't do nothin' 'bout it?" Eddie asked.

"I really don't know—I kinda doubt it. It's been over thirty-six years, Eddie, there's probably some sort of statute of limitations on a crime like that." Jake put the chain in his coat pocket.

"Too bad," Eddie said as he hung his head. "It just ain't right."

Suddenly the ceiling tile below the leak in the roof gave way, and about five gallons of moldy roof water came cascading down on the three.

"Could it get any worse?" Dan asked.

"Don't worry, we'll help clean things up here, Eddie," Jake said.

Then Dan pointed to the broken beer glasses on the floor and said, "Eddie, my good man, I believe ya owe us a couple a beers."

CHAPTER 30

▼

On Tuesday afternoon Jake came to see David to go over the contract he'd received by fax the night before. There, Jake was introduced to Janice McKay, a seasoned entertainment attorney who David brought in to help with the negotiations. She immediately took charge and began the meeting by explaining that MBP was a celebrated enterprise, well known in the music industry and that she'd, in the past, represented artists being sought by MBP. She expounded on the importance of crafting the agreement so that each clause worked in concert with the others. She pointed out some items that should be questioned and negotiated at the meeting on Friday while Jake listened intently. Her dissertation included terms such as royalty cap, creative control, advance payments, controlled composition rate clauses, performance royalty cap, and more. It was, for the most part, well over Jake's head, but he felt that those matters he didn't understand were in good hands. But waiting to see how Friday would turn out was maddening. Jake asked many questions in order to better understand how things should go on Friday. Janice asked Jake why the contract was in the name of a Sonny Dixon. He explained that he had entered the American Songwriting Contest with a pen name because he thought it would be fun. But now they knew him as Sonny Dixon. She told him not to worry about it and that she'd handle that issue when it was appropriate. "But for now, I guess you're Sonny Dixon," she quipped.

As the meeting wound down, Jake told David about the episode with Eddie and asked if he could check on the statute of limitations for a robbery like the one Eddie had suffered. Jake didn't go into the fact that he and Dan had their suspicions about who the culprit might be though. One of David's associates was a criminal attorney who just had a case of that nature. Having been just exposed to the law regarding his question, David recited the answer to Jake on the spot. "Six years."

Surprised, Jake responded, "Man, that doesn't seem right. Commit robbery and avoid being caught for six years and you're home free. A guy could leave town after the deed on an extended vacation to avoid the cops, and come back in six years as if nothing happened. Unbelievable."

On Wednesday morning Jake showed up for his weekly meeting with Jenny. It was a short meeting. She had a few questions, but for the most part everything was under control. Since he had taken time off, Jenny had hired six new salespeople and all the office numbers were up significantly. Just before the meeting came to a close Jenny said, "Oh, by the way, have you picked up your messages from voice mail lately? I took a call from some crackpot, or maybe it was just one of your friends playing a joke on you. The guy said his name was Tom Tyler. I didn't offer your home number to him because I figured if he was a friend playing a joke on you, he'd have your number and if it was some nut, he shouldn't be getting your home number anyway. Hope that was OK."

"No problem," Jake said calmly.

"You wouldn't happen to actually know Tom Tyler would you?" she asked. "I love his music. My dad would play his album all the time when I was growing up."

"Yep. I know him. We went to high school together," he reported with a sad look in his eye that she didn't notice. "He and I were pretty good friends back then."

"I was actually talking to '*the* Tom Tyler'?" she yelped. "I can't believe it. And you know him?"

"It's no big deal Jenny. Almost everyone my age who went to school at Kettering, knows Tom," he claimed.

Jenny fired off a string of questions. "Well, have you picked up his message? What did he say? Have you called him back yet? What do you think he wants?"

"No, I haven't picked up his message. I've been a little lax lately. But I'll get to it soon enough," he pledged. It was refreshing for Jake to see someone of Jenny's generation be so interested in someone from his generation.

"Look," she said with the serious voice of authority as she rose from her seat and started poking Jake in the chest with her index finger. "If that really was Tom Tyler on the phone, I want to know. And I want details. Do you hear me? Details."

Jake held up his right hand to wave off her finger poking and said, "OK, OK," as he laughed. "Dan says he's moving back to town soon. I'm sure that's all he wanted to tell me. If there's more, I'll be sure and report back to you, boss," Jake mocked. "I'll check my messages today for sure. It's just that I've had my mind on other things since I've been off."

"Speaking of which. You've been off about seven months, Jake. Have you decided when you're coming back?"

Thinking about what the future might hold for him after Friday's meeting, Jake said, "I should know more on that by our meeting next Wednesday."

She quickly informed him, "Your mind really is somewhere else. We're not meeting next Wednesday, that's Christmas and the following Wednesday is New Year's Day."

It wasn't that unusual for Jake to be caught by surprise when it came to holidays. One of his big shortcomings was that he was usually so focused on making a living that watching the calendar for days off was never a priority. Now that he was concentrating on making songs, he still wasn't watching the calendar. "Oh, no kidding? Well, I'll give you a call to keep you posted," he promised. "Jenny, you're doing a fantastic job here. How are you doing handling the pressure?"

"I've learned that a little pressure is a good thing. It helps me stay sharp."

Jake was grateful to hear that note of pride in her voice. "OK, I'm outa' here. I'll call you soon," he said as he got up to leave.

As he put his coat on and stepped toward the door, she called after him, "I appreciate what you've done for me, Jake."

He turned toward her and smiled, "Likewise, my dear." At that, he turned and headed into the snow.

On the way to his guitar lesson with Luther, Jake picked up his cell phone to check his voice mail. "Hey Jake, it's Tom. I called Dan to let him know I was movin' back to Waterford for the time bein'. My tour was canceled and I thought I should let ya know that I think I was a little out a line with ya at the golf course. Hope there's no hard feelin's. No need to give me a call. I've sublet my apartment and I'll be in town Sunday the twenty-second and I'll be stayin' with Dan until I get a place. I'll call ya when I get in town and maybe we can get together. I hope ya had time to look at those old songs. See ya."

Jake thought as he hung up the phone, *"It's gonna be great having Tom in town for Christmas."* But he wouldn't allow himself to confront the guilt he felt about getting a break with his songwriting. Songs, by the way, that if not for Tom, would probably be lunch for the worms in some landfill right now.

At dinner that night Jake told Joyce that Tom was going to be home on Sunday and suggested that it would be nice to have a get together on Christmas Eve, since it seemed like it was their turn to host something. She agreed and said she'd get with Patty and Carolyn to help her plan. The conversation turned to the pending meeting with MBP Inc. "Do you have any idea how that'll turn out?" Joyce wondered.

"I wish I did. All I know right now is that they seem to want to buy limited rights to all my songs. For how much, I don't know exactly. I got the impression that they wanted to have one of their groups use them all on one CD, but I could be wrong. So we'll just have to wait and see. David and this entertainment attorney will be there with me to see that it all gets done right, if it gets done at all. Joyce, I'm so excited about this that I couldn't play one thing right at the lesson with Luther today."

"What does he think about all this record business?" she asked.

"I haven't said anything to anyone but Dan and Dave so far. I don't want to jinx the whole thing and then have to tell everybody it was a false alarm. So I'm just keeping quiet for now."

"Good idea," she said.

It was early Thursday morning in California when Maurie Best's phone rang. The voice on the other end of the line was Ken Darby. "Maurie, we've met with Sonny Dixon. We've faxed a contract to his attorney and our next meeting is set for Friday. I've been researching since the Monday meeting. It's my opinion that all his songs are original. Everything—the melody, the lyrics—all of it, original. This Sonny Dixon is the real deal. Did you listen to the song files I emailed you?"

"Yes. You're right, this is the exact material we want. I've been thinking that 'Its About Time' could pull it off convincingly enough to sell a lot of CD's. In any event we have to acquire the rights to record them. We've been working on this 'roots of rock and roll anthology' idea for too long. Every songwriter we've hired blew it. They just couldn't put the right flavor of the 50's and 60's in their product. How is it a guy like this Dixon fella can write fifteen songs to the note, as if we had ordered them directly from him?"

"I don't know, boss. I think we just got lucky. I've done a little snooping around and I don't think he's been talking to anyone else. He doesn't have an Internet site either. No competition that I can see. This could be a big break for us if we act fast to tie it up."

"That's what I wanted to hear. I'm sending Bev there today so she'll be ready for the meeting on Friday. If anyone can wrap this up quickly, it's her. I've called

John Klein to see that we have a valid contract signed on the spot. The last thing I want to face is competition on this deal."

"Well, good luck, boss. Anything else I can do?" Ken asked.

"No. You've done well, Ken. You can fly back home now."

With an unsteady hand, Maurie Best hung up the phone. His aged fingers trembled as he dialed his right hand negotiator, Beverly. "Are you ready for the flight to Detroit?" he asked.

"Yes, Dad, I'm all set. I was just going out the door to the airport. Don't worry about a thing. I'll have this deal wrapped up in no time," she assured him.

"Well, I hope so. This is really a big one for us, honey. I'm counting on you to make it all come together."

"You know I'm not going to let you down? I'll see you when I get back…with the contract. Love ya. Bye for now."

Maurie hung up the phone and sat back in his plush office, savoring the fact that he had a daughter who was so loyal and devoted to him and the firm. It wouldn't be long before he would entrust her with complete control of his company. He thought back to that first time he realized she had given up her wild ways and settled down to business. It was 1966, and he needed money. He started to put his dream band together, but the process stalled and he was looking for a way to entice the musicians he had targeted to join his dream team. He decided he needed a song. Not just any song, but a great song, written by a well-known writer in order to make his offer appealing enough to win them over. But to do that he needed money. Money he didn't have, and had no means of obtaining. That was when Beverly Elizabeth came through for him. She showed up one day on his doorstep with the money he needed. She'd explained that it was from her divorce settlement and that she wanted him to have it. At first he refused, but she insisted, saying she wouldn't have it any other way and that the most important thing in her life was to see that his dream was fulfilled. Ever since then she had been his key business manager, orchestrating all of his music deals and stopping at nothing to get the job done.

CHAPTER 31

▼

Friday afternoon Jake and his attorneys appeared on schedule at the same Fox Theater suite where Jake had his initial meeting with MBP Incorporated. They were shown into the suite and seated by an attendant who informed them that Ms. Best would be in directly. Jake thought, *"Ms. Best? Would that be Maurie's wife meeting with them?"*

They were all shedding their winter coats when a tall, well groomed, woman dressed in an all black business suit with a name tag that read "Beverly E. Best" appeared at the door and surveyed the three seated at the conference table with a trained eye. "Hello. My name is Beverly Best and I represent MBP Incorporated." She held out her hand to Jake who happened to be closest. "Are you Mr. Dixon?" She made the assumption because he was the only one in the room who didn't look like a lawyer.

"Uh, yes I am, and this is Janice McKay and David Williamson, my counsel."

"She nodded a hello to David and said, "Hello Janice," in a warm tone. "It's nice to see you again." She went on to inform Jake and David that she and Janice had hammered out a few contracts in the past.

"How's your father doing these days? Is he still involved in the business?" Janice asked.

"He's doing very well. He still has a great passion for the music business and he never stops surprising me with his enthusiasm and drive for these projects," she said with a look of reverence in her eyes. Changing the subject, she turned to Jake and said, "I must apologize for my counsel. He hasn't yet arrived but I think it wouldn't hurt to begin by asking what you thought of our offer." Jake immediately turned to Janice and David for their input.

Then the talks began in earnest. It was talk that Jake couldn't comprehend enough to be of any use, so his focus drifted from the big words being tossed around to Ms. Beverly E. Best, the person. She seemed to be in her late fifties—trim for anyone at that age, he thought. She wore her hair up. Lots of black hair embroidered with gray strands here and there. No glasses. Her mannerisms exuded confidence and control. Her voice had a southern flavor. Her eyes were dark. *"Brown,"* he thought. But they looked much darker and overpowered any other feature except perhaps her lips. Then he remembered someone from his past that fit that very description. Although age had compromised her beauty, age could not conceal features so distinct. *"Lizzie Turner. This couldn't be her,"* he thought. *"Or could it? But her name was Beverly Best not Lizzie Turner. What if it is her? Turner could have been her married name. Probably was her married name."* Then Jake found himself, quite involuntarily, interfering with the legal exchange that was taking place. "Ms. Best," Jake interrupted.

The previously dynamic contract discussion fell silent. She turned to him, imitating a look of tolerance for the interruption. "Yes, Mr. Dixon. Do you have a question?"

"What does the 'E' stand for?"

She wrinkled her brow, betraying confusion. "I'm sorry. I'm not sure what you are referring to."

Jake apologized for the interruption. "I'm sorry, I was just curious—in your name—the middle initial. What does it stand for?"

Still, she displayed confusion. Confusion about how he could be interrupting a meeting of such magnitude with trivia. The look of confusion changed just enough to show that there was a limit to her patience. "The 'E' is for Elizabeth," she answered with one eyebrow raised. "Now was there anything else?"

"No. That was all," Jake responded sheepishly. He went back to his musings as the contract negotiations continued. *"Elizabeth. Elizabeth, Beth, Liz, Lizzie. Lizzie? It is her. Well, It could be her. According to Janice's exchange with her earlier, this woman was Maurie Best's daughter and according to Dan, she was last seen leaving the 'Silverbell' with Maurie. Hmm."*

Jake was seated with his back to the door so he didn't notice MBP's attorney, John Klein, standing in the doorway. Beverly interrupted the discussion to introduce Mr. Klein to the group. He shook Jake's hand as Beverly said, "This is Sonny Dixon, our songwriter, this is David Williamson and you know Janice McKay, they represent Mr. Dixon."

Jake's pulse faded and his face turned white as if he had seen a ghost. He suddenly realized that John Klein was the attorney who represented the buyer in the

Big Lake Road deal—Klein—the dirt bag who thought he could extract a major part of Jake's commission. He wondered if the dirt bag would remember him. *"How could he not remember me? He's probably got a voodoo doll of me on his desk that he's using as a pin cushion."*

"Sonny Dixon?" Klein asked as if someone was playing some kind of inappropriate joke on him. He turned to Beverly and said, as if he'd solved the crime of the century, "Lizzie, this is *not* Sonny Dixon. This man's name is Jake Strong. He's not a songwriter, he's a real estate broker."

Jake was listening to the dirt bag but all that registered was that the dirt bag called her Lizzie. "You are Lizzie. I knew it. Lizzie Turner."

Lizzie hadn't forgotten Jake, she just couldn't see deep enough through over thirty years of aging, wrinkling and thinning hair to find that naive, impressionable seventeen-year-old sucker she once used perfecting her father's dream band. But when her attorney called out Jake's name she made the connection and knew it was him.

"Jake Strong. How long has it been? She said as she shook her head in amazement. So you're not Sonny Dixon, but I'm guessing you *did* write these songs. Sure took you long enough." Her affectionate tone told Jake that she expected time to have healed any wounds she might have inflicted by walking out on him. But at the same time Jake was wondering if she expected Eddie to be as forgiving. Jake also wondered if she'd be as warm to him if she knew that he knew about her scheme to break up 'The Phogg', 'Crossroads', and the rest.

"You know him?" John Klein blurted out in disgust.

Lizzie turned toward her attorney and then back toward Jake. "Yes, I know him," she said to Klein, keeping her eyes on Jake. "I knew him when he thought he was a songwriter. But I can guarantee you he's a songwriter now." It was clear she hadn't lost her touch.

Klein's contempt toward Jake was obvious, but only Jake knew why. Janice McKay outlined the pen name mix-up to Klein but it didn't ease his disdain for Jake or his embarrassment over prematurely making Jake's identity an issue. His job here was to help Lizzie make a deal, but his intent was to make a deal and win something away from Jake to make up for Big Lake Road.

David and Janice were anxious for the discussion to continue and suggested that they bring Klein up to speed and pick up where they left off. Everyone was in agreement and the talks continued. Jake went back to his role of insignificant observer and thought about the course this meeting had taken. He felt as if he were back in the real estate business again. Having to put up with dirt bags like Klein. And as he thought further he realized that Klein wasn't the worst of it. He just found out that the person he was about to become contractually involved with was an old girlfriend who dumped him. No...a con artist working in concert with her father. They both used him in order to break up his band and apparently conspired to rob Eddie of thousands of dollars. Then he thought of Tom and his expected reaction to finding out Jake had made such a contract with the songs Tom had retrieved just for him. A contract with the same company that he turned down in order to remain with Jake, the so-called songwriter, and 'The Phogg'—the company that would have made him famous beyond his dreams. His thoughts progressed and arrived at the question. *"Do I really want to be dealing with this group?"* He started to feel a little sick about the whole thing and wanted to escape from it all, just like he escaped the real estate business. But then he had an idea. He opened the complimentary notepad that had been laid out in front of each of the chairs at the conference table and jotted down some notes. Jake's sudden change in posture didn't go unnoticed by the negotiators, but they forged on in their quest to arrive at an agreement.

Klein was pressing hard to keep any advance money to a minimum and to keep royalties to seventy-five percent of the statutory rate. Feeling that this wasn't uncommon in this kind of transaction, Janice was about to agree in order to obtain other stipulated concessions. When they had finally agreed to terms, Janice turned to Jake and explained in understandable terms what the agreement meant. Jake nodded occasionally, indicating that he understood what she was saying. When she was finished, she said, "If this meets your approval, Sonny," everyone laughed at the Sonny remark except Klein. "Then MBP is prepared to draft the final agreement while we wait."

Jake thanked Janice and David for their efforts and said, "Before I sign the agreement, I'd like to talk to Ms. Best privately if it's not too much trouble."

All three attorneys looked at each other wondering what kind of trouble Jake would create for them in their effort to close the deal. Klein focused in on Jake, looking him straight in the eye and pointing an accusing finger his way. "This is highly inappropriate. If you have something to say, you can say it to your counsel, Mr. Strong or me. I represent MBP in this matter. That means that they have hired me to negotiate this transaction. So you talk to us, not Ms. Best."

Jake didn't expect or need to get a lesson in legal protocol, especially from Mr. Dirt Bag Klein. He didn't know whether to be embarrassed or angry. He decided to go with angry. "Mr. Klein, I owe you an apology. When I first met you, I thought to myself, 'What a dirt bag this guy is', and you know, I kept that to myself," he explained as he hung his head repentantly. Frankly I'm ashamed of myself for thinking it. Because you really are so much more than a dirt bag Mr. Klein. You also qualify for…"

Jake was cut off in mid-sentence by Lizzie. "John, David and Janice, could you please give Mr. Strong and me a moment?" She waved them toward the door to the adjoining suite. David and Janice rose to accommodate her, left their brief cases and papers on the conference table and their coats hanging on the back of their respective chairs. Klein slowly rose from his seat, mouthing a protest that was quickly put to rest by Lizzie. David and Janice initially wanted to offer Jake some advice against this move but only because they felt a loss of control. David knew that convincing Jake to do otherwise was a lost cause anyway. So the three attorneys left the room, closing the door behind them.

Then Lizzie turned to Jake and said, "I remember you, Jake, but I can't place the hostility. Is that something you picked up over the years?"

"Well, your Mr. Klein and I have a little history. Our first meeting was, shall we say, less than cordial."

"What was it you wanted to talk about? Don't tell me you haven't gotten over the night at the 'Silverbell'," she laughed. "I wanted you to come with me, but you said no. So I drove out to California that night, without you. It's been my home ever since."

"Oh, I'm over it alright, but the memory of it all came back to me pretty quickly, now that I find out you're the one who wants to license my songs."

"And you're going to hold that against me?" she asked.

"Shouldn't I? Shouldn't I hold that against you? And shouldn't Luther Washington hold it against you for doing the same thing to him."

The question jabbed her right between the eyes. "Who's Luther Washington?" she said as her eyes darted around the room as if looking for an escape route. Jake surprised her with his knowledge of Luther. Her control of the situation had eroded and she was concerned about regaining it along with her composure.

"Let me refresh your memory. He was the guitar player in a band called 'Crossroads'. You stood him up at the bus station. His band broke up and their drummer was recruited by your father."

"Ok, I remember him. So it was just a coincidence that his drummer ended up in 'It's About Time'. I had no control over that," she reasoned.

"And I suppose that it was just a coincidence that on the night you walked out on me, your father showed up to recruit Tom Tyler away from us," Jake probed as if he were conducting a cross examination of the star witness in a murder trial. "And I suppose that 'Ghosts', 'White Powder' and 'Blues Train' were all coincidental, too."

She felt her knees buckle and found her chair. Jake didn't take his eyes off her as she sat contemplating her response. "OK. Jake, I did it. What do you want from me, an apology? OK, so I'm sorry I tried to use you. Is that what you want to hear? After thirty-six years what does it matter what the *real* truth is anyway? Remember, *you're* the one who didn't take *me* up on my offer, so what's all the fuss about.

"The fuss is that I don't think I want to be associated with a guy like Maurie Best who would have his own daughter go around trying to break up bands so that he can tailor-make a designer rock group. Look at all the people he hurt to get what he wanted. After you walked out on me back then, I spent years wondering if I did the right thing. And until a few days ago, I really believed you loved me." Jake let out a short sarcastic laugh. "I spent a lot of years doubting myself and questioning that decision. And now I find the whole thing was a scam cooked up by you and your father."

"He didn't have anything to do with it. I planned it all on my own," she confessed.

"Of course you'd say that now, when you're trying to make a deal for my songs," Jake countered.

"It's true. When I married Frank, my father was furious with me. He told me I was making a mistake and I did it anyway. I thought I knew what I was doing and I didn't need *him* to order me around. We had a big falling out and I left home, got married and my father and I didn't talk until about a year and a half later when Frank left. My father was right about everything and I vowed that I would do anything I could to make it up to him.

"My father worked two jobs to support my mother and me. He sold advertising for the paper during the day and worked for a talent agent at night. He'd help with getting the entertainers what ever they needed during their shows in the clubs around Detroit. That was a pretty dirty job and I hated the way the entertainers would treat him. But, for as long as I can remember, he had a dream to put together a rock and roll band and make them famous. After my marriage ended I came back home. He told me all about the bands that he'd seen and which members he wanted. He told me that he'd talked to some of the musicians he wanted, but couldn't entice them away from their groups. So that's when I got the idea to see if I could sort of 'help things along'. Well, as it turned out, I was pretty good at it. I'd just let him know about a band breaking up as if I'd heard it around the clubs. He had no idea what I was doing, Jake…and that's the truth," she insisted. "How did you find out about…?"

"About your con game?" Jake injected. He didn't think he owed her the tedious details of the story so he gave her the abridged version. "I met Luther about seven or eight months ago when I decided to take up the guitar again. He's a music instructor now. His relationship with you came up in conversation about the old days. As I asked more questions, I saw that his story was the same as mine. With the help of a friend, I put two and two together and realized what you were doing and why. Imagine my surprise when I found out today that you're Maurie Best's daughter."

"According to John Klein, you're in real estate," she said.

Jake thought this was an attempt at changing the subject and said, "That's got nothing to do with this."

"You told me back then about your father. He was in real estate, wasn't he?"

"What's that got to do with…?"

"As I remember it, you told me he wanted you to go to college and be in business instead of being in the band and all you wanted to do was play music. Well, it would appear that you did go to college, got into business and not just any business. You got into the real estate business. Just like your father."

"And your point is?" Jake said sarcastically

"My point is that you gave up your music for your father. You went on to college for your father and you even took up real estate for your father. I bet he was happy about that. Maybe you don't realize it, but you fulfilled his dream, not yours. You see. You would do anything for your parents. And so would I. And I did. Don't you understand?"

That shut Jake up for a moment even though he didn't agree with her argument. Then he said, "Well, I know one thing for sure. I wouldn't commit robbery for my father."

"What the hell are you talking about?" Lizzie erupted.

"I'm talking about the night you robbed 'Eddie's Place' in Detroit. You needed money to buy the rights to that first song for your father's band. Why else would those guys join up with him, unless he had something extra to offer."

"You're right about the song. We needed the song to make it work. But I didn't rob anyone. The money came from my divorce settlement," she maintained.

Jake looked down by his chair and remembered something he had left in his coat pocket, put his hand in and fished out the silver chain with the buffalo head nickel and hid it in his fist. "The night Eddie was robbed he remembered only one thing. The person who hit him over the head was wearing this." Jake let the chain slip through his fingers and dangled it in front of her as she stared at the blue nickel swinging back and forth.

"And that's supposed to prove I was there? You've got your nerve, coming in here and accusing me of being a criminal. Anyway, how long ago was that? Thirty-five years? I know for a fact that after six years the police can't do anything. There's a statute of limitations," she responded.

"Funny you should be so up on the statute of limitations for robbery in Michigan. How did you happen to become so familiar with an obscure fact like that living in California all this time?"

"It's not important. What is important is that you can't pin that on me." Her face was flush and her hands were shaking. "Now look, our attorneys have agreed on all terms of the deal and I say we put the past behind us, and you tell them it's a go. We can make you a lot of money, Jake," she appealed.

He paused to consider her request. He did stand to make a lot of money. He put the chain in his pocket and slid the pad of paper he had been writing on across the conference table. "The deal our attorneys struck is fine, except I'd like you to meet this list of additional demands. If you think you can, we'll have a deal."

Lizzie examined the neatly printed words that covered a full legal-sized sheet. When she was finished she said, "I'm sorry Jake, but there's no way we can agree to these terms. We're not running a charity here."

Jake paused and stared at Lizzie, trying to pierce the present reality and get a glimpse of the Lizzie he used to know. He wondered, *Was she as "all business" back then as she appeared to be now? Was there the slightest chance that she once loved me? What was the 'real truth' as she put it?* Her eyes locked on his at that same moment. After a brief silence, Jake said, "What if I'd said yes?"

Lizzie blinked out of her stare and said, "If you'd have said yes to what…this contract?

"No, I mean, what if I'd said yes to you, when you asked me to go to California with you?"

The silence and the staring resumed as Jake waited for her response. Jake thought he could detect a tear building up in her eye, as she turned away without answering. With her back to him she said, "I guess we will simply have to agree not to agree on this one. Let me know if you change your mind about any of these stipulations."

So they did simply agree to disagree and the attorneys were called back in and informed. Without much fanfare, the negotiators disbanded. David and Janice were disappointed to hear that Jake made further demands in his private meeting with Lizzie and said little in the elevator on their way down to the main floor. To break the silence, David said, "Oh Jake, by the way. With regard to that statute of limitations question you had. Remember, you were surprised that the limitation of six years was so short. Well, I looked into it a little further and found that the statute of limitations is suspended or 'tolled' if the perpetrator leaves the jurisdiction. I have a copy of the statute right here." He pulled it out of his brief case and handed it to Jake. "So if someone robbed you and left the state, the clock on the statute of limitations stops ticking, so to speak."

The door opened to the ground floor. David and Janice got out but Jake remained in the elevator. "Can you wait a minute for me? Something I forgot to tell Ms. Best," Jake asked as the elevator doors closed. Jake walked back into the conference room where Lizzie and John Klein were standing. He approached Lizzie and handed her the statute that David had copied for him. "Lizzie, here's some information on that legal question we discussed in our private meeting today. I thought it might be of some help to you in the future." She took the document without a word and Jake made his exit.

John Klein watched as Lizzie examined the document. "What is that?"

"Nothing," she said and she folded it up with shaking hands and slipped it into her coat pocket. "Can you stay on here for a while?" she asked nervously. "I want to go over a few more things with you before I catch my plane."

CHAPTER 32

▼

It snowed during the entire drive back from Detroit. It was really piling up by the time he got home. As he turned the corner toward the driveway, there was Joyce, dressed in her office clothes, leather dress boots, and calf length wool overcoat shoveling the heavy layers of snow from the driveway. This was nothing new. Even though they lived in a community development where streets and driveways were plowed by the subdivision association, she enjoyed the challenge of trying to complete the clearing of snow before the association snowplow could arrive. She usually won. If the truth be known, she felt she did a better job of clearing snow than those trucks with the plows on the front. Jake, on the other hand, did his best to discourage her from shoveling the snow. He had two reasons. The first was that he didn't see the point in shoveling a driveway that you had already paid someone else to clear. It wasn't like they would deduct the cost of the push if Joyce got to it first. And the second was that he was concerned that the neighbors would think that Joyce was the one doing all the heavy lifting around the house. Even though the thought of her out there shoveling snow frustrated him, this was who she was and he loved everything about her. Even the way she shoveled the snow.

Jake got out of the SUV and grabbed another shovel and helped her. "Joyce, I swear we're gonna have to move to Florida, so I can keep you off that shovel." She ignored him as she continued shoveling with a smile. She didn't mind the help.

"How did your big meeting go today?" she asked.

"It was big alright, but we couldn't come to terms," Jake began. "You'll never guess who was negotiating for the MBP guys."

"Who?"

"Remember that attorney that tried to shake me down at the Big Lake Road closing?"

She stopped her shoveling even though she knew it could mean losing the race with the snowplow guys. "No. Not him? Did he remember you?"

"Oh yeah. He remembered me, and I hadn't told them my real name yet. So when I was introduced to him as Sonny Dixon, he kinda blew the lid off that. But that's not the worst of it. The representative of MBP was Lizzie Turner. Come to find out she's Maurie Best's daughter. Joyce, I was totally blown away." Jake spun the tale of the contract meeting and its ultimate collapse as they persevered with their self imposed snowy chore until the driveway was clear. Together they walked toward the garage amidst the still hovering snowflakes to put down their shovels as the plow arrived with a honk and a wave.

"You know, I was thinking about the party on Christmas Eve," Jake began as he shook the snow off his coat. "I was thinking we could invite a few more people over. You know, I've got a couple people to thank for helping and putting up with me these past months. I'd like Jenny and Luther to come."

"That's a great idea, I'll give Jenny a call right now, and why don't you call Luther?" she suggested as she walked off to the bedroom to change out of her office attire. "You should call that Eddie guy too," she hollered from the bedroom. "I bet the bar won't be open on Christmas Eve."

That evening they both were a little worn out from the crazy week, not to mention the driveway shoveling, so they vegetated in front of the TV until it was bedtime.

That weekend was filled with preparations for the party. There was lots of calling, shopping and decorating to be done. Dan called Jake to find out what happened at the meeting and was disappointed for Jake but relieved that Tom wouldn't have to be slapped in the face by Jake's success in his hour of despair. David called to ask what Jake could have possibly demanded in his meeting with Lizzie that could have blown the deal on which he and Janice worked so hard. Jake said, just as he had told him in the car on the way home, "I'm sorry Dave. I guess I just let the situation get a little out of hand. I guess I just got carried away, trying to set a few too many things right."

"Janice thought that it might be best to shop your songs around to some of the other music people, but she said not to expect a package deal like they were offering. That was a once in a lifetime opportunity. The idea of having all your songs on one CD—that apparently is pretty uncommon. And to have an organization like MBP behind the whole thing—she says they're the most reputable company in the industry today."

Jake couldn't explain his behavior to David as he tried and failed to find some words of comfort for him. He knew he'd given way to impulse again and it was indefensible. "Sorry man," was all he could say.

Monday afternoon brought more snow and Joyce, like clockwork, was out in the thick of it shoveling again. Jake decided to hit the woodshed to relieve some of the remorse that had crept into his system from the opportunity that he let slip by. He admitted to himself that the feeling was not at all unlike the disagreeable feelings that plagued him during his real estate career. As he stood playing his guitar and recording the sound on the computer, he watched Joyce through the window in his office. Every pass she made with her shovel was painfully straight leaving a perfectly cleaned strip of cement in its path. She liked things to be neat and perfect. That's how she kept the house too. It was her way of doing her part to make the world a better place. But Jake was far from perfect and he knew, *"the world never gives you perfect, no matter how hard you try or how straight you shovel the driveway."*

As he played on, he saw the UPS truck pull into the part of the driveway that Joyce hadn't yet shoveled. He grinned at the thought that she probably would get upset from the truck compacting the snow with its tires. Sometimes she couldn't get the tracks of compacted snow up with her shovel and it usually made her mad. *"See you try to make the world perfect and just when you think you can make a difference, a big truck comes along and reminds you that it ain't possible,"* he mused as he played on.

As the driver got out, Jake could see Joyce pointing to the tracks he made. Jake laughed out loud as he thought, *"That poor bastard. He doesn't deserve it."* He was carrying a package that Joyce had to sign for. As he drove off, Joyce stood solemnly holding the package and staring at the indelible blemishes of compacted snow he left on her otherwise perfect driveway.

She turned and saw Jake standing in the window and pointed to the package then to the front door, signaling that she would leave it for him there so he could get it without having to put his coat on. Jake put down his guitar, opened the front door, and retrieved the package. It was a very heavy thick cardboard legal sized envelope with MBP's return address posted in the customary spot. He took it to his big green chair, turned on the lamp, opened the package and examined its contents. On top was a letter from Ms. Beverly E. Best indicating that her firm had reconsidered his "post negotiation stipulations" and that "the enclosed documents should accurately reflect same". The enclosed documents were contracts. A big stack of contracts, each agreement was in triplicate complete with the little red marker tags indicating where the parties and witnesses needed to sign. He looked them over and immediately called David who was just walking out his office door for home. "I'll meet you at the Coney in ten minutes," he said.

As Jake pulled out of the driveway he explained to Joyce where he was headed and why. She was elated and said, "Looks like it's gonna be a merry Christmas."

The Coney was overly warm with the furnace blasting, the grill in high gear and throngs of hungry people populating the place. Jake splashed through the small foyer of melting slush and snow then on to the booth that David appropriated for the occasion. "Thanks Dave," Jake said as he handed the package to him, hung up his coat and sat down. Jake quietly sipped the iced tea David had ordered for him while the documents were scanned. The waitress came to take their order and they both ordered pie. Neither planned to eat the pie but didn't want to take up a booth in the crowded restaurant ordering only the tea.

After David went through the contracts he looked at Jake and shook his head. He verbally outlined every important clause of each and every document. "So, is this what you and Beverly talked about in your private little meeting?"

"Essentially," Jake answered with a smile.

"Well, Jake," David admonished. "This is not a better deal for you. In fact it's a worse deal for both you and MBP," he said as he held up a small stack of disheveled papers in each of his hands. "And this is how you want it to be?"

"Yep, I do," he answered still smiling.

"OK. I'll have Janice take a look at these right after Christmas but I don't see any hidden surprises, except those that were self inflicted, so to speak," he jabbed.

"OK if I give these back to you at the party?" Jake asked. "I want to make more copies."

"Fine with me. Now if you will excuse me, I'm gonna go home and try to associate with some sane people for a change and you can get the bill," David demanded.

"Thanks again for meeting me," Jake called out, as David headed down the aisle carrying his coat. He didn't turn around but raised one hand in acknowledgment as he left in haste. Jake stacked the papers, snuck a taste of pie, left the tip and headed for the cash register.

CHAPTER 33

▼

Christmas Eve arrived and Joyce had the house ready for the party. The Christmas decorations adorned both the inside and outside of the house. The flames flickered in the fireplace and warmed the two-story living room. The familiar smell of a Christmas spruce filled the house so that there was no mistaking the holiday. Joyce presented a spectacular spread including a variety of hors d'oeuvres and other delectable finger foods. The bar was fully in operation right down to the eggnog just in case there was a taker. And yes, the driveway was perfectly shoveled.

Every invitee had arrived and the party was in full swing. Christmas music drifted through the halls reminding the guests of the season. Eddie and Luther were enjoying a beer and getting to know Joyce, while Tom was humbly listening to Jenny. She was telling him how much she loved his music and what an honor it was to meet him and how surprised she was when she heard that Jake was a friend of his. Patty, Dan, Rick and Carolyn were surveying and sampling the hors d'oeuvres with David and Janet. It was a great party and Jake was secretly celebrating inside.

Jake tapped Jenny on the shoulder and asked if he could steal her away from Tom for a minute. She reluctantly agreed and followed him to an unoccupied corner of the dining room. He presented her with an envelope. "I wanted to give you a Christmas bonus but I thought this might be more useful to you, given your accomplishments at the office." She opened the envelope. It was a single piece of paper signed by Jake conveying the controlling interest of the real estate company to her. The price was one dollar to make it legal. She looked up from the paper with a tear emerging from each eye. She didn't know what to do so she slugged him in the arm and started to cry. "Thank you," she blurted as she put one arm around his neck and tried to find a tissue with her free hand.

Next Jake walked over to Eddie and asked for a moment of his time. They proceeded to the dining room where Jake presented him with an envelope. In it Eddie found an agreement drafted by MBP that stipulated they would co-sign for a loan to renovate 'Eddie's Place' up to three-hundred-thousand-dollars, plus an additional one-hundred-thousand in cash along with free use of their business consultants to help line up blues and rock and roll acts from all over Canada and the U. S. The document was signed by Maurie Best and Beverly E. Best of MBP, Inc. along with a note saying, *"We heard about your robbery and how it left a void in the music market in Detroit. We wanted to help bring the blues back to 'Eddie's Place'. We will await being honored by your acceptance of this token of our appreciation for your dedication to the music we both cherish."* Eddie wiped a tear away as he turned back to Jake and said, "She's the one who robbed me, ain't she?"

Jake couldn't conceal his emotion as he said sadly, "I'm pretty sure, Eddie."

"I think this makes us square," Eddie said as he looked down at the paper. "In fact, I may owe her a little change back. I know you and Dan had sumpthin' to do with this, man. And I thank you two. You guys won't be able to pay for a thing at 'Eddie's Place' from now on, ya hear me?"

"I hear ya, man," was all Jake could get out without choking up.

Jake's next target was Dan and Rick. Fortunately, he caught them over by the bar in the basement by themselves. "Hey you two, I got some Christmas gifts for you," Jake said as he walked toward them.

Dan greeted him with a bottle of beer and said, "Here's my Christmas gift to *you* Jake."

Rick joined in and said, "Hey, that's from the both of us."

Jake took the beer and downed half of it in one gulp, while Dan and Rick opened their envelopes. "This is a contract of some kind," Rick remarked. "A contract to do the photography for a CD cover and inserts?"

"Yep," Jake acknowledged.

"They want me to play harmonica on one of your songs?" Dan questioned as he scanned his contract.

"Well, *they* didn't want you to, but *I* wanted you to," Jake jabbed.

"What about Tom?" Dan asked.

"Don't worry, I think I got that covered," Jake responded.

Jake stuck around and answered as many questions as he could for the elated pair before he headed upstairs for his next Christmas victim. Jake buttonholed Luther and Tom and asked them to come with him into the master bedroom that was customarily off limits at any of Joyce's parties. They followed Jake with confused looks as they were ordered to close the door behind them. As he entered to see the bed covered with the coats of all the guests, Tom joked, "Jake, I like ya but I think ya got the wrong idea about me. Hey, is Luther tellin' me the truth about you takin' guitar lessons and finishin' all those songs? Man, Jake, that's so great! I was goin' to say I was sorry for how I talked to ya last summer, but if it helped ya to finish the songs, then to hell with the apology," Tom said, starting to feel the beer making a small adjustment to his attitude.

"Tom, I'm really proud to call him my student. Never had one his age. But never had one so dedicated either," Luther explained as the two of them sat on the edge of the bed wondering why Jake wanted to see them. Jake was holding two envelopes in his hand and he gave them each their respective package. "What's this?" they both wanted to know.

"You'll see. Just open it."

They simultaneously ripped the envelopes open to find their separate contracts with MBP, Inc. to cut an album called the 'Phoenix Project'—fifteen songs written by Sonny Dixon. Luther and his band would back up Tom. Both contracts provided advance payments, equitable royalties, a fair amount of artistic control, and best of all, the ownership of the masters to be shared by MBP, Tom, Luther, his band and Jake.

"I assume *you* are Sonny Dixon," said Tom as he pointed to Jake.

"Yeah," Jake laughed. He could hear Don Henley singing his Christmas song on the radio in the next room. He always liked that song. But tonight, for some reason, he couldn't remember any of the words or even the name of it.

"I can't believe what I'm readin' here. Are you jokin' with me? Because it wouldn't be a very funny joke right about now if ya get my drift, bud," Tom warned.

"Trust me, Tom, it's for real and I want you two to get started on this as soon as you feel ready. Luther, all the preliminary work can be done at Gil's studio so neither of you have to travel for now. I expect they might want to master it in California but we'll see."

Then both Luther and Tom jumped up from the bed as if they had won the lottery. But they hadn't won anything. They earned it, because they had paid their dues. And finally...so had Jake.

THE END

EPILOG

▼

February 8th 2004

Lizzie opened the small brown paper envelope in the comfort of her California penthouse as she was preparing for the evening's festivities. She tipped up one end to dump the contents. A silver chain with a buffalo head nickel painted blue, fell out onto her dressing table. She smiled as she stowed it away in her jewelry box.

Jake, Rick, Dan, David and their wives stepped out of their rented limo to attend the big event at 'Eddie's Place'. They were pleased to see a freshly paved and packed parking lot, a fully refurbished building and a new sign that read 'Eddie's Phoenix Lounge'. The Best in Blues and Rock and Roll.'

Tom and Luther were in California. They were seated with the rest of the band and surrounded by contemporary as well as legendary icons of music. The event—The National Academy of Recording Arts and Sciences 2004 Grammy Awards.

"And now in category two, Album of the Year. Nominees are:
Missy Elliott; Under Construction
Evanescence; Fallen
Justin Timberlake; Justified
The White Stripes; Elephant and
Tom Tyler; The Phoenix Project
*And the winner is…*Tom Tyler; The Phoenix Project."

978-0-595-35684
0-595-35684-2

Made in the USA
Monee, IL
05 August 2024